The Summer of the Crow

The Summer of the Crow

By

EUNICE BOEVE

LEATHERS
PUBLISHING

A division of Squire Publishers, Inc.
4500 College Blvd.
Leawood, KS 66211
1/888/888-7696

Copyright 2001
Printed in the United States

ISBN: 1-58597-059-X

Library of Congress Control No. 00-134035

A division of Squire Publishers, Inc.
4500 College Blvd.
Leawood, KS 66211
1/888/888-7696

For my husband, Ron, and granddaughter, Emily, and in memory of Louis Boeve, the sheriff of Phillips County, Kansas, 1962-1972

1

BRADY DROVE THE STAKE through the ring at the end of the trap and into the ground. Opening the wide jaws, he set the trap carefully in front of the prairie dog hole. The stake would keep the animal from dragging it down into its burrow and out of his reach.

He had started trapping the small brown rodents when the county began paying two cents for each tail. With the drought turning their land to dust, they couldn't afford to have a worthless animal digging holes in their fields and eating what little did manage to grow, and he liked having a few coins to jingle in his pockets and spend on root beer floats when he got to town. Besides, his dog sure enjoyed their twice-daily rounds of his trapline.

Brady had tossed aside an old broken stake. Now picking it up, he called, "Hey, Taggart. How about a game of catch?"

The black dog, so big his dad once said it was like having a yearling calf in the house, jerked his nose up out of a straggle of weeds where he'd been investigating a scent, started toward him, and then stopped to sniff the prairie dog carcass Brady had thrown aside. "Come on, boy." Brady held up the stake and pretended to give it a toss. "Leave it for the coyotes and crows." The dog bounded toward him, his dark eyes fastened with eager anticipation on the stake. Brady grinned and threw the stick high and wide. Taggart charged forward, leaped and caught it in mid-air. A small cloud of dust puffed up as his paws hit the ground.

"Great catch!" Brady called. Taggart trotted back to him, the stake poked out from one side of his huge jaw. He looked as pleased, Brady thought, as if he were a big league baseball player who had just made the winning catch in the World Series.

Brady loved baseball. Last fall when Mrs. Guilder brought her radio to school so they could listen to the Series, Brady had imagined himself a part of the roaring, cheering, heckling crowd. He could almost see ol' Dizzy Dean when he pitched that final fireball to strike out Detroit's Hank Greenberg and win the 1934 World Series for the St. Louis Cardinals. He thought Mrs. Guilder acted like she was right there in the stands, too, the way she jumped around and hollered. She was kind of old and a little bit fat. Lumpy was how Brady thought of her. But she sure loved baseball. She had sided with the Detroit Tigers because Eldon Auker played for them and he was from her old home town in north central Kansas. She thought they all ought to be for Detroit since they were Kansans, too. He'd told her his Grandpa Bud was the sheriff at Sentinel, and she said it wasn't more than a hundred miles from Norcatur where she and Eldon Auker had once lived.

She even got Jim Conners, his best friend, to side with her. In fact, all five of the boys, including Jim, had rooted for the Tigers, along with Mrs. Guilder. He was the only one who had been for St. Louis. Mrs. Guilder said she'd heard the students in town had a radio set up in the auditorium. He bet there'd been a lot of St. Louis fans in the town school. There others would have joined him in cheering the Cardinals' win.

This spring his graduation would end his eight years at this little country school. In the fall he'd start high school in town. He hoped his dad would get him a car to drive back and forth. Otherwise, he'd have to board in town through the week and get home only on weekends. He was sure counting on a car. It would be great, too, if Jim Conners would change his mind about going on to high school and would ride with him.

As he threw the stake one more time, Brady glanced up at the morning sun. "I've got to go, Taggart," he called. "If I'm late, Mrs. Guilder will give me an extra assignment."

He started off across the fields in an easy run, his footfalls kicking up dust. Taggart trotted beside him. In his head, Brady could see how these fields had once looked before the drought and the dust storms. By now a lush carpet of green should have sprouted from the seed sowed last fall and in late June or early July be a golden sea of grain that stretched as far as the eyes could see. But the once fertile soil was gone. Dried out under the relentless sun, it had all blown away in the wind. This spring, instead of a carpet of deep green, the little wheat that had survived was a pale, sickly color. Only the dusty weeds were undaunted by the lack of moisture and the suffocating dirt storms. This summer there would be little or no wheat to harvest and the knowledge made him sick with worry.

He had hoped, when he was grown, to farm this land his great grandfather had homesteaded. His plans had always been to follow in his dad's footsteps with a degree in agriculture from Kansas State.

"Maybe you'll even find a wife there, like I did," his dad said one time, teasing him.

His parents had met in college when his dad was a senior and his mother a freshman. After his dad's graduation, they had married and come back to the farm, where his mother had shared the household work with her mother-in-law, and his father had farmed with Grandpa Foster. Brady wished he could have known his dad's parents, but they had both died the year before he was born.

Brady's grandfather and his father had added more land to the original homestead. His dad had been so proud of his acres and acres of land and "pleased," he said, that Brady wanted to farm, too. But now the once rich soil had given way to barren desert and he was beginning to doubt that even if the rains came, the land could be saved to pass on to him.

A sudden gust of wind whipped around Brady and he scanned the horizon, hopeful for signs of rain. But the pink-hued morning sky held only wispy drifts of clouds. He quickened his footsteps. It was getting late and he still had to get his lunch pail and run upstairs and empty his pockets of the five prairie dog tails he'd taken this morning.

He grinned to himself, the memory of the time he'd forgotten to empty his pockets lifting his spirits. He had dropped his overalls in the basket to be washed and his mother, checking the pockets, had stuck her hand into the mass of hairy tails.

"Brady Lee Foster!" she'd yelled at him. "If I ever find another mess like that in your pockets, you're washing your own overalls!"

He hadn't left any more tails, but he and his dad were doing the washing now and most of the rest of the housework, too. His mother just seemed to cough harder and get weaker every day. About all she could do were sitting down jobs, like mending. But sometimes, if it was a clear day, she could cook an easy meal. Everything else soon had her coughing and gasping for breath.

Brady kept his own room now, and to help keep out some of the dirt and grit when a dust storm came up, he'd been hanging a blanket at his window. And either he or his dad tried to stay close enough to the house that if a dust storm came up, they'd have time to run in and grab up some sheets and blankets, douse them in a tub of water and hang them, heavy and dripping, at the windows downstairs. It was impossible now for his mother to lift the water-soaked blankets, let alone hang them up on the nails they'd driven into the window frames.

"Mom," he called now as he stepped through the back

door and into the house.

"I'm here." His mother's faint reply ca parent's bedroom. He knocked and opened the door. in bed, propped up on a couple of pillows, her dark hair about her shoulders, a crochet hook and some blue yarn in her hands. In a corner of the room, his little sister sat crosslegged on the floor. Her blonde head, capped in curls, was cocked to one side and tilted upward, her eyes fixed on a corner of the room near the ceiling. She was humming a faint tuneless sound.

Brady smiled at his mother. "Sarah looks happy this morning," he said.

"Yes." Her dark eyes warmed with her smile. "I expect you are on your way to school."

"As soon as I run upstairs and get my books." He withdrew from the room, closing the door behind him so his little sister wouldn't escape. The house was pretty well "Sarah proof," but he knew his mother worried that she might somehow get outside, wander away and get lost. She probably wouldn't be scared. But who really knew with Sarah? It was doubtful she'd even realize she was lost. Her little mind was more two-year-old than six. But when she got hungry and tired, she'd scream bloody murder and throw seven kinds of a fit. Probably then they could find her.

Upstairs, Brady deposited his morning's collection of prairie dog tails in the sack on his dresser. With these five, he now had twenty tails to turn in at the County Clerk's office for the two-cents bounty they were paying to get rid of the pesky animal. He hoped to get at least five more before Saturday when Mrs. Brewster came to stay with his mom and Sarah while he and his dad went into town.

The Miller twins always cut their prairie dog tails into two pieces, unless they were extra short ones, and got double their money. They bragged about how easy it was to fool Miss Cornish because she always took a fella at his word.

ut Brady knew he could never get away with it. He knew the minute Miss Cornish, who was so pretty she about took his breath away, looked up at him and said, "How many tails do you have today, Brady?" that he would get red in the face and start to stammer. She would know then that he was lying.

Brady imagined his sack of tails dumped out on her desk. Probably she'd spread out a newspaper first and use her pencil to poke through the tails to count them. She seemed pretty squeamish about those tails. He thought she'd probably give him a big lecture on lying, or report it to his dad ... or the sheriff.

His dad never yelled. But he had a look that always made Brady feel lower'n a snake's belly. And when his dad was good and mad, if he spoke to him at all, it would be in short, curt sentences like he was biting off his words. If Miss Cornish told the sheriff, he might tell Grandpa Bud, even though Grandpa Bud was the sheriff of Bunch County up near the Nebraska line while they were the southern-most county in Kansas, right next to Oklahoma. But sheriffs were always calling other sheriffs about stolen cars, or runaways, or something. He remembered his dad and Grandpa Bud talking about it when they were in Sentinel for Grandma Barbara's funeral two years ago. If Sheriff Bills had to call Grandpa Bud, he just might mention that they had caught his grandson trying to cheat the county.

Not that he'd ever try to cheat anyway. Even if he got away with it, he would always feel guilty, and the two cents extra he would get for each tail sure wouldn't be worth his conscience nagging him, even as scarce as money was these days.

He knew he didn't want to make his dad mad at him, and he was pretty sure he'd not care to have Grandpa Bud find out anything bad about him either. Grandpa Bud was a big man, well over six feet, with thick gray hair and pale blue eyes that looked to Brady like he could maybe see inside a fella's head.

Grandma Barbara had been tall, too, her blonde hair so pale it hardly showed the gray, and her warm blue eyes were always crinkly with smiles. It was hard to believe she was dead.

He remembered how astounded he'd been when Grandpa Bud broke down and cried at her funeral. He had cried a little himself, especially when his mother had started crying. But Grandpa Bud was a grown man. He'd never imagined such a big man, and the sheriff to boot, to ever cry. But he guessed Grandpa Bud missed her as much as they all did.

She used to come down on the bus to see them several times a year. The last time just before she got cancer. Grandpa Bud never ever came with her and she always made excuses for him. Usually she laid the blame onto his sheriff's job, but his mother always said it was because her dad didn't like to sleep in any bed but his own. "Besides," she had added, "Dad has been the sheriff there so many years now, he thinks the county would fall apart without him."

He knew his mother missed her dad, but he could sort of understand how Grandpa Bud felt about Bunch County. He had been born and raised there, just like Brady had been born on this farm. In just one more week, it would be thirteen years ago. Dr. McKinley still mentioned coming out to deliver him on that dark and windy April night.

Although he and Grandpa Bud didn't look anything alike, they did share this feeling for home.

Brady wished his Grandpa Bud would have taken more notice of him when they were there for Grandma Barbara's funeral, but he guessed he was just too sad. Besides, he'd probably been too upset over Sarah. He must not have ever realized before just how different she was from other kids.

He was so sure his own doctor could help her, but his mother had explained to her dad that they'd been to all kinds of doctors.

"Most of them were no help at all," his mother said. "Then a doctor in Kansas City gave us a name for it, and a reason to quit searching for answers. He told us Sarah was probably born this way and nothing we did would ever change her condition. He told us he had just read about a doctor, back in 1911, who called what she has, autism."

"Well, I can't see that one more doctor would hurt anything," Grandpa Bud said.

But in a way it had. His mother had come back from that doctor madder than he could ever remember seeing her before.

"An institutional setting!" she'd yelled, jerking her hat off and slamming it and her pocket book down on the kitchen table. "An institutional setting, he says. My Lord, she's only four years old!"

She had burst out crying then, and Brady had about drawn blood biting down on his lip to keep from crying, too.

When his mother had finally stopped sobbing, she had looked up at his dad, her face splotched and reddened, her dark brown eyes swimming in tears. "Oh, Jack," she'd whispered. "Remember when she was a baby? She was fine then." Suddenly the soft, pleading look in her eyes had given way to anger again and she had spit out the rest of her words like they were pieces of poison in her mouth.

"She was fine! Fine! Until this horrible drought came!"

Then she'd cried again and his dad had drawn her into his arms. "Hush, Liddy. Hush," he'd said.

Grandpa Bud had smoothed and pulled at his mustache like he was nervous and uncomfortable. Feeling uncomfortable himself, Brady had turned away to look at Sarah.

She had been as unconcerned as ever. Standing in the corner of the kitchen, she had been smiling her soft, secret smiles and flipping her little hands over and over in front of her face.

That was what made it so hard. Sarah paid no attention

to anything or anyone. She was so pretty with her blonde curls and clear blue eyes, her coloring like their dad's, while he had dark hair and eyes, like their mother's. She was a beautiful little girl, but whatever made one connect with people was missing in her. She seemed to care for no one. No one, except maybe herself.

A surge of anger had coursed through him. Anger at her indifference while their mother cried and their dad kept repeating, "Hush, Liddy. Hush, girl."

His dad always called his mother Liddy, instead of Lydia, during those times. His tone of voice gentle and soothing. It reminded Brady of how his dad used to talk to their team of mules, Buck and Barney. Brady knew his dad missed those old mules, but like he said, "A tractor does the work faster and doesn't need to rest at all."

It was a mystery to Brady why animals and, he guessed, most people were calmed by someone talking to them and touching them and yet Sarah just got more and more agitated. She hardly ever let anyone touch her, and forget trying to hold her, for all you'd get would be struggles and screams. When you let her loose, she'd run in her funny little galloping gait, and when she was far enough away to suit her, she'd begin the ritual of her fingers, fluttering them, like butterflies, in front of her face. She make little clicking sounds with her tongue when she was upset and hummed when she was content or happy. She had never learned to speak and Brady wondered if she "talked to herself" with her humming and clicking sounds.

Grandma Barbara had called her a *Changeling*. But her words had been more fancy than fact. One evening when she was visiting them, he'd found his grandmother sitting on the edge of Sarah's bed, fingering her tumble of soft, blonde curls and watching her sleep, as his mother often did. "My sweet changeling child," he had heard her whisper.

"What's a Changeling?" he had asked, his voice a whisper, too, although once Sarah fell asleep it was hard to wake her. When she woke, she woke on her own and that might be any time of day or night.

At first she had been reluctant to tell him. He had pressed her, hoping, he guessed, that she had some explanation for Sarah's illness ... her autism ... whatever autism really meant.

It's a kind of a fairy tale," Grandma Barbara finally said. "When I was a child, there was a beautiful, but strange-acting little boy in our neighborhood. An old woman in the neighborhood told me he was a *Changeling — a fairy child.*"

"What?" Brady said frowning.

"A fairy child. She told me these children so perfect in looks, but so different in other ways, are fairy children. She said fairies come in the night and steal the human baby and leave one of their own in its place. Our world is confusing to this fairy child and this fairy child is confusing to us." With a soft smile she had reached out and patted his hand. "I know. It's just a silly old grandma story."

Brady wondered if Grandma Barbara had told his mother that story. He thought not. It was too fanciful, and he was sure it wouldn't make his mother feel any better. It would still hurt her to see Sarah act like she had no feelings at all for her family ... not even for her mother. *Why in the dickens couldn't Sarah be like other kids?*

Sometimes he wondered if this drought had affected her. Had maybe blown something in on the winds. Or was it because the world was ending, like old man Richards kept hollering that day in front of Sim's Grocery?

It was all man's fault, he had yelled. Everything from the stock market crash in '29 which had caused these hard times, to the drought that was plaguing their land. It was all because man had sinned. "Repent," he had screamed. "The world is ending! Repent!"

Sheriff Bills had taken him the next day to the State Mental Hospital at Larned. Brady wondered if that was the hospital where Grandpa Bud's doctor had wanted them to put Sarah.

He shivered. "Someone is walking on your grave," Jim Conners would say. But it wasn't that. It was everything. It was Sarah ... and his mother, so weak and coughing almost all the time now. Dr. McKinley said it was asthma complicated by the drought.

And the drought? Would it ever let up? Would their farm ever grow anything again or was it ruined forever, smothered in silt and dust? Was the end of the world, at least this world he had always known, coming to an end for all of them?

2

THE SERIES OF LONG RINGS of the telephone as he was pulling on his overalls brought Brady down the stairs, shoes in hand.

"What's happening?" he asked his mother.

She shook her head, her eyes on his dad who had lifted the receiver from the telephone mounted on the kitchen wall and was listening intently.

They waited, wondering why Miss Mary Smith at the telephone office had rung the emergency ring. Was someone's house or barn on fire, or had some other calamity struck among their neighbors? But his dad was grinning when he hung up the receiver.

"Well, son," he said. "Mrs. Guilder called Central to let everyone know she was closing school today in honor of your birthday."

"Aw," Brady began.

"Actually she's sick." His dad's grin disappeared. "The flu or something, I guess."

"Oh, I hope it's nothing too serious." Her brow wrinkling with worry lines, Brady's mother fussed about Mrs. Guilder for a while and then began to think of things Brady could do, even though it was his birthday. But she did apologize first.

"I'm sorry, Brady, but I've been wanting to get our sheets and blankets washed and the dust beaten out of the quilts. Although," she added, frowning, "the Lord knows why. I'm sure there will be another storm along soon to get them full of dust and dirt again. But so far, it's a clear day and the wind is warm. The bedding will dry fast."

She paused and looked down at her hands and then back at him, with dark, troubled eyes. "I'm sorry I don't have the strength to help you, son."

Brady started to tell his mom it was okay, but his dad interrupted in a deep, growl of a voice, like he was mad about something. "He'll do it, Lydia."

Anger flashed in Brady. Who did his dad think he was anyhow? Some jerk! Sure, he'd do it! He would do it right now before he even went out to check his traps.

Brady set the wash tubs out under the clothes line and filled one with warm soapy water. The other, the rinse tub, he filled with clear, cool water. After he had the bedding washed and drying on the clothes line, he carried out the quilts and hanging them over the extra line, in back of the house, began beating out the dirt and dust with the rug beater.

He worked as hard and as fast as he could, but it was late morning and well past time to check his traps when he was through with the bedding.

He didn't like to leave his traps so long. He hated to see an animal caught in a trap, even a prairie dog, and he tried to end its suffering as quickly as possible.

Brady wiped the sleeve of his shirt across his sweaty face and hurried into the house to tell his mother he'd return as soon as possible.

His mother was peeling potatoes from a bowl on her lap. Sarah sat on the floor beside her chair, her legs tucked under her, wiggling her fingers and making her little clicking sounds.

A smell he had not smelled for a long, long time filled the room, a wonderful, sweet smell.

"Is that a cake?" he asked, hardly believing it could be true, and yet knowing it was, and she had made it for him.

His mother didn't have the strength to do anything extra and here she had made him a cake. "You shouldn't have done that," he said.

"It's your birthday, isn't it?" His mother smiled and held out a chunk of raw peeled potato. "It's not every day my son turns thirteen."

"Thanks, Mom." Brady grinned and took the potato from her hand. "You shouldn't have done it, but I'm glad you did." He shook the salt shaker over the potato and took a bite. "I've got to go check my traps, if it's okay."

"Of course." She smiled. "You didn't ask, but aren't you curious to know if that's a chocolate cake in the oven?"

"It had better be," Brady answered with a grin. "You know it's my favorite." She grinned back at him. "It is. I'll open a jar of beef and make gravy for your birthday supper. These," she indicated the bowl of potatoes in her lap, "will be mashed with cream and lots of butter. How does that sound?"

"Great!" Brady's mouth watered at the thought of eating chocolate cake and he loved mashed potatoes and gravy. He sure hoped the dust didn't blow today. He would hate to have his birthday supper, especially his cake, peppered with grit.

He took another chunk of potato from his mother's hand and salted it. "You aren't too tired to do all that, are you, Mom?"

"I'm all right," she said, but she coughed a little as she said it. "We'll have a bite to eat here as soon as you get back from tending your traps." Her voice weakened on her last words and she wheezed a little, coughing again, her hand covering her mouth.

"Maybe I'd better wait," Brady said.

"I'll be all right." She smiled a little lopsided smile. "If you would get me a drink of water, please."

She took a few sips from the glass and, waving her hand, dismissed him. "Go," she said. He knew she had tried to speak aloud, but that one little word came out a whisper.

He heard her try to muffle another cough as he went outside. He stood on the back steps and waited, listening. In a few minutes, he heard her cough again and again, and each cough sounded harsher. His own throat tightened. He stood for a minute longer and then opened the door to the kitchen.

"Are you all right, Mom?" he asked.

She was standing, bent over the table, her arms crossed in front of her holding herself tight against the harsh coughs shaking her body. Her eyes teared as she choked and gasped for breath. She looked up at Brady, and her tearing eyes were full of fear.

Brady ran to the cupboard and grabbed up her medicine bottle. His hand rattled around in the silverware drawer, located a spoon, dropped it on the floor and reached for another.

It seemed an eternity before his mother's coughing eased. He helped her into the living room where she sank down on the davenport, still wheezing and coughing. He brought her a wet washcloth to wipe the sweat and tears from her face.

"I'm sorry, Brady," she whispered.

"Don't, Mom," he said. "Just be quiet. I'll get some pillows to prop up your head if you want to lie down."

She was quiet for awhile, and then in the midst of another coughing spell she remembered the cake. Brady ran to pull it out of the oven. It had burned a little at the edges.

When his mother finally quit coughing, she drifted off to sleep. Brady went back to the kitchen and put the potatoes she had peeled in a pan of cold water to stay fresh.

He was slicing a loaf of bread to make a peanut butter and jelly sandwich for Sarah and himself, when his mother pushed open the kitchen door.

"I feel better now," she said. "I'm weak as a kitten, but I feel better." She sat down at the table. "Thank you, Brady."

"It's okay, Mom." He saw how thin she'd become and how the shadows had deepened under her dark eyes. He swallowed a lump of fear. "Do you want a sandwich, too?" he asked.

For awhile they ate in silence. Seeing the food, Sarah had come to the table without protest. Evidently she was hungry.

"Did Dad take his dinner to the fields today?" Brady asked, breaking the silence.

"Yes. He knew you would be home today. I wish he didn't feel the need to check on me so often. She gave Brady that same little lopsided smile she had given him earlier, "But I'm glad you were here today. I'm just sorry I kept you so long from your traps."

"Which reminds me, I'd better get going," he said, pushing back from the table.

Outside, he whistled for his dog and started off toward the fields. Taggart ran in wild, excited circles around him and then raced off to bark his delight to the open fields and the warm sun shining in the bright blue sky.

Brady hurried with his traps, trotting from one to the other. In the distance he could hear the hum of the tractor. His dad was working the north field today trying to protect the wheat there. He was pulling the one-way disk plow behind the tractor making the deep furrows that were supposed to help hold the soil when the winds came. The wheat planted last September had been eaten by grasshoppers, and they'd had to replant in October. Some of that seed had blown away in the wind. Now it was April and they'd be lucky if the little bit of wheat that remained survived into summer.

Their wheat harvests had been increasingly poor the last four or five years. It had been a long time since they'd needed the crews of men and half-grown boys his dad used to hire to work the harvest. They used to cut wheat all day long, working until darkness brought them in from the fields. And if drenching rains or hard-hitting hail didn't ruin the crop, they'd have wagon-loads of threshed wheat, shiny as gold in the sunlight, to sell to the elevator in town. He'd loved it all, but he thought he enjoyed meal time most of all with the crew kidding each other, and him, while they stuffed themselves with his mother's good cooking. They hadn't needed a harvest crew at all the last few years, and they wouldn't need one this year either. This year of 1935, his thirteenth, looked, his dad said, like it might be the worse one yet.

He had heard his dad tell Mr. Conners, Jim's dad, that he'd be lucky to get three bushels this year. *Three damn bushels!* The angry bitterness in his dad's voice had made a knot of fear in the pit of his stomach, and the curse word had shocked him. Brady swore sometimes. Not at home, but around his friends, a kind of showing off, he knew. But it was what fellas did when they got together. He had to be careful not to say those words around home. Mr. Conners cussed sometimes, but his dad never swore. He would have bet anything that his dad wouldn't swear even if he hit his thumb with a hammer. But the wheat ... He had cursed about the wheat.

He thought about how upset he'd been at his dad this morning for cutting in and not giving him a chance to tell his mom he'd do the quilts and bedding for her. He should have thought about how worried his dad must be with Mom so sick and the wheat so bad.

It was no wonder his dad got gruff and butted in sometimes.

A sudden wave of sympathy brought with it the sting of remorse, and he turned toward the sound of the tractor, breaking into a dog trot. He would just get close enough to wave to his dad and then hurry back to stay with his mother.

As he topped a rise and looked down the slope of land stretched before him, he saw his dad riding the tractor in the far end of the field. Brady waved his hand high over his head.

"I guess he didn't see me," he said aloud when his father failed to respond to his wave. Taggart cocked his head and looked up at him. Grinning, Brady scratched the big dog's ears.

He waited, waving every time it looked as if his dad was looking his way. Finally, he decided he'd better get back to his mother and started to turn away when he saw a rabbit break cover and run a zig-zag course across a field. Taggart saw it too, and dashed off after it, barking.

Brady looked to see if his dad had heard Taggart's bark above the whine of the tractor, but his dad kept plowing furrows and gave no sign that he had heard the dog or had seen Brady.

Brady whistled for Taggart, and in a few minutes the dog was at his side.

A stiff little breeze had come up, and tiny whirlwinds of dirt twirled along the rows of sickly looking wheat. Some Russian thistles quivered and began to move with the wind, tumbling end over end across the fields. Old wheat chaff and dry grasses lifted up from the long rows of straggly wheat and sailed through the air. Suddenly, a sharp gust of wind whipped at Brady's pant legs, died down, and rose again, stronger, wilder.

The sky's blue had faded to chalk, and the sunlight looked smoky. Apprehension prickling the hairs on the back of his neck and along his bare forearms, Brady swung around and to his horror saw a wall of black rising up on the horizon. Like a giant thundercloud, it was fast filling the sky.

He stared at the coming storm as the wind eddied little dust whirlwinds about his feet.

He had always been able to get inside when the big storms hit. Now he was at least a mile from home, and so was his dad! Already he felt suffocated, the air growing thicker by the second. He reached for his handkerchief, and then remembered he had left it at home on the dresser in his room. He felt the clammy touch of fear.

He had to get home to his mother! She would need him to hang the wet sheets at the windows for her! But his dad hadn't yet seen the wall of dirt coming toward them. He needed to warn his dad!

Brady looked again at the towering cloud. It was growing fast! Too fast! *He had to act now!* He turned and ran back, waving his arms and yelling, "Dad! Dad!" Taggart ran beside him, barking.

Suddenly the tractor motor died and Brady saw his dad leap from the seat and run toward him in long, loping strides. He stopped and waited. Taggart circled him nervously while the wind swirled dust all around them. He rolled down his shirt sleeves and buttoning the cuffs, raised his arm and buried his nose and mouth in the crook of his elbow. Then his dad was beside him, whipping his handkerchief from his overalls and tying it over Brady's nose and mouth.

Brady felt his face go red with shame. It was stupid of him to leave his handkerchief at home. Now his dad would have to breathe in more of the suffocating dirt. How he wished he could give it back, but he knew his dad wouldn't take it.

They ran, his dad giving him a shove that almost sent him sprawling, and at the same time yelling something lost in the roar of the wind.

The air thickened until his dad was only a hazy shadow running beside him. Taggart ran ahead, disappeared into the storm and then emerged to circle them and bark as if telling them to hurry, before darting off again.

In the distance, Brady could, at times, just make out the shape of the house and the barn. And then, without warning, the storm threw a curtain of black around them. The darkness was so complete that for one panic-stricken moment, Brady thought he had gone suddenly blind. Even his dad had been swallowed up in the dust-filled darkness.

Brady stopped, his heart hammering. He could see nothing, not even his hand held up to his face. Fear gripped him, and then a flood of relief washed over him when he felt his dad's hand take his in a firm, steady grip. With hands joined, they stumbled through the dark mass of the storm.

Brady began to feel disorientated, his legs rubbery and weak. He gripped his dad's hand tighter and felt an answering squeeze. Suddenly, Brady stumbled and fell, breaking loose from his father's hand. He staggered to his feet, frantic with fear. His arms failing about, hit only stinging particles of dirt. Inside his head he was screaming silent screams, "Dad! Dad!" *But his father was gone. He was alone!*

He dropped to his knees and crawled in circles, one hand extended before him, searching, groping. Every few seconds he stopped and raised up on his knees, swinging his arms in wide circles. They hit nothing but stinging dirt.

After awhile he stopped. A wave of hopelessness washed over him and he slumped forward, his forehead hitting the ground. His arms wrapped about his head, he gave in to sobs of despair. He knew that the thick choking dirt would soon cover him ... suffocate him ... but he couldn't get up ... couldn't go on.

Then anger came from somewhere deep inside him, rearing him up on his knees and fueling a silent howl of rage. He raised his fists, swinging wild punches as if those punches might make a hole in the strangling wall of dirt.

Then his fists touched something! *Something!* He reached out again, hope filling him, and his dad's hands gripped his arm and pulled him to his feet and into a crushing embrace. A sobbing cry escaped Brady's clenched teeth. They gripped hands and blindly staggered on.

Now Brady remembered Sammy Johnson, a little seven-year-old neighbor boy, found in his own pasture the day after a dust storm. His body, caught up against a barbed wire fence, had been covered over with dirt and Russian thistles.

Sometimes Brady thought he glimpsed quick, short flashes of light, but they seemed to dance randomly, so they couldn't be the fence line. He had heard people tell of following their fence lines home, guided by the flashes of static electricity bouncing off the barbed wire. He had heard them swear that they would have been lost otherwise.

Maybe little Sammy had tried to follow his fences, too. But being so little, the dust and dirt had overwhelmed him. They needed to find a fence or something to guide them home. If they didn't get to shelter soon, this storm would smother them. Just like the storm last year had smothered Sammy Johnson.

"No!" Silently, he scolded himself. *"Don't think that! Or anything! Just move! Keep a hold of Dad's hand and keep moving!"*

But it was hard not to think of what might happen. Hard to fight the panic trying to overtake him. *If they didn't find shelter soon, they wouldn't make it. Mom and Sarah would be alone.* But even as those thoughts took form in his mind, he bumped into something solid! Something big! *A building!*

He felt his father's hand squeeze his, and a great swelling tide of emotion washed over him. *They were safe! Oh, yes! They were safe! Whatever this building was, it had to have a door!*

They moved along the building. Brady ran his hand over the wall, as he knew his father was doing, feeling for the door.

Suddenly, his father let go of his hand, and a gap opened in the dark swirl of dirt. Brady stumbled through the opening and fell sprawling on the rough barn floor.

3

GASPING AND COUGHING, Brady raised his head up off the floor and pulled the handkerchief, caked with dirt and spit, from his face. Beside him, his dad, up on his knees and bent nearly double, was making harsh, strangling sounds as he coughed and spit and gagged.

Brady struggled to sit up and then was caught again in a fit of coughing and gagging and sneezing. Black dirt came from his mouth and sprayed out of his nose. Something balled up in his throat, choking him, and he coughed again, harder, and brought up a black, muddy mass of dirt and spit. That made him feel a little better and strong enough to get to his feet. He looked down at his dad whose continued coughing and gagging worried him. His dad had probably swallowed twice what he would have if he hadn't given up his handkerchief. Every spasm of his dad's body stabbed Brady with guilt and fear. He hoped he hadn't breathed in so much dirt and dust that he was getting dust pneumonia. Dust pneumonia was another hazard of the dust storms, and it was as deadly as the regular kind.

Finally, his dad's coughing began to ease, and as he struggled to get to his feet, Brady reached out his hand to help him. His dad's unsteadiness worried him, and when another coughing spasm shook his lean frame and he slumped back against the barn wall, Brady was certain his dad was in trouble. But a few minutes later, he wiped his shirt sleeve across his dirt-streaked face and flashed a quick grin at Brady.

"That was some storm," he croaked out in a ragged, whispery voice. "Are you all right, son?"

"I'm all right." Relief made him suddenly weak in the knees and his answering grin slipped from his face.

Relieved now of his fear for his dad, Brady suddenly remembered Taggart. The dog had been with them, at least until the storm had wiped out all sight. Had they shut him out when they closed the barn door?

Brady started toward the door, at the same time realizing how stupid that would be. The minute he opened the door, the swirling dirt would blast in on them, and Taggart, after all this time, would not be waiting outside. He just had to hope that his dog had made it to shelter and wasn't still wandering around in the storm.

He had heard of cattle drifting with the storm, just as they did in snow blizzards. If they ran up against a fence, they stayed there, bunched up together, and there they would die, suffocated, their nostrils packed with dirt. He had heard of cows dying all right, but never a dog.

He looked up at his dad, still leaning against the barn wall and still coughing a little now and then.

"Do you think Taggart got home okay?" he asked.

"I don't know, but I bet he made it to some kind of shelter." He brushed a cloud of dirt from his sleeves and, unbuttoning one at the wrist, wiped his face with the loose sleeve. "It's your mother and Sarah I'm worried about now."

"I know," Brady said.

He knew the dirt was filling the house despite the rags and newspapers they kept stuffed into every crack in the windows and doors and the blanket that hung from his window and the rest of the rooms upstairs, as well as the ones in the parlor and in Sarah's old room. All of those rooms, except his, were closed off all the time now. His folks had moved Sarah into their room just a week ago.

His mother could not have hung the blankets at the rest

of the windows, but she might have been able to stuff the rags and towels under the back door, which was all they used now. He and his dad had nailed thin slats of wood over rags stuffed around the edges of the front door so it no longer opened.

Remembering how his mother had coughed this morning when the sky had still been clear, he thought she must be in terrible trouble now. A shiver of fear coursed through him and quick tears stung his eyes.

His dad was moving about the barn, empty now of livestock and hay. The mules, sold several years ago, had been replaced by the tractor, which now sat in the field at the mercy of the blowing dirt. They would be lucky if the dirt didn't ruin the engine by the time this storm was over.

Spitting out more dirt that had worked up into the saliva in his mouth, Brady looked at the stalls where the cows once stood, chewing hay and giving up buckets of sweet, foamy milk.

They were all gone now. The government men had taken the stronger ones to feed lots. The weak ones, those starved from lack of feed or sick from eating grass and hay peppered with dirt, had been shot. He had helped his dad butcher a young beef cow, and his mother had canned the meat. They had buried the rest of the dead cattle in the now barren pasture back of the barn.

In his mind, Brady could still see those bony creatures crumpling with each rifle shot and the stronger ones, wall-eyed and mooing, being loaded into trucks. At the government feed lots they would be fattened up and then slaughtered, the meat canned and distributed to the needy.

The government check hadn't been much, but it had helped pay off their last field of mortgaged land. Brady had often heard his dad say how much he appreciated President Roosevelt helping the farmer. He approved of the work programs the government was setting up to help folks, not just here in Kansas, but all over the country.

Franklin Delano Roosevelt had won the presidency by a landslide, and his fireside chats on the radio were beginning to give people hope. His programs were helping them keep their homes and buy food for their children. But he wasn't getting help to everyone, not yet.

Every night, the news on the radio was full of problems brought on by these hard times: people out of work, drifting from place to place, some on foot, some in cars, and some riding the freight trains that rumbled across the country. Some of the homeless, the jobless, lived in cardboard and tarpaper shacks, called Hoovervilles, named after the last president, whom people blamed for this depression.

"A chicken in every pot," President Hoover had promised, but, instead, the hard times grew worse and people were starving.

"President Roosevelt is near God to folks," Brady had heard his dad say many times.

"Some of the folks around here — folks we know — have jobs working the roads, instead of having to take to the road, because of the KERC."

Every program the government started was known by initials. The KERC was the Kansas Emergency Relief Committee. The cattle program that had paid his dad for their cattle was the DRS, which stood for the Drought Relief Service. There was a wheat program, too, which paid farmers to leave some of their acreage unplanted. It was called the Triple A, or AAA, which stood for the Agricultural Adjustment Administration. His dad had signed up for that program, too.

"Ordinarily, I'm not for so much government interference," his dad had said. "But these are unusual times. People have got to have help." Brady thought his dad had looked embarrassed. But then, his face had cleared and he'd added, "Well, I've always paid my taxes."

"Brady." His dad's voice brought him back from his thoughts. His dad had gone up into the empty haymow a few minutes ago and now, coming down the ladder, said, "I'm going to try to get to the house."

"But, Dad, it's still blowing." Everywhere he looked, Brady could see the dirt shifting in, deepening the dark, hazy atmosphere of the barn and piling up in little ridges on the floor.

"Up in the haymow, I could see sparks from the windmill," his dad said. "They're shooting off those steel blades like fireworks on the Fourth of July. I'm going to use them as a guide to get to the house."

Several coiled ropes hung on the barn wall. He took them down and, shaking out the coils, knotted the ends together. "I'll feel my way around to the corral and tie this rope to a rail. I'll hang on to the other end, and if I keep those sparks from the windmill to my left, I should hit the house." He paused a moment and then added, "If I miss, I'll have the rope to find my way back."

"What'll I do?" Brady asked.

"I think you had better stay here."

"So I can worry about you? And Mom and Sarah, too? And Taggart?" He had added the dog as an afterthought, but he was pretty worried about him. "This storm could last for hours. I can't stay here, Dad. Not if you don't stay, too."

His dad looked at him for a long moment. Finally, he said, "Okay, You can tie a rope to me to hang on to. That should work."

He handed Brady a short piece of rope and turned his back. "Loop it through my overall straps and tie it tight. Then get a good grip on your end. Wind it around your hand several times because you can't let go."

Brady tied the rope tight. "Okay, Dad, I'm ready."

His dad looked back over his shoulder at him and grinned a small, crooked grin. "Well, let's go then, partner," he said.

Brady's answering grin ended in a grimace as the movement of his face tightened the now cold, clammy and filthy handkerchief his dad had insisted he tie back over his nose and mouth. It had gagged him to put it back on, but his dad was letting him go, so he wasn't about to argue.

They pushed open the barn door and stepped out into the dark pit of swirling, stinging dirt.

Slowly, blindly, they edged their way along the side of the barn until they came to the corner. The corral extended beyond the barn, and as they moved out from the semi-shelter of the building, the full blast of the storm engulfed them. His dad's hazy shape vanished. Brady tightened his grip on the lifeline in his hand.

When his dad stopped to tie the rope to the corral rail, Brady bumped against him, drew back and waited. Now he could see the sparks — quick, flashing, jagged lights — bouncing off what had to be the windmill's big, steel blades. But the windmill itself, like everything else, was obliterated by the storm.

He waited while his dad tied the rope around a corral rail. A job, Brady knew, he was doing blindly. When he felt his dad turn away by the tightening of the rope in his hands, Brady followed after him, his head down against the onslaught of the storm.

Although the storm still blew the dirt relentlessly and the pit of blackness was as dark as ever, this time it didn't seem quite so bad to Brady. Now they had a lifeline. Now they knew which way to go, thanks to the flashes of light from the windmill. In a little while, a faint, yellow glow shone through the darkness, and he knew his mother had set a lamp in the window to guide them.

"Jack! Brady!" his mother cried, yanking down the handkerchief she'd tied over her face and hugging them. "Oh, I was so worried. I put a lamp in the window... And then Taggart came home ... And you ... you ..." her voice faltered and huge tears gathered in her eyes.

With his mother holding him so close, Brady could hear the wheezing sound of her breath and feel the heavy, rapid rise and fall of her chest. Gently he slipped out of her embrace and unwound the rope that tethered him to his father. Bending down, he wrapped his arms about Taggart's neck. "You ol' dog," he muttered, his face against Taggart's black coat. "You ol' dog." It was all he could say without blubbering like a baby. For gosh sakes, what was wrong with him? They were all safe now, weren't they?

Brady and his dad gathered up the sheets and blankets and wetting them down, hung them at the windows. While his dad filled the wash basin and began to wash off the worst of the dirt from his face and arms, Brady waited his turn, scratching his dog's ears and watching Sarah.

She sat in a chair pulled out from the end of the table, her shoulders hunched a little as she studied her tiny hands, flipping them palm side up and then back again. If he strained to hear, he could just make out the soft, repetitious clickings of her tongue. The handkerchief their mother tried to get her to wear during a dust storm was, as usual, pulled down around her neck.

He turned away, wondering, as always, why his mother used to try so hard with Sarah. It had never done the least bit of good. She'd only wasted her time showing her things, like colors from an old box of crayons, or touching an object and saying its name. She used to sing to Sarah, too, but she didn't do that anymore either. Now she struggled just to breathe.

His mother took the lamp from the window and set it back on the table. Its light, a hazy, yellow circle on the table top, barely penetrated the deep shadows in the room. Dust particles, swirling slowly in the circle of lamplight, grew thicker as this storm, that had so quickly changed daylight to darkness, sifted an ever-growing film of fine dirt into the house. And outside, what little white was left of the paint that had once graced their two-story house was being scoured off to blow away in the wind.

"Son." His dad's voice startled him. "You can wash now." His dad's grin flashed in his clean, scrubbed face. "I got enough dirt off of me to plant a small garden. But hurry, your mother has our supper ready."

It was then Brady remembered his birthday and the chocolate cake, and as if his mother had read his thoughts, she smiled a wan, weak smile.

"Your cake's wrapped in tea towels," she said, her words coming out haltingly around her now constant gasps for air. "Potatoes ..." she paused... "meat together." Her last words were barely a whisper, and her chest heaved in her efforts to get enough air. Tears welled up in her eyes. At the table, she tried to eat, but finally laid her fork down.

Sarah wandered the room, showing no interest in food. Brady and his dad dished out their own portions of meat and potatoes in small amounts, each time quickly replacing the lid on the kettle. Still Brady could taste the dust and feel the fine sand-like grit between his teeth, but he was too hungry to let it bother him much.

They had filled his mother's canning jars with water for their meal, unscrewing the lids and drinking, and then quickly recapping them again. A hopelessness, heavy with silence, had filled the room so his mother's breathing and coughing seemed to grow louder and raspier. Brady thought he could not bear it any longer and cast around in his head for something to say to break the heavy silence. Taking a drink of water from his jar and quickly recapping it, he thought of the jokes people told about the dust storms and the drought. Thinking to lighten the mood, he said, "We should get some cheese-cloth to cover these jars so we don't have to strain the water through our teeth."

He had meant it as a joke, but his mother just looked stricken. She started to speak, but a coughing spasm overtook her. His dad jumped up and hovered over her. She had already taken her medicine. He couldn't give her more.

"Sorry," he murmured, but no one seemed to hear him.

He hadn't meant to upset her. He had just been trying to make light of this dust and dirt. Folks were all the time saying things like how the crows had taken to flying backwards to keep the dirt out of their eyes, and how they'd heard of a farmer who had fainted dead away when a drop of rain fell on him and they'd had to throw a bucket of sand in his face to bring him around again.

Brady sat, feeling miserable, willing his mother to stop coughing. He wanted to tell her how sorry he was for making stupid remarks. But when her coughing finally eased, she was so worn out his dad had to help her into bed.

His dad came back to the door of the bedroom a few minutes later and said, "Your cake is in the cabinet. Help yourself, if you want some. Your mother said she didn't get it frosted."

"That's all right." He wasn't hungry any more anyway. Not even for chocolate cake, frosted or unfrosted. Maybe, if it wasn't too full of dirt by tomorrow, they could eat it then. With a heavy sigh, Brady got to his feet, put water from the tea kettle into the dish pan and began clearing the table.

Afterwards, he read awhile, hunched over the table, his book shoved up under the pool of lamplight. Taggart sat on his haunches beside him, resting his big head on Brady's knee. But Brady soon had to close his book, his eyes tearing too much from the dirt and dust in the room to read. He tapped lightly at the door of his parents' room. "Good-night, Dad," he whispered when his father opened the door. His mother lay on the bed, her head propped high on pillows, her eyes closed. Sarah, in her little bed, was sound asleep.

Taggart followed Brady upstairs to his room. Feeling his way across the floor, Brady patted the dresser top until he found the box of matches he kept there. Striking one, he lit the small coal oil lamp on the stand by his bed.

He thought of his traps as he pulled the prairie dog tails from his pocket and tossed them into a sack on his dresser. He would have to search carefully tomorrow, or whenever this storm ended, as most of his traps would be completely covered with drifted dirt.

As usual, he had not made his bed, and knowing his mother wouldn't know if he had or not, he'd not washed his bedding this morning either. He couldn't see that it made much difference. The dust storms probably blew in as much or more than was ever washed out. He brushed the dirt and dust from his bed, sneezing and coughing until his eyes and nose ran. Pulling off his shoes and overalls, he crawled in between the gritty covers. Taggart leaped up on the bed and turned around several times before settling down beside him.

Brady sat up in bed awhile, his pillow bunched up behind his back, and sharpened his jackknife. As he worked the blade over a small whetstone in tight circular motions, spitting on the stone several times to create friction, he thought about the day. It hadn't been the best birthday in the world, but he guessed not the worst either. At least he and his dad had survived the dust storm. Maybe his mother would feel okay in the morning when the storm died down.

That thought had barely formed when he heard his mother begin again her harsh, labored coughing. He waited, listening, hoping ... After a while he laid down his knife and whetstone and blew out the lamp. Curled up next to Taggart, he tried to dull the sound with sleep.

4

TAGGART'S DAMP NOSE and a dream that his dad was calling him woke Brady. He kicked back the covers, forgetting what the storm would have blown in during the night, and was showered with a fine, gritty dirt. Sneezing and coughing, he groped his way across the darkened room and tore down the blanket covering the window. The pale morning light filtered through the dusty window pane.

    He pushed up the window and brushed out the dirt piled up on the sill. Then he scooped up as much as he could off the floor and tossed it out on the desert-like landscape below.

    There was no wind this morning, just a cool stillness, as if the wind, exhausted from the storm, now slept. The sun, not yet over the horizon, was painting the sky with a rosy hue. Dirt lay over everything. Like snow, following a blizzard, the mounds of dirt had been sculpted into swirled shapes by the wind and had banked up against the side of the house and the base of the cottonwood tree outside his window. The tree had not survived the winter. The last few years of hot, dry weather, smothering dirt, and high winds had taken its toll. This spring, instead of green, budding leaves, the branches stretched black and barren against the morning sky.

    Closing the window, Brady crossed the room and pulled a clean shirt from the dresser drawer. Shaking out the fine dirt that had filtered in on all his clothes, he put on the shirt and slipped the straps of his overalls up over his shoulders.

His mother was up, sitting at the kitchen table, when he came down the stairs. His dad stood at the stove stirring oatmeal, a cup of coffee in his hand.

"Good morning," Brady said as he passed through the kitchen and out the back door for a quick trip to the toilet. Taggart ran over to the hedge of lilacs. The bushes had leafed out, but the flower buds had never formed. There would be no scented purple blossoms this spring.

It was a cool morning and Brady shivered a little on his way back to the house. As he entered the kitchen, he realized suddenly that something was wrong. His dad still stood by the stove. His mother still sat at the kitchen table. But they were both looking at him like they had something to tell him. He looked around for Sarah. She was not in the room. Fear grabbed him with an ice-cold hand.

"Here, son, wash and we'll have some breakfast." His father lifted the tea kettle from the stove and filled the washbasin with warm water. *That was odd. His father waiting on him.*

He washed quickly, splashing the water over his face and dampening down his dark hair. Emptying his wash water in the bucket beside the washstand, he turned to face his parents. Taking a deep breath, fear making his voice shaky, he said, "What's wrong? Where's Sarah?"

"She's sleeping," his dad said. "Come. Sit down, son. Your mother and I have something to tell you. We've been up most of the night. We've settled now on what we're going to do."

"Settled?" Brady asked, puzzled.

He sat down at the table with a quick glance at his mother. She tried to smile, but her lips trembled and the smile slid away.

"Son," his dad began. "Your mother's asthma is getting worse. She had a terrible night last night. I would have taken her in to the doctor, but I couldn't, not with the storm so bad. By morning we both knew she had to get out of this country."

"Oh," Brady said, relief coursing through him. He didn't know what he had thought, except that it was something really terrible.

"Where will you go, Mom?" he asked.

She shook her head and looked at his dad.

For a fraction of a second, his dad hesitated. "I'm taking your mother to California."

"California!" Brady was astounded. "How? Are we driving?" He grinned, seeing in his mind the four of them in the Ford sedan traveling across the open plains to the mountains and down to the beaches and the rolling ocean waves. His mother would get well in the California sunshine, and when the rains came again they could come back home.

"Yes. That's how your mother and I are going. You and Sarah are going to Grandpa Bud's in Sentinel."

"Grandpa Bud's?" Brady was puzzled. "How is he going to take care of Sarah?"

"His sister, your mother's Aunt Matilda, was recently widowed. She lives with him now and she will see to Sarah."

"But what will you and Mom do in California? And why can't I go? Why can't we just leave Sarah with Grandpa Bud?"

All this time his mother had not said a word. Now she stood and, coming around the table, took Brady's hand between her small, thin ones. "You know I wouldn't do this if I had a choice," she said softly. "I would take you and Sarah both with us, if I could. But Sarah ..." Tears filled her eyes. Tears she blinked quickly away. "You know we can't take Sarah. And it's not fair to Aunt Tilly and your grandpa to have her without any help at all. They'll need you, son."

"Okay, Mom." His defenses melted and he stood and put his arms around her, a lump rising up in his throat. Then a surprising discovery dissolved the lump. Standing there, hugging his mother, he realized he could look over the top of her head.

"Look," he said, patting his mother's dark hair, so near

the color of his own, "I just outgrew you, Mom."

His mother laughed a tiny, husky sound and kissed him.

Brady finished getting breakfast ready while his dad got Sarah up and dressed. As usual, she fought him, screaming as if he were hurting her. Brady saw his mother start to her feet several times and then sit back again, an anxious look on her face. For the first time he realized how hard it was for her to no longer have the strength to dress Sarah.

Sarah's hair, cut short so it hardly even needed a comb or brush, made a halo of golden curls around her head. Her eyes, so blue and innocently sweet, make her look cuter even than Shirley Temple, the child movie star. If Sarah could just have been normal, Brady thought, they could all go to California and maybe, as cute as she is, she could even become a Hollywood star. But Sarah wasn't normal and that was that.

With a heavy sigh, he picked up a tea towel and began taking cups and bowls out of the cupboard for their breakfast, wiping them free of dust and grit before setting them on the table. Earlier, his dad had wiped down the walls and swept the floor, emptying several dustpans full outside the door. Afterwards he'd wiped the dirt from the outside window panes so the morning sun could shine through.

Brady went out to check his traps and help his dad bring the tractor in from the fields. The traps were empty, all but one sprung, and all but that one buried deep under the drifted dirt. The prairie dogs had reopened their holes, drifted shut by the storms, and he reset the traps at the entrances before taking off across the fields to help his dad.

His dad had the tractor shoveled clear and was brushing the dirt from the engine with an old paint brush and some rags he'd brought from the barn when Brady arrived. Together, they changed the oil, drained the gas tank and the water from the radiator, and refilled each from the cans his dad had brought from the storage shed. Brady held his breath as his dad climbed up on the seat. "Hey," he yelled when the engine started.

His dad grinned. "Hop aboard, son," he said. "We're off to the barn."

Brady rode standing on the back of the tractor as his dad drove through the fields past the pale, shriveled stalks of dead and dying wheat poking out of the drifts of dust and dirt.

At the house, Brady's mother met them at the door, an anxious expression on her face.

"I tried to call Dad again. He's not in the office and not expected back until this afternoon. Aunt Tilly's not at home either, so I don't know when they've decided to come for Brady and Sarah."

"I'll call him from town, Lydia." Brady watched his dad put his arm around his mother and draw her close. "Don't worry so much, dear."

"I try not to, " she said, leaning against him for a moment. "But it's hard."

Brady fixed dinner while his dad drove to the neighboring farm for Mrs. Brewster. While he and his dad were in town today, she would stay with his mom and Sarah.

The roads had been graded by the time they left for town, but in a few places the wind had sifted some of the dirt back onto the roads. On their way, his dad filled him in on the rest of their plans.

"As soon as Grandpa Bud comes for you and Sarah, your mother and I will head out for California."

"What will you do when you get to there?" Brady asked.

"I'm not sure. We have a little savings, but I'll need to get work. The Cromwells have a son out there. He's supporting his family by picking fruit." He shrugged. "I don't know. But something will come up."

"Sure," Brady said. There were so many people going west. West where the dust didn't blow and where they might find jobs. It bothered him to think of his parents, especially his mother, joining that throng of ragged, thread-bare people. He saw them in town, sometimes, and on the road going past their farm. Weary looking people in old jalopies with all they owned strapped to the sides and the top, or pulled in a makeshift cart behind. Usually there were several skinny kids peering out from behind the boxes and bundles, and often a gaunt, rangy dog trotted along side.

"Dusted out and flat broke," they traveled the country looking for work and the chance to live and raise their families. Okies, he'd heard they were called. He hadn't liked the sound of the word, or the way it was said, like they were a trashy kind of people that nobody could trust. At first he had thought the word meant just Oklahoma people, but few of them came through here, even though they were only, as his dad said, "a stone's throw" from the Oklahoma line. But his dad said it meant all people down on their luck and hard-pressed to feed themselves and their families. He said folks didn't like seeing them because it made them feel sad and guilty, too, for what they had, even if it wasn't much.

If his dad couldn't find work in California, Brady thought, and they had to use all their savings and maybe live out of the car, would folks in California call his parents O*kies?*

"We'll go south," his dad said, interrupting Brady's thoughts, "and cut across the corner of Oklahoma and the Texas panhandle. We'll hit highway 66 at Tucumcari, New Mexico, and from there go straight west to California."

"It sounds like a long ways," Brady said.

His father nodded. "It is," he said.

At the edge of town, Brady was surprised when his dad pulled off on a rough washboard of a road and stopped in front of a railroad boxcar. Several small children looked up from their play beneath the barren limbs of a cottonwood tree and scrambled to their feet. They darted up the steps and disappeared through the open boxcar door.

"Come on, Brady," his dad said, getting out of the car. "I want you to meet the Harkins family."

As they approached the boxcar, a tall man appeared in the doorway. Grinning widely, he came down the steps and extended his hand to Brady's dad. "Well, Jack Foster!" he exclaimed, "What brings you to these parts?" Then without waiting for an answer, he hollered back over his shoulder, "Rosealee! Jack Foster and his son are here."

Rosealee Harkins appeared at the open door wiping her hands on her apron, her round face full of smiles. Behind her, Brady could see small faces peek at them from around her ample body.

"Morning, Missus," Brady's father said touching his hat brim. Then he turned back to Tim Harkins. "We've decided to leave, Tim," he said. "Lydia can't take any more of this dust. So if you're still willing to move out to our place and look after things, I would sure appreciate it."

"You bet, I'm willing and then some," Tim Harkins said.

"I'll tell them at the courthouse to send the allotment from the Triple A program to you then," Brady's dad said.

"Oh, thank you! Thank you!" Mrs. Hawkins lifted a corner of her apron and wiped at her eyes. "Oh, Tim. Our prayers have been answered."

On the way back to town, his dad told Brady that the Harkins had farmed on the Daley place, renting it from George Daley. But when the Triple A allotment checks started coming to Tim, George decided he had better take the farm back and get the checks himself.

Tim and Rosealee were just barely scraping by and didn't have any place to go. The railroad was selling old boxcars for twenty-five dollars, so Tim bought one and moved his family into it. "It's shelter," his dad continued, "but not much else. It's hotter than the hubs of Hades in summer and colder than the Devil's own breath in winter. They're good people. Tim will do all he can to save our land."

As his dad parked the car into the curb at the courthouse, he added, "Rosealee and the kids might as well enjoy our big house. It's better to keep life in it anyway. An empty house doesn't seem to hold up very well. So they'll be helping us more than we'll be helping them."

As Brady entered the County Clerk's office, Miss Cornish flashed her warm, heart-stopping smile at him. "Well, hello," she said. "How many tails do you have today?"

"Twenty-six," Brady said, setting the sack down on her desk.

He grinned as she picked up the sack with thumb and forefinger and set it on a low cabinet near her desk. She counted out his fifty-two cents, frowning as she handed him the money. "I'm sorry," she said, but the county funds for paying bounties are about depleted." "We can't pay out any more after this month."

Brady opened his mouth to tell her that he was leaving anyway, so it didn't matter to him, but something kind of jumped up and closed off his throat, so he just nodded and turned away.

Outside, Jim Conners was coming up the walk with his sack in hand. "Hi, Brady," he said grinning. "How much money did you get?"

"Fifty-two cents," Brady said, and went on to tell him what Miss Cornish had said as they walked into the courthouse and up the flight of steps to the County Clerk's office.

"Gosh, Brady," Jim said. "If the county's going broke, we must really be in trouble."

"Maybe it's just the funds they allowed for our prairie dog tails," Brady said. "Maybe that's all it is." But he worried that his dad might be finding out right now that the Triple A program had dried up, too. If it had, would the Harkins still live on their farm? It bothered him to think about their house being abandoned. The Moores had left their farm last fall to go to Oregon, and their house looked so forlorn with the dust and dirt banked against it. Every time he and his dad drove by on the way into town, the windows seemed to him like sad, vacant eyes.

Over root beer floats at the Bluebird Cafe, Brady told his friend about going to live in Sentinel, up north near the Nebraska line. Up north in Bunch County where his grandpa was the sheriff.

"Wow!" Jim said. "Boy, that'll be swell! Maybe he'll let you see the jail. Maybe your grandpa will capture some famous outlaw while you're there." He paused, frowning. "Too bad Bonnie and Clyde and Pretty Boy Floyd are all dead."

"Yeah, too bad," Brady said, grinning. His friend's enthusiasm had lifted his spirits. At least until he thought about going to school there. There was only about a month and a half of school left. He'd have to graduate from the eighth grade with some strangers in Sentinel, Kansas. And if his folks didn't get back by September, he would have to start high school there, too.

And what about Sarah? What would those kids, those strangers in Sentinel, say about Sarah? On the farm, not many people saw her. But Grandpa Bud lived in town. Would the *town talk about her? And the kids make fun of her, like they did Lukie Barnes who limped around on his club foot and was said to peer into people's windows?*

They hadn't taken Sarah to town now for several years. When his mother used to go to town, before she took sick, they got Mrs. Brewster to come and stay with Sarah. Now she stayed with his mother, too.

It was funny. Not, ha-ha funny. But funny that his mother was sending both of her children to live in town for at least a summer. Funny, when she had kept Sarah hidden out on the farm and every summer fretted when he went into town with his dad. Polio always seemed to strike in the summer, and it scared her that he'd pick up whatever caused it in town.

Everyone said President Roosevelt had polio. Some said he was in a wheelchair all the time. Others said he could walk with braces. In the newsreels, shown before the main feature at the picture shows, he was often standing. If he was really crippled, Brady couldn't figure out how he could hide it so well. In those newsreels, he sure didn't look crippled.

Brady met his father at Sander's Mercantile as arranged. He and Jim had promised to send each other penny post cards during the summer, or until Brady came back.

"Be sure and tell me if your grandpa catches anyone famous," Jim had flung over his shoulder as he ran across the street to where his dad waited with the family's team and wagon. Mr. Conners had no use for machinery. "One of these days the horse and mule will be gone," he often lamented, "and we'll just have those dang-blasted automobiles and tractors. Would now, if folks like me wasn't hanging on to the old ways of doing things."

"Did you telephone Grandpa Bud?" Brady asked quietly as he carried the box of groceries his dad had purchased to their car.

"Yes. He and Aunt Tilly will come for you and Sarah Friday evening and leave for Sentinel on Saturday. You can finish out the rest of the week of school. Get your notebooks and things." He paused and looked up at the sky as if studying the wisps of clouds. "Your mother and I will leave then, too."

"How long will it be, Dad?" Brady asked.

"How long will what be, son?"

"How long before this is over? Until the dust goes away? Until you can bring Mom back home? Until Sarah and I can come home?"

"I don't know." He opened the car door and paused again, one foot on the running board, and looked across the top of the car at Brady. "I guess when it rains," he said.

"Which maybe means never," Brady mumbled as he climbed into the car.

5

BRADY'S LAST DAY AT SCHOOL was like any other day, and yet it wasn't like any other day at all. For one thing, he just couldn't concentrate on any of the lessons. Not that it mattered much. He wouldn't be here next week to hand in the assignments anyway. The kids all knew he was leaving,and said things like, "Hey, Brady, I hope your new school doesn't have crabby teachers." Or, "Don't put any snakes in the teacher's desk, Brady." He and Jim Conners had done that to Mrs. Guilder last year. But the big bull snake hadn't scared her one bit, and the next Monday she had two books about snakes that she'd borrowed from the library in town and made them each write a three-page report and read it aloud to the class.

"Good luck, Brady," Mrs. Guilder was saying now. She looked a little sad, which sort of pleased him. Maybe she understood how he hated going off to that school in Sentinel where he wouldn't know anyone.

"Thanks," he mumbled, quickly ducking his head. A sudden desire to have her hug him to her soft lumpiness swept over him, and he felt his face go red. He stepped back and stumbled out the door.

Jim was waiting for him outside and they started off for their homes, Jim jabbering away again about Grandpa Bud catching gangsters and outlaws. Brady hardly heard him, seeing in his head the emptiness of their house with everything packed and waiting. If it would rain, he thought again for the millionth time. *If it would only rain.* But the sun stayed day after day in a cloudless sky, the dust piled higher, shifting with each rush of the wind, and the cracks in the parched ground deepened. And, it seemed to Brady, his mother was coughing constantly now.

They parted, he and his best friend, with a handshake, like grown-up men. A sudden stiffness swept over Brady so it was hard to think of what to say or to get his tongue to say it. Finally, he muttered, "See ya," and turned away toward home.

Taggart was waiting for him and bounded out to greet him as he came in sight of the house. He knelt, hugging the dog, his teeth clenched to hold back tears.

If only Taggart could go with him, but his dad had been adamant about that. "No, son," he had said. "Your Grandpa Bud is a busy man, and Aunt Tilly is going to have her hands full taking care of Sarah without the added burden of a dog."

"But I'll be there to take care of him," Brady had protested. "He's a good dog. He minds well."

"No, son. Dogs in town get in fights with other dogs. They bark too much and can be a general nuisance. Besides, we don't know how Grandpa Bud or Aunt Tilly feel about dogs and I'm not going to ask." The worry lines deepening in his sun-browned face, he'd laid his hand on Brady's shoulder. "Tim and Rosealee will take good care of him, and," he smiled a slight, half smile, "he'll be a joy to those little ones of theirs."

Giving his dog a tight squeeze and receiving a warm, wet lick of Taggart's tongue, Brady rose and walked up to the house. He dreaded walking into it ... into the empty feel of it. His gut was already reacting, twisting and churning like a regular cyclone.

Everything was packed and waiting. His dad had built a wooden box to hold food and pots and pans for cooking along the way to California. Two bedrolls lay over the box. His parents planned to camp alongside the road as often as possible to save money. Brady wondered how often that could be. Maybe if his mother slept in the car ... She sure couldn't sleep out in the dirt and dust, but maybe it wouldn't be so bad once they got out of this part of the country. Beside the box and the bedrolls were his parents' two suitcases from their college days and his and Sarah's two pasteboard boxes filled with their clothes.

Even though the house still looked the same, the furniture and the heating stove and kitchen range and almost everything else as it was, those things by the kitchen door made it feel as empty and desolate as the barren fields surrounding it.

"I'm home, Mom," he called as he stepped into the kitchen.

His mother looked up. Her sad, dark eyes had been on Sarah.

Somehow Brady knew that his mother blamed herself for Sarah's illness. He didn't know why, he just knew she did.

Sarah sat on the floor, her legs tucked back under her, rocking from side to side. She never faltered in her rocking or looked his way. He wished she would take notice of him, but unless he got in her way, she rarely did ... Not him, or Mom, or Dad either. Even Taggart could not pull Sarah out of her secret, silent world.

His mother smiled at him, but her smile did nothing to erase the shadow of worry from her eyes. "How did school go today?" she asked.

"Before he could answer her, she started coughing.

Brady tried to give her the medicine that she had sitting on the table, but she pushed his hand away. "Took some," she gasped.

Helplessly, he waited. *Why did this have to happen to his mom? Why did they have to leave their farm ... their home ... It wasn't fair! Oh, why, oh, why couldn't it rain?*

A rash of hot, angry words welled up, tightening his chest and filling his brain until he thought he would burst with

44

the need to spill them. An almost overwhelming urge to slam his fists against the wall and overturn table and chairs pulled at him, but he stood still, clenching and unclenching his fists as he waited for his mother's coughs to subside.

He was calmer by the time she quit coughing enough to speak, her throat muscles working hard at swallowing her coughs as she wheezed out her words.

"Dad's in the barn ... Need to get traps in."

"Did he get supper started?" Brady asked.

"Yes. Stew. Dad and Aunt Tilly will be here to eat with us." She paused, breathed in a gulp of air, and added, "Bread ... butter ... expect you're starved."

"Thanks," Brady said. He wasn't hungry, and he didn't think he could force anything past the tightness in his throat anyway. But he didn't want her to worry about him.

Outside, he gave the bread and butter to Taggart, who woofed it down and looked eagerly at him for more, his tail wagging in anticipation.

A rush of love for Taggart flooded through Brady, and giving the dog's head a rough tousling of affection, he started off at a dead run across the yard and out into the open fields. His dad stepped to the door of the barn as Brady ran past, and he knew he expected him to stop, but he couldn't, not with the turmoil that raged inside him.

He ran, raising clouds of dust with each pounding footstep. When he could run no more, he collapsed on the ground and let the tears fall.

He felt Taggart's nose nuzzling him, and he rolled over and curled up close to the dog, wrapping his arms around the solid, comforting body. Then the vision of his dad standing in the doorway of the barn intruded, and he nudged the dog aside and sat up.

This was enough of feeling sorry for himself. Everyone felt bad. His mother especially. She probably felt it was all her fault. As if she could have helped getting sick. His dad probably didn't want to leave either, and he had to be plenty worried. Only Sarah was unaffected. And Taggart. Would his dog miss him, Brady wondered, with the Harkins children around to play with?

As if Taggart knew he was thinking about him, he scooted closer and licked Brady's hands. Brady bent his head and nestled his face in his dog's thick coat. If only he could take him with him, this dog he had picked out of a litter of squirming brown and black puppies. This dog he had named Tag, but his mother had started calling *Mister* Taggart because she said he had such a solemn face that he looked more like an old man than a puppy. And so Taggart he'd become, the Mister used only in playful times, times that were no more. Times that might never come again.

The old angry, hopeless feelings began to crowd in again, worming their way deep into his belly and rising up to choke him, but he pushed them back. "Let's go get the traps, Taggart," he said, getting to his feet.

Brady pulled up the stake that held the first trap. Carrying it by the ring at the end of its chain, he moved on to the next one. He had killed three prairie dogs this morning and then on impulse had sprung all the traps. He would let the blasted things dig all the holes they wanted and eat anything they could find, but he bet they weren't finding much. It was pretty bad when even the prairie dogs went hungry.

He had let his traps lay this morning rather than try and explain to his dad why he had given the animals a reprieve.

"How many did you get, son?" his dad was asking now as Brady entered the barn to hang his traps on the nails in the barn wall.

He started to say "five," but the words of his lie faltered on his tongue and he stammered out, "N-none."

"That's unusual," his dad said. "But maybe you're about to get them all." A smile warmed his eyes. "I could stand not to see another prairie dog hole in our fields, couldn't you?"

"Yeah," Brady said, eyeing the traps dangling from their chains, "I sure could."

"Well," his dad said, wiping his hands on an old greasy rag, "I've cleaned up the tractor for Tim, as slick as I can. She's under the shed and covered with a tarp. I guess that's all I can do." He sighed heavily, blowing the air through pursed lips, so it escaped slowly. "I guess we had best go on in. Your Grandpa Bud should be here any time now."

Brady walked to the house with his dad, but he didn't go inside. He didn't think he'd be able to stand to see both of them sitting there in the house worrying ... scared of doing what they had set out to do, and just as scared of not doing it. His dad's face would be drawn as tight and as hard as the top of a drum, and his mom's, thin and pale as a ghost's, with tears, not always visible, but there all the same.

Brady dropped down on the top step by the back door, where he could see the road, and waited. The sun had slipped down beneath the horizon, and the evening sky blazed with the red and orange shades of the sunset. He pulled Taggart between his legs and stroked the dog's warm black coat. The waiting filled his stomach with a thousand worms, all gnawing at his guts. He wished it were over. Wished that Grandpa Bud had already come and taken them back to Sentinel. Wished that his dad and mom were already in the fresh, ocean-washed air of California. Then a thin spiral of dust caught his eye. The waiting was about to be over.

Squinting, Brady searched for the car in the midst of the dust moving steadily closer. But all he could see was a high, grayish-white wall like a huge cloud moving along the road. Grandpa Bud's car would be in their yard, stirring up dirt here, before the dust had settled back along the road.

Grandpa Bud eased his big frame out of his dusty black two-door Hudson and shook hands with Brady's dad. His mother went around to the passenger's side and helped Aunt Tilly out of the car.

Aunt Tilly was nearly as large as Grandpa Bud, but

softer looking. She had snowy white hair, and her blue eyes, framed in round glasses, twinkled with humor. Brady felt a sudden rush of relief. *She would be good to Sarah.*

"My Lord, Jack," Grandpa Bud said, looking at the house and then swinging around to look out toward the barnyard and the fields. "And we think we have it bad. You're just about buried in dust."

"You're doing better then?" his dad said, a kind of hopeful look on his face. For the first time, Brady realized his dad worried about him and Sarah, too.

"Some better, but it's not good at all. We've had our share of those dust storms, and very little rain. But it looks to me like you have had it worse. When was the last time it rained here anyway?"

"We had a half inch last fall and about that last month. But we had no snow cover all last winter and we had grasshoppers, thick as fleas, all through the summer and into October. We've not had an easy time of it, Bud."

All the time Grandpa Bud and his dad were talking, Brady thought of how he would greet his grandpa when he finally turned to him. Should he shake his hand? Maybe he'd just nod and say hello. But he needn't have worried, for Grandpa Bud never did really acknowledge him. The dust churned up by his car started his mother to coughing so hard it took all of their attention as his dad hurried them into the house.

And inside there was Sarah. Sarah seemed to put a damper on everyone's tongue for a while. But later, Aunt Tilly whispered aside to him, "Well, Brady," she said smiling. "I expect you and I can handle this little angel all right."

After his mother's medicine had eased her coughing, his dad set her down at the table between Grandpa Bud and Aunt Tilly. He and Brady dished up the stew.

They sat in the front room awhile after supper. Brady noticed his mother brushing at the dust on the floor with her foot as if trying to hide it. He wondered if she was embarrassed about it, afraid her dad and Aunt Tilly would think she was a bad housekeeper. But they ought to know how impossible it was to keep the dirt out of the house any more. They must know, too, that she was in no shape to do housework, or much of anything else.

They talked awhile about Grandma Barbara. Brady listened, liking the memories they brought, but feeling too nervous about tomorrow to add any of his own. Then the talk changed to the death of Aunt Tilly's husband and of her move to Grandpa Bud's house.

"It was good of him to give me a home," Aunt Tilly said. "Ralph was sick so long before he died, I didn't have a thing left. If it wasn't for my brother, I'd be in the County Poor House now, living with strangers."

Grandpa Bud smiled and patted Aunt Tilly on the hand. "We're blood, big sister," he said. "Blood should stick by blood."

Brady felt a little glow of relief at Grandpa Bud's words. He a*nd Sarah were blood, too, weren't they?*

They went to bed early, his mother and Aunt Tilly sharing his parents' bed, his dad and Grandpa Bud in his bed upstairs. Sarah slept in her own little bed, and Brady rolled up in a blanket and lay on the davenport. Taggart wiggled in beside him, his head on Brady's chest.

Brady was sure he dreamed the whole night through, awakening with the first streaks of dawn lighting the dusty window panes. He tried to remember his dreams, but already they had faded.

Climbing over Taggart, Brady got up to pull on his overalls and shoes. The dog yawned and stretched before jumping down to follow him through the quiet, semi-dark kitchen and out into the freshness of the morning air.

"Hello, Brady." The voice startled him, and he swung around to see Grandpa Bud coming up from the barn.

"Hello," Brady said. "I didn't know anyone was up yet."

"I couldn't sleep. I was just checking my car. She was

running all right when we run her in last night. But I got to worrying that the dirt might have blown in on the motor. I've seen cars completely ruined with dust and dirt."

Brady looked up at his grandpa and told him about his dad having to leave the tractor in the field the day of the last dust storm.

Grandpa Bud was a big man, tall and rawboned, with huge hands and feet. Brady bet his chest was nearly as broad as Johnny Weissmuller's, who played Tarzan in the picture shows. Grandma Barbara had been tall, too ... much taller than his mother. Aunt Tilly was almost as tall as Grandpa Bud, and pretty big all the way around. It was funny that his mother was so small. Why, he was already taller than she was, and he wasn't anywhere near as tall as Grandpa Bud, or even Aunt Tilly. He wondered if his mother's brother, his Uncle Lee, had been a big man.

Brady searched his brain for something else to say to this man standing before him. This grandfather who was almost a stranger. He couldn't think of anything else, so he said, "Mom doesn't look like you, does she? She doesn't look like Grandma Barbara did either. I wonder why."

"I ... I ... well, son ..." Grandpa Bud stammered as if he couldn't think of what to say.

"I'll tell him, Dad." At his mother's voice, Brady swung around to stare at her. She was standing on the top step by the back door, one hand clutching her old brown sweater in tight gathers across her chest. She shivered, but Brady didn't think it was from the chill in the morning air.

6

A SUDDEN TINGLING OF APPREHENSION, like the warning rattle of a snake, made Brady suddenly wish that he had not awakened so early. He should have stayed in bed until everyone was up and about, the kitchen fire going and the coffee pot bubbling. But he'd had to get up, and now his mother stood on the top step by the kitchen door about to tell him something he wasn't sure he wanted to hear.

"You've never told him, Lydia?" Grandpa Bud was frowning at her like whatever she hadn't told him wasn't making his grandfather too pleased either.

"I meant to." Her lips quivered and tears gathered in her eyes.

She brought the sleeve of her sweater across her eyes, clearing them. "I meant to," she said, "but the time just never seemed right."

"So you'll tell him now? Now, before we take him home and you go off to California?"

"Yes." Her lips were firm now and steady. "I have to tell him now."

It's like I'm not even here, Brady thought. *Or like I'm invisible or deaf or something.*

"Well, we'd better sit down," Grandpa Bud said. He took Brady by the arm. "Sit here, son," he said, pointing to the bottom step. Letting go of Brady's arm, he eased his own big frame down on the step above.

Brady sat down, and his mother moved past Grandpa

Bud to sit beside him. She looked at him, hesitating a second before she said, firmly, quietly, "You need to know that my parents aren't really my parents."

Brady stared at his mother. *Then they aren't my grandparents either,* he thought, and Grandpa Bud's words to Aunt Tilly suddenly rang like fire alarm bells in his ears. *We're blood, sister, and blood should stick by blood.*

"My brother and I were left on the steps of the courthouse in Sentinel." His mother's voice took on a harsh bitterness. "Like we were a couple of barnyard kittens. Strays that nobody wanted."

Brady wished he could think of something to say that would take away her anger, but nothing seemed to come to mind.

"My brother, your Uncle Lee, was killed, you know," she went on, "in the war, in France. We never got his body back." She shivered and pulled her sweater tighter around her arms. When she spoke again, the anger was gone, replaced by a faraway, hollow sound.

"He was just eighteen. Only a boy. He wanted to look for our family, especially our father, but the war came ..." She sighed a deep, ragged sigh. "He remembered someone he thought was our father. Someone who had cared for us ... loved us ..." Her voice grew wheezy and sudden tears glistened in her eyes.

They sat awhile without speaking, his mother's breathing a harsh sound in the silence. Brady wished he could say something to ease her sadness, but as before, he felt tongue-tied and dull. His brain didn't seem to know anything at all. So he sat still and the cool morning air washed over him, chilling him. He had to grit his teeth to keep them from chattering.

He thought about what his mother had said. Would she ever have told him if they weren't leaving? Why did she tell him now? Did she think he would feel better going home with a grandpa and a great aunt that weren't really his at all?

Behind them, Grandpa Bud started to speak, stopped, cleared his throat and began again. "They were there on the steps when the courthouse opened on Monday. Two little half-starved, dark-haired urchins. They each had an old flour sack they clung to. But there was nothing in either sack, except a change of clothes as ragged and dirty as the ones they wore. There was no identification at all."

"It was your grandpa's first year as sheriff," his mother said. "Just his luck to find two children on the courthouse steps."

"I couldn't put them in jail," Grandpa Bud said, smiling so Brady knew he was teasing. "So I took them home."

"They were just little?" Brady said.

"Your Uncle Lee told us he was six and your mother was four," Grandpa Bud said. "He was so protective of you, Lydia," he added, a softness coming into his face. "He would have braved a pack of wolves for you."

"I know," she said, her voice a soft whisper.

"Didn't you think you might have some children of your own someday?" Brady asked.

"We had been married five years and no sign of any babies. Your grandma longed for babies, and the minute she saw those two, she was hooked. They were hers and there wasn't a thing I, or the county, could do but give them to her." He grinned. "Like you said, Brady, didn't we think we'd have children of our own? I asked her that and she said, 'That would be fine, then these two will have brothers and sisters.' "

"Did you even try to find their parents?" Brady asked.

"Yes, he did." His mother answered for Grandpa Bud. "But we had been passed through several families. I couldn't remember living with anyone but strangers. For me, my brother was my family. But your Uncle Lee remembered this man ..." Her voice trailed away, and she bent forward hugging her arms tight against her body.

"Your mother said prayers for your folks, Lydia, whoever they were," Grandpa Bud said. "But, I know, in her heart, that even as she prayed they'd be found, she hoped to keep you."

"For Lee it might have been best if our parents had come for us." The sadness in his mother's voice made Brady's eyes sting for a moment. "Maybe for me, too," she continued turning to look again at Grandpa Bud. "But I was happy with you and Mother. I'll always be grateful that you took us in and raised us. I hope we didn't disappoint you too much."

"You were a good girl, Lydia," Grandpa Bud said. "You and Lee were both good. It was just that Lee remembered a father he had loved. A father who, for some reason, had abandoned him. He had no explanation for it, and it ate at him and made him restless and dissatisfied."

"He used to get into fights all the time." His mother turned back to him. "You know how it is, Brady. In a small town everyone knows who you are and where you came from. The kids knew our story. They had heard it from their parents. They knew we had the Lewis name only because your grandpa and grandma had taken us in. Lee was always fighting over our parentage. I think sometimes he created those situations out of a kind of anger inside himself."

"I tried to get him to understand that fighting wouldn't change things," Grandpa Bud said. "But he wouldn't listen to anything I said."

Brady's mother turned and laid her hand on Grandpa Bud's knee. "He just couldn't let go of that memory, Dad. For his sake, I wish he could have found the man his heart longed for."

"You were old enough to know your names," Brady said. "You must have known your last name."

"Yes, we did," she said softly, touching his arm. "At least the name we knew as our last name. But whether it was or not is another matter." She smiled. "And to keep it, I gave it to you. Our last name was Brady."

"Really?" Brady said. He couldn't believe she had kept this from him all these years.

He turned this new knowledge over in his mind and wondered if some part of his mother, at least at the time he was born, had still longed for the parents she never knew.

"The people who left us on the courthouse steps," his mother went on, the smile gone from her face, "told us to call them Auntie and Uncle. We never knew any other names for them. We hadn't been with them very long before they left us. Other names and faces sometimes surfaced in my head, a kind of a jumble, so I think we were quite regularly handed from one family to another. But my brother remembered that one man ... the man he was sure was our father. The man he could never forget."

"I think he thought I should have found that man of his memory," Grandpa Bud said quietly. "I was the sheriff, I should have been able to track him down. I think that's what Lee thought. I think he always held it against me for not finding him. But I did try, Lydia. I tried for years."

"I know you did, Dad." She paused, coughing, her hand over her mouth. When the spasms passed, she said, "I wish I could say that Lee understood, but I don't think he did. Somehow, I think he thought you could find him if you would only try harder. He was so obsessed with wanting to find the man he just knew was our father."

"And all that time, the man was probably dead," Grandpa Bud said.

"If he wasn't, I hope he had a good reason for giving us away." Anger fueled his mother's voice. "A really good reason."

"I'm sure he ..." Grandpa Bud stopped, and Brady looked up to see his dad pushing open the back door.

"Are you three ready for breakfast?" Brady knew his father had tried for a light-hearted tone of voice, but his words sounded strained, and even the smile on his face looked forced. I bet he wishes all this was over, too, Brady thought.

Brady's mother stood up, steadying herself with a hand

on his shoulder. "We had better go eat before it gets cold," she said.

Only then did Brady smell the smoke from the chimney and the odors of breakfast cooking. Any other morning he would have been starving, but this morning he wasn't sure if he'd be able to choke down even a bite.

"I'm not hungry, Dad," he said, getting to his feet. "I think I'll just stay outside with Taggart awhile. Maybe go down to the barn."

As he turned away, Taggart at his heels, he heard Grandpa Bud say, "She just told him, Jack. I never dreamed he didn't know."

By late morning, Brady and Sarah and their pasteboard boxes were packed into Grandpa Bud's black Hudson. Sarah had pulled back from her mother's good-bye hug, stamping her feet furiously and flapping her tiny hands as she made a high-pitched, screeching sound. Brady watched his dad force her into the back seat of the car, making her cry. He looked back at his mother before getting into the back seat with Sarah. Her eyes were swimming with tears. He wondered if his dad wasn't close to tears, too, the way his adam's apple kept bobbing up and down like he was having to swallow all the time. Aunt Tilly's eyebrows were drawn together in a worried frown, and she kept pulling out the handkerchief she had stuffed up the sleeve of her dress, to blow and wipe her nose. Grandpa Bud rubbed his mustache and paced around like a nervous horse reined in too tight.

Brady sure didn't blame Grandpa Bud and Aunt Tilly for being nervous and worried. Here they were stuck with a half-grown boy and a little girl who acted like she had no sense at all. Grandpa Bud had told Aunt Tilly that blood should stick by blood. But he and Sarah weren't any blood kin at all. Was Grandpa Bud remembering that now and wishing he'd not been so quick to say he'd take them?

With a sigh, Brady turned to wave out the back window as they pulled out on to the road. His dad stood where they had left him, but his mother had walked a little ways after them, her hand up as if calling, *"Wait! Wait!"* But the dust soon shielded her from his view and Grandpa Bud drove on.

They arrived in Sentinel eight hours later — hours that stretched out so long Brady thought they might ride forever locked in this black Hudson car with Sarah. First she had wet herself. Aunt Tilly had tried to take her into the ladies' room when they stopped at a filling station, but Sarah had fought her, pulling back, stomping her feet and yelling. So Aunt Tilly had put her back in the car. As soon as they were driving away, she'd wet all over the back seat. It wasn't exactly a warm day, so they'd had to ride with the windows rolled up. Grandpa Bud and Aunt Tilly hadn't acted like they'd smelled a thing, but Brady had thought the smell was pretty bad.

At noon, they had stopped by the side of the road to eat the sandwiches Aunt Tilly made from the bologna and cheese she'd bought at the grocery store across from the filling station.

Sarah had refused to eat and kept running out on to the road. Every time Brady brought her back, she'd flapped her little hands and cried angry-sounding tears. People going by in cars always looked back, and one even slowed a little and then picked up speed and went on. Brady figured they were wondering why he was fighting with the pretty little girl.

Brady kept hoping she would fall asleep, but she never did. All the way to Sentinel, she alternated between a pitiful-sounding cry and fits of violent temper when she tried to stomp out the floorboards or open the car's doors as they were going down the road.

When they finally pulled into Sentinel, Brady was never so glad to see a town in all his life.

"Well, we're home," Aunt Tilly said. "I'd better get started on some supper right away." Brady thought her voice sounded dull and flat. He bet supper was the last thing Aunt Tilly wanted to do. What she was probably aching to do was to go to her room, shut the door and flop down on her bed. He wondered if the County Poor House and living with strangers wasn't sounding better to her all the time.

"You go on in, Tilly," Grandpa Bud said. "Brady can carry in their boxes of clothes and our suitcases. I'll open Sarah's door and wait until she's ready to get out on her own."

"If she ever does," Aunt Tilly said grimly.

But as soon as Grandpa Bud opened the door, Sarah jumped out of the car and ran after Aunt Tilly, following her into the house.

Aunt Tilly's bedroom was just off from the kitchen, and Grandpa Bud had moved a cot in for Sarah. Grandpa Bud had a bedroom upstairs, down the hall from the one Brady was to use.

Brady put his box of clothes on the bed of his new room and went over to the window.

It overlooked the back yard, a large part of which had been spaded up for a garden. The yard was enclosed by a board fence. The only tree was a big hackberry, so close to his window that he could have crawled out and onto its thick branches. The tree was beginning to leaf out and would soon provide a deep shade for his room. Visions of the old dead cottonwood outside his window at home sent a wave of homesickness through him. He backed up to his new bed and sat down beside his pasteboard box of clothes.

He wondered how many miles his parents had made today and if they would rent a cabin tonight or sleep in their bed rolls. He hoped the dust wasn't blowing wherever they were so his mother could sleep tonight.

All day he had kept a thought pushed back in his mind. Now it surfaced again, and he knew he might as well face it. He knew good and well that something could happen to his parents. Something could happen, and they would be gone. An accident ... Anything ... Gone like his mother's parents. Gone and he would never see them again.

If they never returned, would Grandpa Bud send him to a boys' home or an orphanage? Would he send Sarah to that hospital where his doctor thought they should send her? He knew if Grandma Barbara were here, they wouldn't be sent away. But Grandma Barbara was dead.

He forced his grim thoughts away by thinking of how he had been named Brady Lee, a turnaround of his Uncle Lee's first name and the name his mother thought was their last name.

Sighing, he lay back on the bed, keeping his feet dangling off to the side, so his shoes wouldn't dirty the white coverlet. In his mind he'd gone over the story his mother had told him this morning, a dozen times. Why hadn't she told him before? Would she have told him then if they hadn't been forced to leave the farm? She said she could never find the right time to tell him. When would have been the right time? When he was sixteen, or eighteen, or would the right time have ever come?

A strange mixture of anger at his mother and guilt for feeling angry filled him, and he jumped up from his bed just as Grandpa Bud called up the stairwell for him to come down to supper.

He crossed the bedroom floor and opened the window, breathing in gulps of the cool air. Then feeling calmer, he closed the window and was about to turn away when a flash of something outside caught his eye.

He turned back in time to see a white-haired boy run across the backyard. As he watched, the boy leaped up and grabbed the top of the board fence, hoisted himself over and dropped from sight. Brady blinked his eyes in surprise, for flying just above the boy's head was a big black crow.

7

BRADY CLIMBED THE STEPS of the big brick building and entered the dimly lit interior of the school. Before him was a long hallway filled with kids laughing and talking. They quieted as they saw him, and Brady could almost hear their whispered voices; "Who is t*hat? Where did he come from?"*

He felt like a freak in those freak shows at the carnivals. *Step right up, folks! See the two-headed monster captured from the wilds of Mongolia! He eats live chickens with both heads, and he'll eat you too, if you get too close!*

A bell rang overhead, startling him, and in a sudden bustle of movement the hallway emptied. Brady heaved a sigh of relief, looked up at the signs over the doors and saw he was standing in front of the principal's office.

Grandpa Bud had dropped him off in front of the school this morning on his way to his office in the courthouse. "I called the principal, so he's expecting you," he'd said. "Come directly home after school."

"Wh*ere else would I go?"* Brady thought the words inside his head, but he didn't say them out loud.

Wiping a sweaty palm across the bib of his overalls and clutching the notebook he'd used in his school back home, Brady knocked on the principal's door.

Mr. Horn was a solemn-looking, middle-aged man with a paunch beginning to develop over his belt. "I've been expecting you, Brady," he said, a faint smile warming his eyes. "Your grandfather called yesterday. He said you would be staying with him for a while."

"Yes, sir," Brady said.

After he had answered a few questions about his old school, Mr. Horn scribbled out a note, handed it to him and ushered him out into the hall. "The third door on the right is your room," he said. "Give the teacher this note and she will assign you a seat."

"Thank you, sir," Brady said, but the principal had already turned away.

The sign over the third door on the right, read, *Miss Winters*. Brady took a deep breath and opened the door.

Miss Winters looked just like a school girl — a very pretty school girl. She had soft-looking brown curls and big blue eyes with long, dark lashes. She smiled warmly at him, scanned the note he gave her, and said, "Welcome to our classroom, Brady. We are so pleased to have you with us."

Brady nodded and mumbled a thank you.

She smiled at him again and turned to rap her desk top with a ruler. "Class," she said, "this is Brady Foster. He has just moved here to Sentinel and is living with his grandfather, Sheriff Lewis, while his parents are in California."

Some twenty pairs of eyes looked at Brady. He felt his face flush red. Then Miss Winters was telling him to take an empty seat in the back of the room.

Aware of the eyes watching him, Brady moved down the aisle between the rows of desks. Midway to the desk that awaited him, a foot suddenly shot out and stopped him.

He looked down at the shiny brown shoe stubbed up against his own scruffy one and then up to gleaming black eyes and a grinning face.

"Hear you got a funny sister." The boy hissed out the words. His grin disappeared and left just cold black eyes.

"Raymond Blackburn. What are you doing?" Miss Winters' voice tried to be sharp, but it wavered uneasily. *She's afraid of him,* Brady thought.

The foot was withdrawn, and the boy spoke to the teacher

in a sweetly mocking voice. "Why, Miss Winters. I wasn't doing a thing except saying hello to our new boy. Sheriff Lewis' grandson, huh? But not by blood, I understand."

"That's enough, Raymond," Miss Winters said in her quivery voice.

Brady slumped down into the only empty desk he could see, his face burning with embarrassment and anger. So everyone knew his mother's story and about Sarah, too.

He thought of the ladies from the church and Aunt Tilly's quilting circle who had stopped by the house with cakes and loaves of bread still warm from the oven and jars of preserves from their pantries.

"They are so thoughtful," Brady had heard Aunt Tilly telling Grandpa Bud. "I told the quilting ladies and Reverend Switzer I wouldn't be such a regular for a while. Not until we all get settled into a routine. They wanted me to know they would miss me and would be so glad when I could rejoin them again."

But had they come to see Aunt Tilly, or had they heard about Sarah? And had this Blackburn's mother been among them?

"All right, class." Miss Winters brought his thoughts back to the classroom. "Take out your geography books. This will be an open book test." She walked down the rows handing out papers. When she reached Brady's desk, she handed him a book along with his paper. "Just do what you can," she said quietly.

Throughout the morning Brady kept his eyes glued to the papers and books on his desk, giving only sideways glances at the class under lowered eye lids. At mid-morning, the class was sent outside for recess. Brady asked to stay in and catch up on his work. It wasn't that he was so anxious to study, but he didn't want to go out where he didn't know anyone and where Raymond Blackburn, no doubt, waited to say things about Sarah. What was the matter with the fella anyway? Did he have something against Grandpa Bud or

Aunt Tilly? Or was he just mean ... just a bully?

They ate their sack lunches in the auditorium. The big room soon filled up with other classes from the little first-graders to their eighth grade class. Brady sat alone. All of the kids, except one boy, sat in twos or more, laughing and talking as they ate.

The lone boy sat at the back of the room near Brady. He was a small boy who looked like he belonged in the sixth grade rather than the eighth, but Brady had seen him in the back corner of his classroom, so he knew he was older than he looked. His light blond hair looked almost white. Brady thought of the boy he'd seen leap over Grandpa Bud's fence. The boy with the crow. He was sure he was the same boy.

He sure was a ragged-looking kid, Brady thought. His overalls had patches over patches, and the tattered shirt he wore had been made out of a flour sack. Brady recognized the print as one his mother had used to make herself an apron. Not that there was anything wrong with wearing a flour sack shirt. He had had several, and at home a lot of the boys wore shirts out of feed or flour or sugar sacks, and the girls' dresses were often made of that material, too. Looking around the room, he now spotted some shirts and a couple of dresses that he was pretty sure had been made from those sacks. He also noted that quite a few of the boys wore patched and faded pants and overalls. They weren't all dressed like rich kids. Like Raymond Blackburn. But this boy's clothes were almost in shreds, and there was something different about him. And why did he sit alone? Maybe, the thought just occurring to him, he was a new boy, like himself, and didn't know anyone yet.

Satisfied that was the answer, he bit into the meatloaf sandwich Aunt Tilly had packed for him and shot a quick glance at Raymond Blackburn. A group of boys and a few girls, too, all leaned in toward him as if hanging onto his every word. They listened when he talked and laughed when he laughed. Several times, Raymond Blackburn looked over at him, and the rest of them turned to look, too, big grins on their faces. Like puppets on a string, Brady thought, feeling his face flush with heat and anger churn in his stomach.

He knew they were talking about him and about Sarah, too. He wished he could just shrink up and disappear, but that wasn't going to happen. He could only hope Raymond Blackburn would soon get bored with making him the butt of his meanness.

He supposed Raymond Blackburn was the king in this school, probably by a combination of meanness and money. He sure was mean, there was no getting around that, and he dressed like he had a million bucks with his new-looking brown pants and matching plaid shirt. The foot that had shot out in the aisle to stop him was shod in shiny brown leather. He wondered where the Blackburns got their money. Most folks were too hard up to dress their kids that well.

One of the things his dad had said about him and Sarah staying with Grandpa Bud was that, despite the Depression, Grandpa Bud had a steady income as sheriff and could afford to keep them. "But," his father had hastened to add, "I'll reimburse him for your room and board as soon as I get a job in California."

The bell rang and Brady smoothed the wax paper that had held his sandwich and put it back in his lunch sack. Folded, the sack fit in his back pocket. Aunt Tilly had cautioned him about throwing away anything that could be used again. "If we waste not, we'll want for naught," she had said.

Brady stood back and let the other kids file out first and go to class. The white-haired boy waited for Brady to go in front of him.

"Thanks," Brady said quietly as he moved ahead of the boy.

The boy nodded, solemn faced.

As Brady stepped into the classroom, he looked to see if Raymond Blackburn was in his seat. He was, a smirk of a grin on his face.

For a moment Brady considered taking another aisle and cutting across to his desk, but he knew Raymond Blackburn would know why. As would the rest of the class. He wouldn't have Raymond Blackburn, or anyone else, thinking he was a coward. They would really make sport of him then. He could see them, hands tucked into their armpits, elbows flapping while they "pluck, pluck, plucked" like chickens. Or one might sneak up behind him and pretend to paint a broad yellow stripe down his back while the rest of them jeered and hooted.

He wasn't afraid of Raymond Blackburn. It was just that he didn't know what the big bully might say about Sarah. He might tell the whole class that Brady's little sister was stupid or retarded or something. He took a deep breath and started toward his desk. Raymond Blackburn watched him with bold black eyes.

"After school," Raymond mouthed as Brady walked past him. "I'll see you after school."

Brady sat at his desk a few minutes after the dismissal bell rang. He could hear the desk tops slamming and the laughter and talking all around him, but the sounds seemed muted and far away. He wished Miss Winters would ask him to stay after, but she didn't. He pretended to study his English assignment, hoping Raymond would go on home. But when he looked up, Raymond Blackburn was standing in the doorway looking back at him, his smirk of a grin plastered on his face. With a sigh, Brady got to his feet.

Raymond Blackburn was in the middle of a group of boys as Brady came down the steps of the school.

"Hey, Roscoe," Raymond called. "Did the teacher say this new boy is ol' Sheriff Lewis' grandson? Well, our pretty Miss Winters was misinformed, now, wasn't she?"

"The way I heard it," the boy called Roscoe answered, "ol' Sheriff Lewis got stuck with this here boy's mama. Found her sittin' on the courthouse steps, ragged and filthy as dirt."

"And now ol' Sheriff Lewis is stuck again." Raymond Blackburn moved out of the circle of boys and toward Brady. "Right, new kid? Now he's stuck with you and your funny sister."

Brady felt his face grow hot. He knew it would do no good to say anything, so he turned and started toward Grandpa Bud's house.

"Say, Freddy," Raymond Blackburn's taunting voice came again, addressing another of his cohorts. "Did you know this new boy's sister is ..." There was silence and then someone snickered, and Brady knew Raymond had finished with the sign for crazy. The circular motion of a forefinger pointed at the head.

Brady clenched his teeth and kept walking.

"Hey, new boy," the taunting voice continued. "I'm saying your sister is crazy. Crazy as a bed bug."

This, finally, was too much for Brady. Turning, he dropped his books and faced his tormentors.

"Okay," he said. "What do you want? A fight? What?"

Raymond Blackburn laughed and, cocking his head, said in a tone of mock fright, "Oh, my, this new boy is a tough one."

"You gonna fight, Raymond?" the boy called Roscoe jeered.

"If I have to," Brady said.

Raymond Blackburn handed his books to the one called Freddie and began to roll up his sleeves. "Well, I think you're going to have to, boy," he said.

Brady waited, clenching and unclenching his fists.

Raymond Blackburn began to circle Brady, fists up, leaning a little forward on his toes, dancing like the prize fighters did that sometimes came to the county fairs back home.

Brady waited, turning, watching the circling, black-haired boy. And when Raymond launched a punch, Brady was ready, except someone snaked out a foot and tripped him.

He fell flat in the dirt, a roar of anger filling his head.

He scrambled to his feet and with head lowered, barreled into Raymond Blackburn's stomach. The boy gave a satisfying "Oohfah!" and went down. Brady leaped on top of him, fists flying.

He got in several good punches before hands grabbed him and, pulling him off Raymond, began pounding him with their fists.

Brady rolled up into a ball, his arms shielding his head. Pain shot through him, and something warm ran from his throbbing nose.

Suddenly the pounding stopped. Brady opened his eyes and looked up into the face of Mr. Horn. "Are you all right, son?" the principal asked, reaching down and pulling Brady to his feet.

Brady nodded and wiped a shirt sleeve under his nose. It came away stained with a stringy, bloody mucus.

Mr. Horn turned to Raymond, who now looked the picture of innocence. His sleeves were rolled down again and buttoned, and his books were back in his arms. There was a touch of dismay in his voice as he looked up at Mr. Horn. "This new boy attacked Roscoe and Freddy here for no reason. Just jumped right on them." He paused, and a painful expression crossed his face before he added with a deep sigh. "Sheriff Lewis is going to have a time with this boy, and did you know, Mr. Horn, there is something wrong with his sister, too?"

"Enough, Raymond," the principal said, scowling. "Now get on home. All of you." He moved toward them as he spoke, and Raymond's friends scattered, but Raymond held his ground, his eyes on Mr. Horn, and a smile played across his face. Then he turned away and called to his friends as he left the school yard.

"You get on home, too," Mr. Horn said, turning back to Brady, "and stay out of his way, if you two can't get along."

"Yes, sir," Brady said. It seemed to him that Mr. Horn should have given that same advice to Raymond.

Brady picked his books up from the ground and headed for Grandpa Bud's house, aware of his torn and bloody shirt, sore nose and a throbbing ache in his shoulder. He reached the edge of the schoolyard and was crossing the street when Raymond Blackburn stepped out from behind a white house. As usual, he was grinning.

Fighting the raging anger swelling up inside him, Brady stepped up on the sidewalk and faced the grinning bully. "What do you want?" he ground out through clenched teeth.

"Oh, nothing, new boy, " Raymond said, the grin deepening on his face. "At least not now. Maybe later."

"Why?" Brady asked. "What have I done?"

"You don't have to do anything once Raymond takes a notion to be mean," a voice said quietly.

Brady turned to see the white-headed boy in the ragged clothes standing beside him.

"Heck," the boy continued. "Even a snake's got a reason for striking. But not Raymond Blackburn. He's even lower'n a snake."

"Say, boy," Raymond Blackburn said. "Getting a little uppity, aren't we?" He leaned in close to Brady, his black eyes mocking. "This raggedy little whelp is Eddie, *New Boy*, the son of the town drunk."

"Maybe he wouldn't be if your old man wouldn't sell him his bootleg rotgut," Eddie said, his voice still even and quiet. But anger snapped in his blue eyes.

"Say, punk," Raymond Blackburn snarled, "you had better watch your mouth. One word from me and your old lady is out of a job."

"Hello, boys." Miss Winters had crossed the street unnoticed. "I'm on my way home, and I would suggest you do likewise."

"Yes, Miss Winters." Raymond's voice was sweet and mocking. "We'll see you tomorrow." Grinning broadly, he turned to Brady and Eddie. "I guess I'll see you two tomorrow, as well, won't I?"

Neither boy answered and both turned and began walking in the direction of Brady's Grandpa Bud's home.

8

THEY WALKED A WHILE in silence; then Brady asked, "Does he always act like that?"

"Most of the time," Eddie said.

"The teacher is afraid of him ... and Mr. Horn ... he's sort of afraid of him, too, isn't he?"

"Miss Winters is too young. She doesn't know how to handle him. We had Mrs. Blake last year. She's been teaching for years, and she's not afraid of anything. Not even Raymond Blackburn's daddy. Raymond didn't act up so much last year."

"How come Mr. Horn is afraid of him?"

"Mr. Horn has eight kids. His wages, along with the teacher's, have already been cut because the school is short on tax money. There's talk that they might have to delay opening school next fall. All Mr. Horn needs is for Sam Blackburn to decide his little Raymond is being picked on and Mr. Horn will be out on his ear."

"Really?" Brady said. But when he thought about it, he wasn't at all surprised.

"Yeah, really," Eddie said. "Sam Blackburn not only owns the bank, but nearly everyone in this county, except maybe your grandfather."

Suddenly Eddie stopped and, squatting, untied a strip of leather shoe string wrapped around one shoe. With a start, Brady realized the string was actually holding the shoe together. The other shoe, the leather cracked and misshapen, wasn't much better, but it didn't yet need more than its regular laces, although they had been broken and retied many times.

Slipping out of the shoes, Eddie picked them up and laid them on top of the books in his arms. "I'm trying to make them last until school's out," he said.

"Oh," Brady said, only then realizing that Eddie wasn't wearing socks. He tried not to look at Eddie's feet, reddened and blistered from the shoes.

He thought of the boy who had climbed over the fence in Grandpa Bud's backyard. The boy with the crow flying overhead. "Did you cut through Grandpa Bud's yard last Saturday?" he asked.

Eddie grinned. "That was me," he said.

"Was that your crow?"

Eddie's grin grew wider. "That was Blackie. I found him in a nest when I was hunting crows with my brothers." He looked up at Brady, his blue eyes squinting against the glare of late afternoon sun. "The county used to pay a bounty for crow heads, but they ran out of money."

"Our county used to pay us for prairie dog tails," Brady said. "They ran out of money, too."

"Before Pop sold his old gun for booze, my brothers and I used to take it out and shoot prairie dogs and crows. That's how I got Blackie."

"Did you shoot the mother bird and then realize she had a nest?" Brady asked.

"Jimmy Joe did. It was his turn to use the gun. I climbed up in the tree to get the babies. It doesn't matter if they're grown or not. To the county a crow head is a crow head, big or small. Besides, they die anyway when we kill the mother."

Brady nodded, remembering how the Miller twins, who doubled their prairie dog tails by cutting them in half, had complained about not being able to get to the babies who would die underground after the mother was dead.

"So you kept one of the babies. How come?"

Eddie shrugged. "I don't know. I guess for one thing he was the only one in the nest. The others had fallen out, or the mama had pushed them out after they died. There were two of them on the ground under the tree, bugs crawling all over them.

"Blackie just about had all his pin feathers, but he wasn't looking too good, like maybe he was going to be dead in a minute. I don't know why ..." Eddie shook his head. "But that little bird just suddenly seemed to be mine. I picked him up and stuffed him inside my shirt and took him home."

"Do you have a cage for him?" Brady asked.

"Sometimes I keep him in an old chicken coop. Pop doesn't like him much and raises a ruckus when he sees him, so I try to keep him out of his way."

"Could I see him sometime?" Brady asked. He was beginning to wonder where Eddie lived. They were getting close to Grandpa Bud's house, and he hoped Eddie wasn't going that far with him. Aunt Tilly might have Sarah out in the yard. Aunt Tilly tried to take her out at least once a day for fresh air and sunshine. The house — he still had a hard time calling it *his* house — was just around the corner and down at the end of the block. The big white house and yard took up the whole corner lot.

"Sure," Eddie said. "I'll bring him around sometime."

"Oh, that's okay," Brady said. He had meant, could he go to Eddie's house, not have Eddie come to his. He didn't want Eddie, or anyone else, to see Sarah.

"I bet your aunt is going to be upset about your clothes being torn and dirty," Eddie said. "You've got blood on your shirt, too."

"Probably," Brady said, but right now he wasn't worried about what Aunt Tilly was going to say. He was worried now about Eddie seeing Sarah. Inside his head, he began a chant. Go *straight, Eddie. Go straight. Don't turn. Don't turn.* But when he turned the corner, Eddie did, too.

"Where do you live?" Brady asked.

"About a mile and a half on past your grandpa's."

"Where do the Blackburns live?" Brady's eyes searched the part of the yard that had come into view. No Aunt Tilly. No Sarah.

"They live east of town two miles. They have a big limestone house. The place used to belong to Mrs. Blackburn's folks."

"Does Raymond walk home?" Brady asked. Somehow he couldn't see Raymond walking two miles.

"Walk." Eddie snorted. "I should say not. He hangs around town as long as he wants and then calls his mother to come and get him, or else he stops at the bank and has someone there take him home."

Brady stopped at the sidewalk that led up to Grandpa Bud's front door. He was thankful there was no sign of Aunt Tilly and Sarah. "Thanks, Eddie," he said. "I guess I'll see you tomorrow."

But Eddie didn't answer him. He was looking past Brady, his eyes wide and startled-looking.

Brady swung around, a jolt of fear shooting through him. Then he saw Aunt Tilly and his fear changed to embarrassment. Aunt Tilly was stepping out of the house, and in her hand was a broom. *Gee,* he thought. *Aunt Tilly is really mad!* He braced himself for the swat of her broom, but she just looked at him, her face more surprised or puzzled than angry.

"My land, Brady," she said. "What in the world happened to you?"

"Well, I've got to go," Eddie said, turning to walk away.

"Not so fast, young man," Aunt Tilly said. "You come on in the house with us. I've got a piece of pie in the kitchen with your name on it. Except..." she paused, a smile deepening the wrinkles in her face, "I don't know your name."

"Eddie," they both said together, and then Eddie added, "Peel. Eddie Peel."

"Well, come on in, Eddie Peel," Aunt Tilly said. "Let's

have that pie and find out what happened at school today."

As they stepped inside the house, Brady darted a quick look around for Sarah. At least she wasn't in the living room. He hoped she wouldn't be in the kitchen either, but she was. Standing in a corner, she was fluttering her little hands and humming. Brady felt his face flush with shame.

"I expect you had better go to the bathroom to wash up, Brady," Aunt Tilly said. "Eddie, you can wash here at the sink. I'll get you a towel."

As Brady closed the bathroom door behind him, he heard Aunt Tilly say, "And this is Sarah, Eddie. Brady's little sister."

Brady grimaced at the face that looked back at him from the bathroom mirror. Boy, was he a mess! Dried blood and dirt streaked his face, and a purple bruise covered one cheekbone. Gingerly, he touched the puffy swelling around his left eye and winced when he saw the cut on his bottom lip. He washed his face carefully and brushed at the dirt and dried blood on his torn shirt and overalls. He wished he hadn't worn his best clothes today. Maybe Aunt Tilly could get his overalls clean again, but his shirt would probably have to go in the ragbag.

When he came out of the bathroom, Eddie was sitting at the kitchen table watching Aunt Tilly fill two large glasses with milk. In front of him was what looked to Brady like a slice of chocolate pie. He hoped it was chocolate anyway. Chocolate anything was his favorite.

"Well," Aunt Tilly said with a grin. "When you change your clothes, you'll look about half normal again." She made a small gesture toward him. "But never mind that now. Come, let's eat our pie and you can tell me what happened."

When Brady finished telling his story around mouthfuls of smooth, creamy pie, he added with a grin, "Boy, Aunt Tilly, when I saw you with that broom, I thought I'd had it for sure."

Aunt Tilly laughed. "I was just going out to sweep off the sidewalk," she said. Then sobering, she added, "I think we should tell your Grandpa Bud. Maybe he can straighten out this business with the Blackburn boy."

Eddie made a soft sound before quickly ducking his head and appearing to examine his hands in his lap.

Aunt Tilly looked at him. "I take it you are well acquainted with this Blackburn person," she said.

Eddie squirmed in his chair. "I didn't mean ... " he began.

"Mean what?" Aunt Tilly said.

"Well, " Eddie began slowly, his eyes still looking at his hands. "Mom works for Mrs. Blackburn ... washes, irons, things like that. She doesn't hardly ever get paid for it. Mrs. Blackburn finds too many wrinkles or a spot or something and docks her pay." He lifted anger-filled eyes to meet Aunt Tilly's. "Mom irons smooth as glass and cleans and washes good, too. But she don't dare argue, or Mrs. Blackburn will fire her ... and ... and ..." he stammered, "we need the money. Even the little she pays her."

Eddie looked back at his hands again, took a deep shuddering breath, and said, "You know my pop can't hold a job. He drinks too much of Sam Blackburn's bootleg liquor."

"I'm sorry, Eddie," Aunt Tilly said. "I could speak to Sheriff Lewis about the liquor. You know, it is illegal in the state of Kansas."

"It won't do any good," Eddie said.

"It might," Aunt Tilly said.

Brady changed his clothes after Eddie left and helped Aunt Tilly clear the table, drying the plates and glasses after she washed them. The first time he had helped her, without even being asked, she had been surprised. "Your mother is blessed to have a child like you," she said. "Not many boys would help with the dishes if they could get out of it."

"I guess I'm used to it," he'd told her. "I didn't even think about it. Since Mom's been so sick, Dad and I have had to do most of the housework." He'd grinned then, teasing her, "But if you don't want me to, I could quit."

"Not on your life," Aunt Tilly had said, smiling back at

him. "But maybe you won't have to do as much as you did at home."

He'd nodded, suddenly swept with a rush of homesickness and worry. Where were his parents now? Was his mother doing better? He wished there was some way he could know.

"I met Mrs. Peel the other day at the grocery store." Aunt Tilly's voice brought him out of his thoughts. "I feel sorry for folks like the Peels. I doubt if Mrs. Peel could find another job, and I'm sure the few dollars she does get are sorely needed. Nowadays few folks can afford to hire household help. Most folks are doing well if the man of the house can hold on to his job. President Roosevelt, bless his heart, is helping folks all he can, but until these hard times are over and the weather straightens up ..." She sighed and, taking the tea towel from Brady's hand, hung it up on the towel rack by the sink.

"I like your friend, Eddie," she said, turning back to look at him. "His mother seems nice, too. She's a pretty woman. Eddie looks much like her." A sudden sparkle danced in her eyes. "Now don't go telling Eddie I said he was pretty," she said, smiling.

"I won't." Brady smiled back at her. "I've got enough cuts and bruises to last me awhile."

Grandpa Bud came home tired and hungry long after supper was over. Aunt Tilly warmed up the roast beef and potatoes she'd set aside and filled a plate heaping full for him. She cut a large slice of chocolate pie and set it beside his plate, filled her coffee cup, and sat at her place across the table from him. Brady eased into his place at the end of the table, opposite Grandpa Bud, and waited.

Grandpa Bud ate silently and slowly as if he were almost too tired to eat. When he had finished his plate and turned to his pie, he began to talk about what had happened that day.

"We found old Mrs. Nelson dead in her bed this morning. The poor soul was skin and bones. There was nothing in the house to eat. Not a thing!" Grandpa Bud's eyes clouded, and for a minute he looked as if he might burst out in a rage of anger. Or, Brady thought with surprise, tears. Then he made several deep, clearing sounds in his throat and continued. "If she'd have just let someone know, the county could have bought her groceries. Now it will have to bury her instead."

"Pride is a hard thing for some folks to get past," Aunt Tilly said.

Grandpa Bud nodded. "I picked up a couple of short-change artists today, too." He grinned suddenly, his mood lifting.

"They were slick. A husband and wife team and both of them as bold as brass. They took Fred over at Sentinel Grocery, and then instead of getting out of town like they would have been smart to have done, they decided to try Cope's Hardware. As soon as John caught on, he told them he'd have to send his boy to the bank for more cash. Johnny ran over to the office and got me."

Grandpa Bud took a deep swallow of coffee and held out his cup for Aunt Tilly to refill. "I have them in jail, Tilly. Do you want me to get their meals at Molly's cafe?"

"No," Aunt Tilly said. "I can manage. The county's allowance for food won't cover too many restaurant meals. And who knows but what you'll have several more tomorrow or the next day."

"I expect you're right," Grandpa Bud said.

True to her word, Aunt Tilly brought up Brady's fight with Raymond Blackburn after Grandpa Bud had finished his supper and was settled in his easy chair by the radio. But she didn't mention Eddie's folks or Sam Blackburn's bootleg liquor. He thought maybe she meant to do that later when he wasn't around to hear. Sometimes grownups were like that.

"I thought you looked a little worse for the wear,"

Grandpa Bud said. "So that's what happened. I'm sorry, son, but I expect Sam Blackburn's boy was given instructions to razz you some. Sam Blackburn hates me over something that happened a long time ago. Probably his boy doesn't even know the whole story. But if his daddy says to do something, I expect he does it. Sam's wife, too. Although she's turned out to be about as mean as he is ... too bad. Her old daddy's probably spinning in his grave." Grandpa Bud shifted in his chair. "From what I've heard about the boy, he's a chip off the old block and then some. If he grows up, he'll put his old man in the shade when it comes to meanness."

"If he grows up?" Brady said. "Is something wrong with him?"

"No." A flicker of a smile touched Grandpa Bud's face. " I just meant that boys like him, who fight at the drop of a hat and generally cause trouble, are usually unhappy boys. Unhappy boys, when they get old enough, usually drive too fast, drink too much and get into too many fights. In a way, they are to be pitied."

He leaned over and began turning the dial on the radio. "Don't let him get your goat or he'll keep at you." He paused, his fingers on the dial, and looked back at Brady. "I guess you held your own with him today, didn't you?"

"Yes, sir. I guess so," Brady said. But he wouldn't have if the principal hadn't intervened. Otherwise, Raymond Blackburn and his gang would probably have beaten him into mincemeat. But he wasn't going to tell Grandpa Bud that because, well ... maybe because Grandpa Bud wasn't listening to him any more. He had turned up the volume on the radio, and President Roosevelt's voice was filling the room.

9

THE WIND BLEW day and night all the rest of the school week. The wind kept the dust stirred up, so no one wanted to be outside. Recess was held in the auditorium, and after school they were told to go straight home. No one needed to be told twice.

That week Raymond Blackburn's mother brought him to school and picked him up afterwards in a 1932 Ford Coupe of dark green. Some of the other parents picked up their kids, too, but most, including him and Eddie, ducked their heads against the wind and dirt and hurried home as fast as they could.

Brady was almost glad for the miserable weather as it gave Raymond less of an opportunity to harass him. But he knew it wouldn't last forever. Now and then he would look up and find Raymond's black eyes staring mockingly at him, and several times each day Raymond, or one of his buddies, would "accidentally" bump him and whisper something about Sarah.

It was hard to ignore them, but so far Brady had kept his anger in check. He knew they were just waiting for him to explode. And if he did, he would be giving them just what they wanted. And when it was over, if there was anything left of him, he would be the one kicked out of school — not Raymond — but him.

He hated to think of what Grandpa Bud would say if that happened. "You held your own, didn't you?" he had asked. And after telling him he had, although not telling him the whole truth of it, Brady sure wasn't going to let it prove out otherwise, if he could help it.

He guessed Raymond had gotten to Eddie, too, for Eddie had been avoiding him all week. He always seemed to be fiddling with his books or something at his desk so he came late for recess and sometimes didn't show up for lunch at all.

At noon on Friday, Brady picked up his lunch sack and walked over to where Eddie had suddenly lifted the top of his desk and appeared to be extra busy doing something with the papers inside. Brady knew he was pretending not to see him.

"What's the matter?" he asked. "Did I do or say something you didn't like, or is Blackburn threatening you if you hang around with me?"

Eddie looked up at him and then slowly closed the top of his desk. "You don't want to be friends with me," he said.

"Why not?" Brady demanded.

"Gee. You're the sheriff's grandson and have that nice, big white house to live in. My family's not much ..." His voice trailed away and he looked down at his desk top.

But I'm not the sheriff's grandson, Brady thought. *I don't know who half of me is.*

For the hundred millionth time he wished he could have known his dad's folks. He wished they had lived. They would have taken him and Sarah. At least he knew they were blood. His dad had a picture of them, and his dad looked exactly like the man in those pictures.

Brady stared at Eddie, unable to think of anything to say. A part of why he wanted to be friends with Eddie was because Eddie had already seen Sarah. And because Eddie had said something that had made him think, for the first time, more about Sarah than himself and the shame he felt over having her for his sister.

They had just finished the chocolate pie when Sarah

had come up to Aunt Tilly, her little fingers making tiny, plucking motions at the sleeve of Aunt Tilly's dress, a signal that she wanted something, and generally meant she had to go to the bathroom.

When they left the room, Eddie said, "Gosh, Brady, but your little sister is so beautiful. It's too bad life played such a mean trick on her."

Eddie's words had shocked him, but he had seen the truth in them, too. Sarah would be a regular little girl if fate hadn't decided otherwise. However Sarah was, it wasn't her fault, and he had been acting like it was.

The other reason he wanted Eddie as a friend was because he didn't plan to stay here long. As soon as his dad found work in California and his mom got better, they would come back for him and Sarah. Or maybe the rains would start soon and things would begin to grow again and his mother could come home. No, he wasn't planning to stay long, and one friend was all he needed, all he wanted.

"Maybe some of the fellas will be friends with you," Eddie spoke quietly. "Some of them don't much care for Raymond Blackburn."

"I still think he would pick on them," Brady said. "I guess he wouldn't care if we're friends, so ..." He stopped. Shoot, he thought, now I've probably hurt Eddie's feelings.

Eddie gave a little snort of a laugh. "No," he said, "I don't guess he would. Not a Peel. Not the town drunk's son."

"Then I guess you can eat lunch with me," Brady said.

"I didn't bring any lunch."

"I can share," Brady said. "Aunt Tilly always packs plenty."

Again he felt embarrassed. The Peels must not have enough for Eddie to take a lunch, leastwise not every day. And here he was bragging about having plenty.

Eddie studied him a moment, and then a quick grin flitted across his face. "Did she put in any of that pie? I've been remembering that pie all week."

Brady laughed. "How about chocolate cookies?" he said.

"Good enough," Eddie said, grinning. "Let's go eat."

Saturday morning dawned clear and sunny with no wind. Aunt Tilly announced at breakfast that she needed Brady's help planting a garden in the back yard.

Brady had planned to ask Grandpa Bud if he could go with him to the office to see the jail, but Grandpa Bud had already left by the time he got up.

"Some fellow called this morning," Aunt Tilly said. "Found evidence that one of his calves had been butchered out. Nothing left but the hide and hooves, I guess," she added, setting a bowl of oatmeal down in front of him.

After washing the breakfast dishes, Aunt Tilly put on a wide-brimmed, floppy hat and sort of herded Sarah out into the backyard. "A little sun will do this child good," she said. If there was one thing Aunt Tilly believed in, Brady thought, it was fresh air and sunshine.

David Hager, a boy in Brady's class, lived across the street. Brady had seen him outside a few times. He hoped he wouldn't come over, and he didn't think he would. David Hager was sure to know that he was Raymond Blackburn's enemy, and to go against Raymond would just make trouble for himself.

He did wish Eddie would come over, though. Maybe Aunt Tilly would let him out of planting the garden if Eddie came by. Maybe they could walk out of town and look the country over a little bit. A sudden vision of the fields at home, as they used to be, brought the sharp sting of homesickness to him. He pushed it aside and turned to Aunt Tilly to see what she wanted him to do first.

Aunt Tilly planted her garden just like his mother used to do. Using string tied to stakes at each end of a row and drawn taut across the soft dirt, she hoed a straight furrow along it. Behind her, Brady dropped in the seeds and patted the soil firmly over them. After a while, Brady began to enjoy himself. In a way, it was kind of like farming, he thought.

At mid-morning, Aunt Tilly wiped her flushed face with the hem of her apron and announced that it was lemonade time. And almost as if he'd been waiting for just such words, Eddie appeared with his pet crow riding on his shoulder.

Aunt Tilly exclaimed over the crow and, cautioning Eddie with a grin on her face not to let that crow into her garden, crossed to where Sarah sat on the ground, her legs tucked under her, picking at an imaginary object. Quickly raising the little girl to her feet, almost before she had time to protest, she followed behind her, and sort of herded her ahead of her and into the house.

"So this is Blackie," Brady said.

The crow cocked his head and stared at Brady with black, shiny eyes. "Say hello to Brady," Eddie said, grinning.

The bird opened his beak. "Hello, hello," he said, his raspy voice a strangely human sound.

Brady laughed. "Have him say that again."

But, although Eddie coaxed and coaxed, the bird refused to say the word over again.

"Does he know any other words?" Brady asked.

"I've been trying to teach him to say my name," Eddie said. "But so far, no luck. It took a long time to teach him to say hello, so maybe one day he will."

"My sons shared a pet crow," Aunt Tilly said, coming out of the house carrying a tray with two glasses of lemonade and a stack of cheese and crackers. "He loved shiny things. I lost my wedding band once and the boys found it in George's stash in the corner of the hayloft."

"That sounds just like Blackie," Eddie said. "He likes Mom's clothespins, too. Once he unpinned all of her wash, and when she came out to gather it in, it was all laying on the ground." Eddie grinned. "She was pretty upset."

"What happened to your boys' crow," Brady asked, looking up at Aunt Tilly.

"I don't know. My boys were twins. They did everything together." She sighed and a faraway look came into her eyes.

"They drowned swimming in the river the summer they were ten. I don't know what happened to their bird. I thought about him months later when my grief wasn't so strong, but by then he was no longer around."

She stood still for a moment gazing out beyond the backyard. Out, Brady thought, into another time and place. Then she shook herself a little and looked back at them.

"Mercy sakes," she said, "here I go running off at the mouth and you two boys are probably half starved. Go ahead." She motioned toward the tray. "Eat your fill. If you want more, come in and get it." She grinned. "But don't bother me. I'm going to be sitting in my easy chair with my feet up on the ottoman."

They sat down on the back steps. Brady could tell Eddie was pretty hungry. He didn't stuff his mouth full of cheese and crackers or gulp down the lemonade, but Brady saw him swallow a time or two like he was pushing back a rush of saliva. He wondered when Eddie had eaten last.

Eddie finished helping them plant the garden, and Aunt Tilly invited him to stay for dinner. They waited awhile for Grandpa Bud to come home, but he never showed, so they ate the thick stew and fat slices of buttered bread without him. Blackie waited in the hackberry tree in the back yard.

After they had eaten, Aunt Tilly put a covered bowl of stew and some buttered bread in a box and turned to Brady. "Your grandpa has a fellow in jail, and I need to see that he gets his dinner. Could you take it for me?"

"Sure," Brady said. "Can Eddie go with me?"

"What about the crow?" Aunt Tilly said.

"I don't like to take him up town," Eddie said frowning. "I guess I had better go home."

"There's an old chicken coop out in the shed," Aunt Tilly said. "Would he stay in that?"

Eddie grinned. "That's what I put him in at home when I go to school. Mom lets him out after I'm gone."

They set the chicken coop under the hackberry tree, and

Eddie pulled off the ragged bill cap he wore and put it inside with the bird. "For company," he said, "so he'll know I'm coming back."

The sheriff's office and jail were in the courthouse in the middle of town. Eddie said he had been there before, but he didn't say why.

"Your grandpa is still out on a case," Mr. Shiller said, taking the box containing the jailed man's dinner. "Don't know when to expect him back."

"That's okay," Brady said. "Aunt Tilly just wanted us to bring the prisoner's dinner."

The slightly stooped, gray-mustached Mr. Schiller nodded. He was an old man hired by the county to sweep the jail and keep an eye on things when Grandpa Bud and his deputy, Pete Peters, had to be out. Now he squinted at Eddie. "You a Peel?" he asked.

"Yes, sir," Eddie answered.

"I thought so," the old man said.

A slight flush colored Eddie's cheeks, and he turned toward the door.

He's embarrassed, Brady thought. He's ashamed of being a Peel on account of his dad. Brady thought of how Sarah had embarrassed him, just being who she was. But like Eddie said, she was the one who got the bum deal. She couldn't help being how she was, but Eddie's dad could, couldn't he?

"Come on, Eddie," Brady said. "Let's go. We'll see you, Mr. Schiller," he called as they went out the door.

They walked back across town, past Wint's Barber Shop, Cope's Hardware, the Sentinel Grocery and Porter's Drug Store. In every store window was a sign announcing a rabbit drive to be held the Sunday after next.

"Are you going?" Brady asked.

Eddie shrugged. "Maybe," he said.

"Have you been to one?"

"A couple of times. I went with my brothers. It's exciting. Boy, do you kill a lot of rabbits. But it takes some getting used to."

"I wonder if Grandpa Bud will go," Brady said. "I guess I'll ask him. If we go, do you want to go with us?"

"Sure," Eddie said. "I'll ..." He broke off with a sudden, sharp intake of breath and his whole body stiffened.

Looking up, Brady saw a man coming toward them, and he knew instantly that it was Eddie's dad. The man, weaving back and forth on the sidewalk, looked as ragged and dirty and skinny as an old scarecrow left out in the fields through a long winter.

As they met, the boys drew aside to let him pass. Neither Eddie nor his dad spoke. Brady doubted if Eddie's dad even saw them as he stumbled by mumbling to himself, a smoky sourness lingering after him.

They walked a block in silence and then Eddie said, "That was my old man."

"Yeah, " Brady said. "I thought so."

"I suppose he's out of cigarette makings," Eddie said. "When he runs out, he staggers down to the grocery store and has them put on the bill for Mom to pay. Then they put him out the door and point him towards home. If he don't fall off the sidewalk or have to stop and throw up or pee in some alley and get disorientated, he'll get home before dark."

Brady nodded. In the distance came the long, drawn-out whistle of a train. "Sounds like a train coming into town," he said, hoping Eddie would stop talking about his father. It made him feel half sick, seeing Eddie so shamed.

"That's Number Eight coming in from the west," Eddie said. "She comes through here every afternoon at this time." He looked over at Brady. "Do you want to go watch her come in?"

"Sure," Brady said.

They broke into a trot, Eddie taking them through alleys and catty-corner across several streets. They arrived at the depot just as the train pulled into the station, the engineer pulling on a big yellow bell so it clanged loudly as the billowing, hissing steam dissipated in the air.

Excitement shown in Eddie's face. "Man," he said, "when I grow up, I'm going to be an engineer."

"Well, wave to me as you go by," Brady said, grinning. "If this drought ever lifts so a fella can grow a decent crop, I'll be back in southwest Kansas working our farm."

The two boys watched the train empty out its passengers. Suddenly, Eddie grabbed Brady's arm. "Look there," he said. "See that fella with the black hat and suit and tie? That's Sam Blackburn, Raymond's daddy. Don't they look alike? My brothers say they just chopped a hunk of meanness off Sam Blackburn to get Raymond. Said there couldn't be no baby born that mean."

They watched the man walk across to the parking area to a big black car. A Plymouth, Brady decided, and brand new at that. He thought Raymond walked just like his old man, a kind of swaggering strut that put him in mind of a big ol' cocky rooster.

"I bet he's been to Denver," Eddie said. "Folks say he goes out there to play poker with some of the big-shot fellas he knows. I guess he must be good," he added. "Or else he wouldn't keep going."

As the boys turned away from the train yard and started back along the dusty streets, Eddie said, "My brothers left home to ride the freights last year. They'll be back when school is out this year to take me with them."

"Are you going to go?" Brady asked, already knowing the answer.

"Sure. It'll help Mom. She won't have to worry about feeding me if I'm gone, and maybe I can make a little money, too. My brothers send Mom all the cash they can, but it's never much, times are hard all over." Eddie shrugged. "I sure miss them." And then as if to change the subject, he said, "I wonder how Blackie's doing."

When they got back to Grandpa Bud's, the crow seemed

perfectly content. Aunt Tilly had given him some clothespins and a tin bowl, and he was busy dropping them into the bowl and taking them out again.

"We talked," Aunt Tilly said, smiling. "He says he likes it in there. I gave him some water and a little bread soaked in milk. He kept saying, 'Hello, hello,' every time I started back to the house."

"Thanks, Mrs. Johnson," Eddie said. "It was nice of you to feed him."

"It was my pleasure," Aunt Tilly said. "But, please, call me Aunt Tilly, like Brady does, won't you?"

"Okay, Aunt Tilly," Eddie mumbled, ducking his head shyly, but when he looked up again, Brady could tell he was pleased.

As Eddie and Blackie were leaving, Grandpa Bud arrived home tired and hungry. "We found a couple of boot prints and where they loaded the beef on a horse," he said when Aunt Tilly asked him about the butchered calf. "There's some rumors out, too, we aim to follow up on."

"Do you suppose you'll ever catch them?" Aunt Tilly asked, putting a full plate of beef stew in front of him.

Grandpa Bud shrugged. "I don't know," he said.

Later, after he had listened to the news on the radio, Grandpa Bud mentioned the rabbit drive. "Could you fix us a take-along dinner, Tilly? Everyone is meeting at the old Vermillion schoolhouse as soon as church is over."

Aunt Tilly looked over at Brady and winked. "Maybe Brady could ask Eddie Peel to go with us," she said.

But Grandpa Bud didn't answer her. He had fallen asleep in his chair and was snoring softly.

10

THE SUNDAY OF THE RABBIT DRIVE dawned bright with sunshine in a cloudless blue sky. The past week of school had gone fairly well for Brady, even with Raymond Blackburn and his henchmen goading him every chance they got. He had managed to avoid them most of the time by constantly watching for them and ducking out of their way when they came near. But a couple of times he'd been caught and shoved and taunted about Sarah, and several times, when Eddie was with him, scorned and ridiculed for having Eddie for a friend.

After one encounter, when the boys mocking him about being Eddie's friend — and totally ignoring Eddie, as they always did — had had their fun broken up by the presence of Mr. Horn coming down the hallway, Eddie had said in a matter-of-fact voice, "Have you noticed that being the town drunk's kid, I get spoken about, but never to? I guess that makes me not good enough even for their words."

Not knowing what to say, Brady had only nodded. Later, he wished he would have said, "Their *words aren't good enough for you, Eddie.*"

He wished he could say it still, but he didn't know how to bring it up now without hurting Eddie's feelings all over again. Maybe he would have the chance this afternoon during the rabbit drive.

Because Aunt Tilly was getting along so well with Sarah, she had announced the Saturday evening before last that she would like to go to church and take Sarah, if Grandpa Bud would drive them. "Otherwise," she said. "I guess we can walk."

"If nothing's going on," Grandpa Bud said, smiling a little, "I'd be glad to drive you and I'll go myself."

That meant, Brady knew, that he would be expected to go, too. He hoped there wouldn't be any kids from school at Aunt Tilly's church. Even though he felt better about Sarah now, he knew if she acted up and started running around, flipping her little hands and yelling like she did when she got upset, he'd be embarrassed. And if Raymond Blackburn and his friends were there, he hated to think of the misery he'd have to suffer at school on Monday.

"What if Sarah gets upset in church?" Brady asked Aunt Tilly, hoping she would reconsider what he thought was a rash notion.

"I'll take her out until she calms down," Aunt Tilly said. "We can't stop our lives because of Sarah. Folks will get used to her, and perhaps she will get used to them."

I wouldn't count on that, Brady thought.

But Sarah did very well.

The Methodist church, a big, white, tall-steepled building, had most of the pews filled, but there were no Blackburns, nor did Brady see any of Raymond's friends.

David Hager, from across the street, sat with his parents. Brady saw David look over at him several times, but he pretended not to see him.

After church, Brady hurried out ahead of Aunt Tilly and Grandpa Bud and climbed into the car. Looking out of the back window, he saw David and his family drive away in their old black Ford.

Later, Brady asked Eddie where the Blackburns went to church, if they did.

"They're Presbyterians," Eddie said. "Edna Blackburn's daddy was big in the church, folks say, and Sam Blackburn just followed in his footsteps, only Mr. Crandall's footsteps were real and Sam Blackburn's aren't even poor imitations. Everyone liked Mr. Crandall, and maybe Edna, too, until she turned mean from living with Sam Blackburn."

When Brady asked Eddie what church his family attended, Eddie said he didn't remember ever going to church.

The Sunday morning of the rabbit drive, Sarah had behaved especially well in church, and on the way home Aunt Tilly couldn't seem to quit talking about her. "I think it was the music. She just listened and then began humming along right with it. And I swear to goodness that she had the tune just perfect." Her face beaming, Aunt Tilly turned her head to look back at Brady and Sarah in the back seat. "If she could talk, I bet she would sing like an angel."

Her praise of Sarah reminded Brady again of Eddie's words, "*It's too bad life played such a mean trick on her.*" A rush of affection for his little sister made his eyes sting. Quickly he turned his head and looked out of the car window, turning his thoughts ahead to the rabbit drive that afternoon.

At the house, Aunt Tilly changed Sarah's dress and finished getting the food ready to take to the rabbit drive. Grandpa Bud eased the car back out on the street and headed for his office, assuring Aunt Tilly he would return for them in a little while.

The last few days, Brady had searched for something to use for a rabbit club. He had been about to give up when Grandpa Bud suggested a leg off an old broken table in the shed.

"I've got an axe handle in the car I use," he said. Then he grinned. "Actually I keep it there in case some would-be tough gets too big for his britches."

Brady grinned back. He knew Grandpa Bud also kept a gun under the front seat, instead of on his hip like Sheriff Bills back home did. Down at the sheriff's office, locked up in a case, were several rifles and a shotgun. He thought of how excited his friend, Jim Conners, would be to see all those weapons, and his grin widened.

Brady was pulling on the table leg when Eddie appeared at the door of the shed. "I got us both a club," he said. Brady looked up from the jumble of boxes, old tires, magazines, newspapers and other discarded items, and let go of the table leg. He climbed over a stack of wooden boxes and jumped down beside Eddie.

"I brought my brothers' clubs for us," Eddie said. "They're old wagon spokes." He held one out to Brady. "You can use Jimmy Joe's and I'll take T.J.'s. Okay?"

"Thanks," Brady said, taking the club Eddie offered and giving it several trial swings.

"Hey, this is all right," he said with a grin. "Let's go get us some rabbits."

They rode in Grandpa Bud's Hudson. Aunt Tilly had fried mounds of golden chicken and had mixed big bowls of potato salad and coleslaw which she sat on the back seat beside them.

The smell of the fried chicken made Brady's mouth water, and he wondered how Eddie could stand to sit beside that delicious aroma. Aunt Tilly had made biscuits and eggs for breakfast this morning. Eddie probably hadn't eaten any breakfast at all.

Sarah sat up front between Grandpa Bud and Aunt Tilly. It still bothered Brady to have his sister going along. She had done well in church, but this was different. Church was quieter, and Sarah had liked the music. That was probably what had kept her so calm.

Outside, with people milling around and laughing and talking, Sarah was sure to get a little agitated. Especially if she got tired, which she was bound to do with all the excitement and everything.

He worried, too, that Raymond Blackburn would be there and would see Sarah. He had no idea what Raymond would say or do when he saw her. Maybe nothing with Grandpa

Bud around, but at school he was sure to be all mouth and then some.

Grandpa Bud hadn't been too pleased about taking Sarah to the rabbit drive either. But Aunt Tilly had overridden his protests. "My friends will help me with her," she'd said. "Just don't you worry, Bud. She'll do fine."

Brady hoped she was right.

As they drove out of town and along the dusty roads, they were sandwiched in a line of other cars all heading for the old schoolhouse and the rabbit drive, and all stirring up clouds of gray, choking dust. They rolled up the windows, but the dust still sifted in, and the car soon grew stifling hot.

Sweat rolled off Grandpa Bud's face, and Aunt Tilly kept dabbing her upper lip and forehead with her handkerchief. Brady's skin itched as the sweat trickled down inside his shirt and overalls, but Eddie and Sarah looked as if the heat and dust didn't bother them at all.

Brady envied those riding horseback across open fields, trotting along or putting their horses into long, easy lopes, the wind fanning away the heat and dust. But he wouldn't trade places with those who rode in the buggies and wagons they slowed to pass along the way. If anyone ate dust, it was those folks.

At the school, Grandpa Bud parked the Hudson beside the other cars and trucks. All around them, doors opened and smiling, sweating faces emerged, calling out good-natured greetings.

Brady and Eddie carried the food for Aunt Tilly to the long tables set up in the sparse shade of two small trees beside the school house. Aunt Tilly shook out a blanket and laid it close to the building and out of the direct rays of the sun. Brady held his breath as Sarah walked on the blanket, turning in little circles. He just knew she was going to raise a fuss, but Aunt Tilly reached into her apron pocket and took out a cookie. Smiling, Sarah took the cookie and sat down. Brady released his breath in a swoosh of air so loud that Eddie gave him a quick, startled glance.

While they waited for the women to set out the food on the tables the men had made of boards laid over sawhorses, Brady and Eddie listened to the talk around them. Most of the talk centered on past rabbit drives and how the animal, especially the jack rabbit, had multiplied in the last few years.

"I bet we'll get more jacks than cottontails," one of the men standing close to Grandpa Bud said. "Leastwise, I hope so. A dozen of those big critters can eat near as much as a yearling heifer."

"That's right," a man standing next to him said. "My pastures are in bad shape anyway. If it don't rain soon, I'll have to start selling off my stock."

"I set out a windbreak last year," another man spoke up. "What the drought didn't kill, the rabbits did. They chewed the bark off as high as they could reach. I replanted this spring. I've got chicken wire around them now. I tried wrapping gunnysacks around the trunks first, but the darn things started chewing up the gunnysacks. I hope we get a passel of them this time."

"If we don't," the man beside Grandpa Bud said, "they'll eat everything ... every blade of grass in our pastures, our crops, gardens, everything ..."

"If it don't rain soon," another said, " there won't be a crop anyway." He paused and, pulling out a red bandanna from his hip pocket, began wiping his sweaty, florid face. "Getting mighty hot for so early in the year, and I'm seeing twice the grasshoppers already."

Grandpa Bud acknowledged the man and then added, "Looks like the women have the food all set out and Reverend Jamison's got his hands folded like he's warming up a prayer. I believe we're about ready to eat, fellas."

Eddie plucked at Brady's sleeve as a white-haired old man called for everyone's attention. "That's the Presbyterian minister," he whispered, "Blackburn's minister."

Brady bowed his head for the prayer, and when he looked up again, Raymond Blackburn's black eyes were staring at him from several feet away. A swift, sudden anger shot through him, and he stared back. In that moment he knew he was through hiding from Raymond Blackburn and his toughs. He would not run any more. Let them taunt him about Sarah. Let them scorn him for being Eddie's friend. He didn't care. Eddie was worth the whole lot of them and then some.

No. Today, at this moment, he had quit running!

He narrowed his eyes and directed a hard, mean stare back at Raymond, who laughed and turned away to begin filling his plate.

When Brady and Eddie had their plates heaped full, they sat down on the running board of Grandpa Bud's car. From where they sat, Brady could see Aunt Tilly put a plate down in front of Sarah. The little girl picked up a spoon and began eating. Brady grinned and turned to his own food. He felt good. Better than he had felt in a long, long while. He sure wished he would hear from his parents though. But maybe a card or even a letter would be in tomorrow's mail. Maybe. He sure hoped so.

After they had eaten, Sam Blackburn stepped up on the back of a truck and called for everyone's attention. The talk ceased.

"You men know who your captain is," Sam Blackburn said. "Listen to him." He pulled a shiny watch out of his vest pocket and looked down at it. "It's two o'clock now. We're covering nine sections with the pen set up in the middle, taking up the corners of Murdock's and Swartz's land. At two forty-five, we expect everyone to be on the line and ready to move forward. Any questions?"

"Let's go get 'em!" a voice called out, echoed by several others shouting in agreement.

Brady and Eddie rode with Grandpa Bud the three miles

north and two miles east to take their place in the line. Leaving the car by the side of the road with the vehicles of the other walkers, they stepped up to the long line beginning to form. Brady was surprised to see several women and girls in the line.

He groaned inwardly, feeling his cheeks go hot, when two girls from the eighth grade class came running up to stand next to him and Eddie. Back at the schoolhouse, Sarah had suddenly jumped up, knocking over her plate, and started running about like she did sometimes, in her little galloping gait, up on her tiptoes, her hands flapping. Aunt Tilly had eventually coaxed her back to the blanket, but not before she had bumped into these two girls.

Sarah's actions had made him angry with Aunt Tilly. Why had she thought it was all right to let people see how Sarah acted? Why didn't Sarah ever embarrass Aunt Tilly? Was it because she wasn't really related to her? Because she wasn't blood kin?

"Hello, Brady. Eddie," the girl, named Mary, said. The other one, whose name was Sue, just giggled.

He figured she was remembering Sarah, and a surge of anger coursed through him. "Hello," he muttered and turned to look down the long line of people stretched out across the flat, open land. He did not look at the girls again.

The mid-afternoon sun was hot. Brady lifted his cap and ran his fingers through his sweaty hair. A little breeze, picking up swirls of dust at their feet, cooled his head, and he pulled the cap back down and waited.

Grandpa Bud looked at his pocket watch. The line of people grew quieter. Most of them were watching the captain now, a short, stocky, sandy-haired man whose own eyes were on the watch in his hand. Then the man looked up and, raising his club overhead, called out, "All right, folks, let's go get 'em!"

The line surged forward chanting and whooping, their clubs swinging at weeds and bushes and thumping the ground, raising dust, like dry mist all around them. Suddenly, the first rabbit, a big jack, leaped out of a bush and dashed ahead of the line. At the sight of the jackrabbit, the yelling and whooping and hollering grew louder and the clubs swung harder and faster.

"The taste of blood," Eddie shouted.

"War cries!" Brady shouted back, the excitement building until he was yelling whooping war cries of his own.

Soon other rabbits, both jacks and cottontails, were running in their zig-zag pattern, trying desperately to escape the mob of shouting humans. Some of the rabbits tried doubling back, but the mob closed up ranks and few escaped.

Brady and Eddie worked side by side, moving sideways at times to keep the rabbits from darting back and escaping between them. The physical exertion, the shouting and the feeling of unity in this crowd of people swept over Brady in an exhilarating rush of excitement, and he swung his club at the weeds and laughed and yelled at the mass of weaving, darting rabbits.

Suddenly, to Brady's surprise, a flock of crows landed in among the running rabbits. Flying up as the walkers drew close, they would light again a little farther ahead in the midst of the wave of moving rabbits.

"Look at that!" he shouted to Eddie.

"I see them," Eddie called back. "I've heard they sometimes do that." He moved quickly sideways to head off an escaping rabbit. "I don't know why. Some kind of a fascination, I guess."

"Probably glad we're after rabbits this time and not crows," a man beside them said, grinning.

"We'll go after them next time," another shouted.

"Already have," another man called. "You ought to see my boy, he can shoot the eye out of a crow at fifty paces."

Brady darted a quick look at Eddie.

"It's okay," Eddie said. "Maybe I'd hunt them, too, if they still paid a bounty. It wouldn't have anything to do with

Blackie. He's different. He's a pet."

As they drew near the large square pen made of chicken wire and snow-fence lath, with an open gate of fencing fanning out on either side, the walkers stood shoulder to shoulder, and the rabbits, Brady thought, had to number in the hundreds.

He had lost sight of Eddie and Grandpa Bud as the circle of walkers tightened. The girl, Mary, was a few feet away, but she was dropping back. Some boys and men were moving in ahead of her as they drove the rabbits on toward the pen.

The line that had started out so orderly had dissolved into a moving, yelling mob as it pushed the rabbits into the enclosure. Brady looked for Eddie and Grandpa Bud as he moved forward into the pen. He didn't see them, but not more than two feet away was Raymond Blackburn. He was staring at Brady, his black eyes glaring out of his sweaty, dirt-streaked face. Brady narrowed his eyes and glared back.

And then he was in the midst of the slaughter with clubs swinging all around him and rabbits squealing as the blows connected. It was a madness ... a nightmare ... Brady swung his club, and a rabbit squealed and died. He swung again and again.

Sometime early on in the midst of the killing, Brady saw the girl, Mary, swinging her club hard and fast, but tears were making streaks through the dirt on her cheeks. He thought he knew how she felt, and he remembered Eddie's words. "*It takes some getting used to.*"

Mounds of rabbits soon lay against the fence, dead piled upon dead, and the swinging clubs began to lose their momentum. Brady realized he wasn't ducking the others' clubs quite so much and that the noise level, the grunts and squeals and yells of humans and animals, was decreasing. Then, without warning, something whacked him across the back and he fell, face down, in the dirt. A hand reached for him ... Eddie's ...

He was pulled to his feet. His back felt like it was on fire. "Look behind you," Eddie hissed.

Brady turned, spitting dirt and rabbit fur from his mouth. Standing several feet away, an evil-looking grin on his face, was Raymond Blackburn.

A wild, fierce anger surged through Brady and, with a hoarse cry of rage, he raised his club and charged toward him.

"Brady!" Grandpa Bud's voice thundered in anger and his hand grasped Brady's arm in a strong grip. "What in the devil is the matter with you, son?"

Brady could not answer. Rage choked off any words. He struggled against Grandpa Bud's gripping hand, intent only on reaching Raymond Blackburn.

Raymond Blackburn stood watching, grinning his evil grin. Then he turned and disappeared into the crowd.

"Brady," Grandpa Bud shook him. "What's got into you, boy?"

Brady stopped struggling. "Raymond Blackburn," he said through gritted teeth. "He clubbed me across my back! Knocked me flat in the dirt! And he did it on purpose!"

Grandpa Bud's face was set hard and stern. "Are you two still having run-ins at school?" he asked.

"Yes, he calls Sarah a retard, a dummy."

"Well, it's best to ignore folks like that," Grandpa Bud said. "They're ignorant and unless it happens in their family, they usually stay that way." The stern set of his face relaxed and a small grin touched his lips. "Even," he added, "if you beat the thunder out of them." He turned from Brady to survey the carnage strewn before them. "Well," he said, "we've still got work to do. So let's get with it."

Grandpa Bud moved away and bent to grab up the legs of the dead rabbits and fling them up into the bed of an old Ford truck that had just been driven into the pen.

His back hurting as if every bone in it had been broken, Brady moved toward Eddie, and together they began to pick up the dead rabbits. As he worked, Brady kept the anger pushed back — anger at Raymond Blackburn and Grandpa Bud as well. It was fine for Grandpa Bud not to take offense over Raymond Blackburn's words and actions. Sarah wasn't related to him. .. not by blood. He didn't have to worry that people would think something was wrong with him, too. Everyone knew Grandpa Bud wasn't really his and Sarah's grandpa.

When the pen finally emptied of rabbits, the walkers began leaving to go to their cars, trucks, wagons or saddle horses. Most of the cottontails would provide meat for a lot of tables tonight. The big jack rabbits would go for chicken and hog feed. Eddie had four cottontails, and Brady carried four more for him. He would skin them as soon as he got home, he said, and his mother would can the meat.

"I could come over and help you skin them," Brady said.

"That's okay," Eddie said, "I can do it."

"That's a lot of rabbits to skin," Brady said.

"I'm pretty fast," Eddie answered.

Brady started to say more, but Grandpa Bud interrupted. "You're walking like an old man now, Brady," he said. "You had better stay home and let Aunt Tilly take a look at that back of yours. She'd never forgive me if I didn't let her practice her doctoring skills on you, boy."

There was a warning sound in the tone of Grandpa Bud's voice. Suddenly Brady realized that just as he was embarrassed over someone seeing Sarah, so Eddie was embarrassed about having him in his home. But why, Brady couldn't figure. He had already seen Eddie's father at what had to be his very worst.

11

GRADUATION WAS ALL anyone could talk about as the end of May drew near. All of the eighth graders were excited, except, Brady thought, himself and Eddie. During practice he was lined up to sit between Freddie Evans, Raymond Blackburn's friend, and Sue Goodwin, one of the girls Sarah had bumped into at the rabbit hunt. The girl who had giggled when she saw Brady afterwards. Next to her sat David Hager from across the street. Because of the alphabetical listing, Raymond Blackburn was in a first-row seat.

Eddie had asked to be excused from attending the ceremony, so he didn't come to practice at all. "They'll mail me my diploma," he said.

At first Brady had considered asking to be excused, too, but Eddie had changed his mind.

"So, Blackie," he'd said, caressing the shiny, black feathers of his pet crow. "Brady has a pair of shoes, pants without holes and a new shirt, too. Seems funny he's not going to graduation."

"Hello," Blackie said, cocking his head to one side and staring up into Eddie's face. "Hello."

Brady felt his cheeks redden with embarrassment. He should have known that Eddie wasn't going because he had nothing but ragged overalls to wear and broken-down old shoes that hurt his feet.

Aunt Tilly had taken Brady to the J.C. Penney store to buy him a new white shirt and a tie. His Sunday pants, she decided, were good enough, and she thought his shoes, after polishing, would be presentable, too. Brady wished he could go back home and look in the attic for some clothes he had outgrown and give them to Eddie. But even if he could go home, his old clothes probably weren't there any more. His mother was certain to have given them away. "*There are too many children needing clothes to save things you've outgrown,*" his mother once told him when he'd protested about giving away a favorite, but too small jacket.

On graduation night, Brady marched across the stage and received his diploma along with the rest of the class. His new shirt and tie and polished shoes made him feel conscious of himself, but good, too. He liked the feeling and could understand even more how Eddie would have felt dressed in his ragged clothes.

Raymond Blackburn had swaggered across the stage in a new gray suit. Only Raymond and his dad, Mr. Horn and the superintendent wore suits.

Grandpa Bud and Aunt Tilly were in the crowd. Aunt Tilly had left Sarah at home with one of her church friends, for which Brady was grateful. Walking back to his seat, his diploma in hand, Brady thought of his parents. Would they return before high school started in the fall? If they didn't come or send for him and Sarah to come to California, who would he have for a friend next year? Eddie wouldn't be here to go on to high school, but it was doubtful that he would go anyway, even if his brothers didn't come for him. But Eddie was certain they would.

"They said if I would finish the eighth grade, they'd come for me," Eddie said. "So I know they will. They know our sister, Mayrose, got married last year and is trying to get Mom and my little sister to come and live with her." Sighing a heavy, deep sigh, he added, "Mayrose's husband just does odd jobs and works some on people's cars. Mom thinks three extra mouths are too much, but maybe if I'm gone with T.J. and Jimmy Joe, she'll take Lilly and go."

Aunt Tilly had invited Eddie for ice cream and cake following graduation. She had insisted, too, on Sarah eating with them. But Sarah, flighty and cross, refused to eat. Yelling and hitting at Aunt Tilly, she jumped up from the table and knocked over her glass of milk, spilling it all over her dress. Sighing, Aunt Tilly changed Sarah's dress and washed it out to hang it on the clothesline.

When they finished eating, Brady asked to be excused, and he and Eddie went out to sit on the back steps in the shade of the hackberry tree. Blackie poked in the grass around them and then flew to the branches of the tree.

"Will they let you know when they're coming?" Brady asked as they talked about Eddie's brothers.

"I don't ..." Eddie suddenly jumped up and ran toward Aunt Tilly's clotheslines, shouting and waving his arms.

Brady laughed when he saw what was happening. Blackie had flown down from the tree and, balanced on the clothes lines, was pulling out the clothespins holding Sarah's dress. With the last pin in Blackie's beak, the dress fell to the ground.

"You rascal, you!" Eddie scolded, jerking the clothespin out of Blackie's beak and shoving him off the clothes line. "Aunt Tilly's going to be mad at both of us!"

Blackie flew to the top of the fence and watched as Eddie picked up the wet dress and tried to brush off the dirt. Then cocking his shiny black head first to one side and then the other, he mimicked Eddie's words. "You rascal, you!" he said, strutting the length of the fence. "You rascal, you!"

They laughed so hard that Aunt Tilly came to the back door to see what was going on. She laughed, too. "I guess I'll hang it over the bathtub," she said, taking the dress from Eddie and, still smiling, she went back inside the house.

When she was gone, Brady asked again about Eddie's brothers. "Have you heard from them lately?" he asked.

"Not lately. Mom usually gets a penny postcard every couple of months."

"Maybe they're on their way home right now."

"I hope so," Eddie said wistfully.

But Brady hoped they wouldn't come. At least not until the end of summer.

The Monday after graduation, Aunt Tilly, as usual, filled the washing machine and rinse tubs from the kitchen sink and began the week's wash. Brady helped hang the clothes on the lines in the back yard. He was conscious of David Hager in his front yard across the street. He hoped he wouldn't come over and see him doing "girls' work." It wasn't likely David Hager helped his mom with the wash, unless she was sick or something, like his mom. If by chance he did come over, he could say that Aunt Tilly was too busy taking care of Sarah. Except he didn't want to say that either. He still didn't want to say much about Sarah, even though he had pretty well told the whole school the day after the rabbit drive.

That Monday, Raymond Blackburn, trailed by his gang, all grinning like idiots, had come up to him in the hallway at school and had shoved him up against the wall.

"Saw your stupid sister yesterday," he jeered.

Taking a deep breath, Brady had looked from Raymond to each one of Raymond's friends. Behind them a group of kids were gathering. Remembering his pledge to himself that he would no longer run from Raymond, he'd swallowed a rising swell of fear and looked deep into Raymond's black eyes. Then an odd kind of calmness came over him and suddenly the words were there. Words he had had no idea he was going to say.

"My sister has something called autism," he said. "It's like a disease or something."

"Well, whatever," Raymond said. "She's still stupid."

"She's just different. But she's not stupid. If you were around her very long, you would know that."

"Oh, would I?" Raymond thrust his face close to Brady's. "So are you calling me stupid?"

"No," Brady said. The calmness had left him and his heart had thumped in his chest like it might break through his skin. A sudden need to wipe his damp, shaking hands on his overalls came over him, but he had held his ground. "You can't understand what you don't know," he said.

"Geeze." A bored look came over Raymond's face. "What a sissy idiot. Come on, boys. Let's go to class." He'd jerked his head in a "come with me" motion and swaggered away, his friends trailing after him.

The rest of the kids had followed, all but David Hager. "Raymond's a big bully," he'd said solemnly. "It's time someone stood up to him."

"Thanks," Brady had said, conscious of the praise, but too shaky to really take any pride in it.

The rest of the day Brady had walked where he wanted to and Raymond had left him alone. In class he continued to make snide remarks about Brady, remarks for which Miss Winters reprimanded him, but not too hard. But a line had been drawn, it seemed to Brady. A line Raymond Blackburn wasn't sure what to do about.

Brady need not have worried about helping Aunt Tilly with the washing because the only one who came over was Eddie, and Eddie would never tease a fella about anything. Eddie knew all too well what it felt like to have someone make fun of him. Besides, Eddie pitched in and helped, after sticking Blackie inside the old chicken coop so he wouldn't steal Aunt Tilly's clothespins again and let her clean wash fall on the ground.

After the washing was finished, the boys carried the big galvanized wash tubs of rinse water out and poured it down the long rows of Aunt Tilly's garden. It hadn't rained since she had planted her garden, and, like his mother had done before she got so sick, Aunt Tilly saved the rinse water for her garden.

The last few years his mother's gardens had produced little, but so far Aunt Tilly's was coming up nice and green and even. They had already had radishes and lettuce and peas and tiny sweet carrots thinned from the rows.

"Do you want to go hunting?" Eddie asked, as they poured the last of the rinse water down the garden rows.

"Sure," Brady said, grinning, "but what are we hunting and what'll we use for guns?"

Eddie's blue eyes danced. Going over to the chicken coop, where earlier he'd put Blackie, he reached behind it and brought out two slingshots. Handing Brady a cleanly whittled fork of wood, he said, "I made yours last night. Cut the sling from an inner tube out of an old tire we had laying around. I've got a bunch of rocks, too," he added, patting the front pockets of his overalls.

"Gee," Brady said, admiring the slingshot. "This is great! Thanks."

Eddie grinned, looking pleased.

They let Blackie out of the coop and headed out of town. At first Eddie led him in the direction Brady knew was towards Eddie's house. He was both surprised and curious. But soon Eddie turned and headed off across an open, unplanted field of straggly weeds.

They topped a rise and dropped down through a stand of sumac and other brush, climbed a hill and came out again on open land. The sun glared down on them, and Brady unbuttoned his shirt, wishing he had left it at home, as Eddie had his. He considered taking off his shoes and tying the laces to hang around his neck, but decided against it. His feet weren't quite as tough as Eddie's yet.

They used the rocks Eddie had in his pockets, Brady's shots flying wild, but Eddie's often hitting their targets of trees and twigs and leaves. Eddie knew of an old dump, and they spend some time there shooting at the rusty tin cans they unearthed from the dry, dusty soil.

"Hey, I think my aim's getting better," Brady said as he let fly another rock and it resounded loudly on a tin can, knocking it over.

They dropped down beside a creek bank to eat the sandwiches Aunt Tilly had sent with them. They were mashed flat from being in Brady's pocket, but they tasted okay.

The low waters of the creek flowed past an area where layers upon layers of limestone rock jutted up from the ground making a jumble of high, rugged hills. Small pieces of the rock had broken off the crumbling limestone cliffs, and they picked up some for their slingshots.

Brady remembered some fences he had seen on the way to Sentinel. The posts, holding the barbed wire, had been hewn from this brownish-yellow rock.

"The Blackburns' house is made of limestone," Eddie said, squinting against the glare of the sun. "Do you want to see it?"

Brady had to admit he was curious, but apprehensive, too. "What if they see us?" he said.

"They won't." Eddie grinned. "I've been there lots of times."

The Blackburn house towered three stories high. Rectangular blocks of limestone rock, perfect in size and shape, had been used to build the massive structure. It reminded Brady of the pictures he'd seen of stone castles in Europe.

"Mom's here today," Eddie said as they stood looking across at the house. "She comes over early to do old lady Blackburn's wash. Tomorrow she'll be here ironing all day." He squinted up at the slanting rays of the sun. "I can't see the clotheslines from here, but she should be about done." He turned to Brady. "Do you want to meet my mom?"

"Sure," Brady said. He hoped Eddie's Mom wasn't like the staggering, rank-smelling man they had encountered on the streets last month. "But we aren't going to Blackburns' house, are we?"

"Sort of," Eddie said. "At least close enough to tell when Mom leaves." He looked at Brady, a sparkle in his blue eyes. "Come on, it's fun to see how close you can get."

Brady started to protest, but Eddie was already moving toward the house. Bent nearly double, he was headed toward the cover of a row of lilac bushes. Brady took a deep breath and ducked down to follow him.

They skirted the lilacs, coming to the end of the row

several hundred feet from the back door of the Blackburn house. Peering around the bushes, Brady could see a chicken house with a flock of white chickens inside a wire fence, pecking and scratching in the dirt. Beyond the chicken house was a storm cellar. The rounded mound of earth was covered with sparse brown grass and green weeds. A white painted door marked the underground entrance.

As they squatted there in the protection of the lilacs, a little breeze brought the odor of the chicken house past their noses. The rank, ammonia-like smell reminded Brady of the Rhode Island Reds his mother used to raise before she got sick, and for a moment he was back on the farm pulling eggs out from under a clucking old hen. The memory brought a rush of homesickness to him, and the worry he had been holding back hit him full force. Why hadn't they heard from his mom and dad? Why? It had been over two months now. Even Aunt Tilly and Grandpa Bud were getting worried. He could see it in their faces now when Grandpa Bud brought the mail home.

"See that storm cellar?" Eddie whispered. "That's where Sam Blackburn keeps his liquor supply."

"Really," Brady said. "Isn't it risky to keep it here at his house?"

"I think Blackburn likes taking risks," Eddie said. "He likes money, too. I guess he doesn't get enough at the bank, so he sells bootleg liquor." Eddie made a small snorting sound. "He thinks he's so high and mighty that he's above the law. I wish your granddad would catch him."

"Where does he get his liquor?" Brady asked.

"Oh, he has a regular set-up here. A fella from Nebraska is his supplier and he brings it down. Nebraska is what they call wet, which means they can buy and sell liquor there. A couple of other fellas come out and buy from Blackburn to resell to their customers. Oscar Stevenson, who lives over west of here, gets a whole carload."

Suddenly Blackie, who had flown to a nearby tree, began his loud cawing sound.

Brady felt a chill run down his spine.

He looked quickly at Eddie. "Blackie's going to give us away," he whispered.

"No, he won't," Eddie said. "He's just a crow to them. If they even notice."

"Oh." Brady still wished the bird would be quiet. And he wished Eddie's mother would hurry up and finish her work, so they could go. This hiding here on Blackburn's property was making him really nervous.

"Pop gets his here, too." Eddie whispered. "It's rotgut stuff. Sam Blackburn's not going to waste good liquor on Pop."

"Does your dad come here to get it?" Brady asked, surprised that the man who had walked past them without even noticing his own son could find his way out here.

"Yeah, he has to. Mom won't bring it to him. She pays for it though. Old lady Blackburn takes it out of her pay. But she doesn't say that's what it's for. She makes Mom feel inferior instead."

"What does she say?"

"*Now, May. You see these wrinkles in my husband's shirt? You're not doing as good a job as you used to do. I'm going to have to deduct a few dollars on account of I'm going to have to redo these shirts of Sam's.*" As Eddie whispered the words in a high, nasal tone of voice, his eyes filled with anger, and, Brady thought, a hurt, too.

"Your Mom told you that?"

"My brothers. I ..." he broke off as a door in the Blackburn house opened and a woman and a little girl stepped out on the porch and walked down the steps. "That's Mom and Lilly," he said. "They take a short cut home. The one Pop uses, only he comes at night, like the fella from Nebraska and Oscar Stephenson. They drive along real slow and shut off the headlights before they get here." He suddenly grinned. "I bet you think the Blackburns don't have a dog."

"I didn't hear any barking," Brady said, a prickle of fear

raising the hairs on his arms.
He hadn't thought about a dog!
"They have one all right," Eddie said. "A big one. But Sam Blackburn would kick it into the next county if he barked when Sam didn't want him to. Mostly they keep him in the house. But," he looked over at Brady and grinned, "he likes me. You're safe with me. Otherwise..." He curled his lip, showing his teeth in a mock snarl. Then he laughed. "Come on," he said, "let's go see Mom and Lilly."

They made their way from the Blackburn place using the lilac bushes again for cover. But even with Eddie's assurance, Brady kept expecting the Blackburns' dog to suddenly appear with Sam or Raymond Blackburn behind him.

Brady followed as Eddie circled back the way they had come. He tried to smother a sigh of relief as they dropped down over the creek bank and out of sight of the house, but Eddie heard it and flashed a grin at him.

At the limestone rock hills, a squirrel darted up along a ridge a few feet away and stopped to sit up and chatter at them. Slowly Eddie reached for his slingshot and, fitting a rock in the sling, took aim and let it fly. The squirrel fell from the rock and lay still.

"That's supper," Eddie said, walking over and picking it up by its tail. "Have you ever eaten squirrel?"

Brady shook his head. "No," he said, holding back the surge of distaste he felt, "I never have."

From the rock hills, Eddie changed courses, taking them down to a wild plum thicket, one side of it edged by a well-worn path. "Mom will be here in a minute," he said, dropping the dead squirrel and sitting down cross-legged beside the trail. Brady sat down beside him. In a few minutes, Eddie got to his feet. "I hear them coming," he said.

Listening, Brady could just make out a faint rustling sound.

"Eddie!" his mother said as she rounded the plum thicket and came suddenly upon them. Surprise colored her voice.

"You always give me such a start."

"Hi, Mom," Eddie said grinning. "I want you to meet my friend, Brady."

"Hello, Brady," Mrs. Peel said. She was a small woman with the same white-blonde hair as Eddie's. Her blue eyes looked tired, but friendly. She smiled and put her arm around her little girl, drawing her close. "This is Lilly," she said, "my big five-year-old."

Lilly pressed her little face against her mother's leg so all Brady could see was her tousled head of blonde hair. Her thin little arms and legs were covered with bug bites.

"Hello, Lilly," Brady said, thinking of Sarah.

"So you have Blackie with you," Mrs. Peel said as Blackie swooped down and landed on the ground beside them. Cocking his head, the bird stared up at Mrs. Peel. "You rascal, you!" he said.

Brady thought Mrs. Peel would laugh, but she didn't. Instead she turned to Eddie and her voice was stern. "Have you been hanging around the Blackburns again with that bird?" she asked.

"Some," Eddie said.

"Mrs. Blackburn has lost her key to the storm cellar," Eddie's mother said. "She went out to get some of her canning jars, and she thinks she laid it down to take the padlock off. But she's not sure if she picked it up again." She paused and took a deep breath as if she had suddenly run out of air. "I know you are on the place sometimes, Eddie, waiting for me, and I hear a crow now and then. I know how Blackie loves shiny things."

"I don't think Blackie took it," Eddie said. "She probably just misplaced it."

"Maybe," Mrs. Peel said. "But she thought she remembered hearing a crow when she was out there." Her brow wrinkled and she peered hard at Eddie. "I don't want you going there ever again, Eddie."

"Sorry, Mom," Eddie said. And then his face brightened,

and he picked up the squirrel and held it out toward her. "Look," he said, "I got this for supper. If you'll take it, I'll go a little ways with Brady, and then I'll come home and skin it out for you."

The worried frown stayed on Mrs. Peel's face even as she reached for the squirrel. Clearly, her mind was still on the missing key. "Edna doesn't dare tell Sam that she's lost it, and she's about beside herself. I feel so sorry for her."

"I wouldn't waste my time," Eddie said dryly.

Mrs. Peel sighed. "Everyone has their troubles," she said.

After Mrs. Peel and Lilly left them, Eddie said. "I bet Raymond lost that key. When Sam's gone, he has drinking parties down by the creek with those kids he hangs out with. I've seen them. I always figured his old man gave him a key of his own, but I bet he steals Edna's. I bet he's the one that lost it."

"You've seen them?" Brady asked. "Raymond and his friends, I mean. Do you come out here at night?"

"Sure. I follow Pop sometimes. They get so drunk and make so much noise, I wondered how Edna keeps from hearing them. But," he added quietly, "maybe she does."

They were quiet as they walked back toward town. Suddenly, Eddie said, "I wish I could find that key. I'd go there some night and take a club and smash his whole stock of liquor."

Brady nodded, but he didn't say anything. He hoped Eddie never found the key. If he did, he might ask him to go along, and that was one thing he sure didn't want to do, even if Blackburn couldn't turn them in, not with liquor being illegal. Still, he had that big dog ... the one trained not to bark. Maybe he should tell Grandpa Bud about Blackburn selling bootleg liquor. But didn't he already know it? Hadn't Aunt Tilly told him? So maybe he just wasn't going to do anything about it. And maybe he'd be mad at them for trespassing on Blackburns' property. No, he wouldn't say anything to Grandpa Bud. Not now anyway.

12

"I'LL HAVE TO BE at the foreclosure sale of Anna's farm next week." Grandpa Bud spoke quietly to Aunt Tilly. Even though Brady was hunched up close to the radio listening to the Lone Ranger, he heard every word.

"If you want to go," Grandpa Bud continued, "you could leave Sarah with Brady."

"I need to go," Aunt Tilly said. "Our quilting club will all be there. We want to give Anna the last quilt we pieced to take with her, although Lord knows where she'll go. She has no children or anyone." Aunt Tilly sighed heavily and waved a hand at the fly that had been pestering her about the face. "It makes me so sad I could just bawl."

"There's talk among the neighbors of bidding low." Grandpa Bud leaned over and picked up his newspaper. Folding it, he held it up, his eyes following the buzzing fly. "If they do, it will be perfectly legal, and Anna won't have to move."

"That would be a blessing," Aunt Tilly said.

Grandpa Bud took a swat at the fly and missed. "Anna's had a tough go of it." He leaned back in his chair. The fly circled Brady's head.

As the thundering hoof beats of the Lone Ranger's horse faded away, Brady turned on his chair and swatted at the fly with his hand. "I can stay with Sarah," he said.

"I think you should go," Aunt Tilly said, frowning a little. "You and your Grandpa haven't had a speck of time together yet."

"What about you, Tilly?" Grandpa Bud said.

He doesn't want to take me, Brady thought. *He never acts like he likes me very much. I guess because I'm not really his grandson.*

"I'll just take Sarah," Aunt Tilly said.

Brady groaned inwardly. Now he would have to go with Grandpa Bud, who didn't want him, and with Sarah who would likely do something really dumb and embarrass him. He thought about asking if Eddie could go, too, but then decided against it. Eddie wouldn't want to go now that his brothers were here. They had come in on a freight a couple of nights ago, and he hadn't seen Eddie since. Grandpa Bud had seen the brothers walking through town and had talked to them. Brady wondered how long it would be before they were gone again, and Eddie with them. Boy, it was going to be lonely without Eddie around.

It seemed like everyone he cared about was disappearing from his life. First his folks, and now Eddie. He'd even had to leave his dog. He sure missed Taggart. He wished he could have him, just for tonight, to curl up on the bed beside him. A sudden lump came up in his throat. Swallowing it, he muttered a quick "good night" and went upstairs to his room.

The day of the foreclosure sale was hot and windy. Grandpa Bud drove with the windows down through town and out on the highway, his arm resting on the open window, the sleeves of his brown shirt rolled back a few turns. Sarah had flopped over on the seat, humming contentedly. She liked riding in the car now. Aunt Tilly thought she probably liked the sound of the motor, and heat and dust never seemed to bother her at all.

When they started out, Brady had hoped they would go past the Peels' place to get to Anna's farm. If they did, he hoped that Eddie and his brothers would be outside and he'd get a glimpse of them. But at the first street corner Grandpa Bud stuck his arm out straight to signal a left turn. Disappointed, Brady slumped back on the seat.

They were among the first ones to arrive at the sale. Grandpa Bud parked by the barn, backed in so his car faced the road. Two milk cows stared inquisitively at them as they got out of the car, and an old collie dog barked half-heartedly, tail wagging.

Makeshift tables set up in the yard were filled with household goods. Underneath the tables were wash tubs, crocks, a cast iron kettle and pasteboard boxes of dishes, and pots and pans. One table held a stack of books and an old phonograph with a pile of black records in paper sleeves. Next to the records were picture frames, needlework and other items. A pint jar of buttons made Brady think of Blackie. He wondered if Eddie's brothers would let him take Blackie with them when they left.

"I don't think they'll care," Eddie had said when Brady questioned him about it. "He can fly in and out of a freight car faster and easier than we can climb into one."

The collie dog nuzzling Brady's hand brought him back to the present. He grinned and bent down to take the dog's head between his two hands. "Hey, boy," he said, working his fingers through the old dog's thick coat, "I bet you're wondering what's going on here?" The dog wagged his tail, obviously pleased with the attention.

Others were coming now in a steady stream. Cars, old trucks, and horse and mule teams pulling wagons and buggies. It looked like the whole county had turned out for this foreclosure sale. Brady hoped what Grandpa Bud had heard was true about bidding low and giving everything back to the lady. It pleased him, too, that Sam Blackburn was going to get "skunked."

Brady had asked Eddie why people didn't just take their money out of Sam Blackburn's bank.

"Well, for one thing," Eddie had said. "It's the only one in town. And also because he's smart enough to hire good people. People like David Hager's dad across the street from you."

"Why do they work for him?" Brady asked and then felt stupid as soon as the words were out of his mouth.

"They'd be fools to give up a job these days," Eddie had said, echoing his own thoughts. "Besides, with Mr. Hager it's sort of a tradition. Mr. Hager's dad and maybe even his granddad worked there before him when Mr. Crandall and Mr. Crandall's father were still alive."

It amazed Brady how much Eddie knew about people in Sentinel. Eddie had told him a lot of people didn't think Mr. Crandall had embezzled money at the bank or committed suicide either. "Lots of folks put the blame square on Sam Blackburn for the embezzling, and they think that if he didn't pull the trigger, he knows who did."

"Why do they think that?" Brady had asked.

"He was working at the bank, and he had just married Edna Crandall. They say he just didn't want to wait to inherit."

Now, thinking of what Sam Blackburn might have done made him shiver despite the hot sun, and he squatted and rubbed his hands along the dog's coat. The old collie wagged his tail, his milky eyes on Brady's face.

Brady watched the people as he petted the collie. The men stuck close to the barn looking at the machinery and the little bit of stock Anna had left. Which was, as far as Brady could tell, two milk cows, a team of mules and the few chickens that were scratching and clucking in the barn lot.

He had seen Grandpa Bud walk up to the house when they first arrived. A white-haired woman had answered the door. He assumed she must be Anna. Funny, he had never heard her last name, and yet he knew a lot about her. She had no children and her husband had shot himself, depressed, Grandpa Bud said, over getting old and not being able to grow enough of a crop to keep them going. He had hoped to pay off the mortgage, and when he couldn't, he'd rigged up a shotgun to blow his head off.

As Brady watched the women pick up an item from a table and then put it back, nod to each other, and then stop to visit, he was sure they were just making a pretense of looking at Anna's things.

He saw several boys and girls from his school, but none of Raymond's friends or Raymond himself. Grandpa Bud had said that Sam Blackburn would stay home today, if he wasn't out in Denver wheeling and dealing with the big shots. It didn't sound like Grandpa Bud liked Sam Blackburn one little bit.

Aunt Tilly stayed near the car where she had decided it was best to keep Sarah.

The auctioneer, a big man with sharply creased pants stuffed into cowboy boots and a white Stetson hat tipped back to show his face, began his sing-song, urging folks to bid on a set of table and chairs.

"What am I bid?" he called out. "Five dollars? Who'll give me five?"

"Five cents," a voice called out. And before Brady realized it, the table and chairs had sold for a dime.

Several items later, Brady saw how they were doing it. Everyone was bidding really low, and if someone tried to raise the bid, that person was "accidentally" bumped or suddenly engaged in conversation with a couple of men. Or sometimes their voices were simply drowned out in loud, boisterous laughter. And once it appeared that two of the men were about to engage in a fist fight. But afterwards, these same two men were laughing and talking together.

When the sale was over, everyone seemed to be in a good mood as they gathered around to pay for the items they had made a pretense of purchasing. Even the auctioneer and the bank's representative seemed as cheerful as the rest of the crowd.

"That was some sale," Grandpa Bud said, his eyes twinkling as he came over to the car. "The fellow who bought the land told Anna he'd sign over the deed to her first thing on Monday morning. Anna took the rest of the names. Vowed she'd pay everyone back as soon as she could."

"She was pleased with the quilt," Aunt Tilly said, smiling. "At first she said she just couldn't take it. She said there were folks needing it worse than she did. But we said it was a gift and so she had to take it or she would hurt our feelings." Aunt Tilly laughed, and forgetting that Sarah didn't like to be touched, drew her close and hugged her.

Sarah yelled and pushed away, stamping her feet indignantly.

When they got back to town, it was well past supper time, and Brady was starving.

The lunch Aunt Tilly had brought to the sale was now a distant memory.

But when he saw who waited on the front porch, all thoughts of food fell from his head.

"Evening, Raymond," Grandpa Bud said as he opened the car door and stepped out on the ground. "Do you have a problem?"

"Sure do," Raymond Blackburn said. "Dad's over at the Peels holding a shotgun on them. Caught them red-handed with some of our chickens."

"And just who took your chickens?" Grandpa Bud said. "May, or Cliff, or Eddie ... Surely not little Lilly?" A touch of something in his voice made Brady give him a quick look. But his face was calm, unreadable.

"T.J. and Jimmy Joe are back. Dad says he supposed they came in on a freight. They've been bumming the country and probably stealing as they go. Now they're home, he figures they're giving Eddie stealing lessons."

Raymond Blackburn's words jolted Brady. Had they really stolen the chickens, and was Eddie in on it? Was Sam Blackburn holding a shotgun on Eddie, too? And Mrs. Peel? And Lilly? A shiver passed through him as he remembered Eddie's words about Sam Blackburn and his father-in-law's death. If he didn't *pull the trigger, he knows who did.*

"Help Aunt Tilly get Sarah and her things into the

house," Grandpa Bud said, turning to Brady. Then come out and go with us."

When Brady got back to the car, Raymond was sitting in the back seat. He hesitated a moment, not wanting to sit with Raymond and not sure if Grandpa Bud would want him to sit up front. Then Grandpa Bud motioned him around to the front of the car. "Come on, son," he said. Brady hurried around the car and slid in beside him.

The Peel house sat back from the road a few hundred yards. It was a shabby little house covered with peeling tarpaper, the edges flapping in the hot dry wind. Behind the house were a couple of sagging old buildings of gray weathered wood. The front yard was hard-packed dirt with a few straggly weeds.

Raymond jumped out the minute Grandpa Bud stopped the car. "Follow me," he said and started up the dirt path to the house.

"Now, hold your horses." The coldness in Grandpa Bud's voice stopped Raymond. "You'll walk behind me, with Brady."

Raymond glared at Grandpa Bud, but he stepped aside and let him pass. Then he gave Brady a squinty, curled-lip look and stepped in front of him. Brady was so glad Grandpa Bud hadn't made him stay in the car that he gave ground without protest.

"Hello," Grandpa Bud called out as he stepped up on the broken and sagging front steps. "It's Bud Lewis."

"Come on in, Sheriff," a deep voice called. "Raymond bring you?"

Without answering, Grandpa Bud pushed open the door. It groaned and creaked on loose leather hinges. Raymond followed and Brady slipped in behind him.

The stifling hot room seemed airless. Brady took a deep breath and looked at Eddie.

Eddie's eyes darted toward Brady and then back to Sam Blackburn. His face was a mask of anger.

Mrs. Peel, with Lilly on her lap clinging tight, her little

face hidden against her mother's shoulder, was sitting on a sagging, old davenport. Eddie sat beside her, and beside him were two boys. One had a blood-stained bandage on his foot.

Brady was surprised to see that Eddie's brothers were only a few years older than he was. Somehow he'd gotten the idea that T.J. and Jimmy Joe were grown men.

Sam Blackburn sat on a chair facing them, a shotgun across his lap. The white handkerchief in his hand had been well used to mop his sweating face. Brady thought it was probably a lot cooler in the Blackburn house at this time of day.

Mr. Peel was nowhere in sight.

For a moment a heavy, angry silence filled the room. Brady watched a fly stuck to a curl of flypaper hanging from the ceiling. It fluttered and twisted and buzzed in its efforts to escape the sticky strip. He noticed a broken window pane stuffed with old newspapers and thought it was probably no better at keeping out the cold than it was the heat.

Then Grandpa Bud spoke. "Where's Cliff?" he asked Mrs. Peel, his tone of voice respectful and gentle.

"He's asleep," she said.

"Mom, he's passed out," one of the boys said. *Was it T.J. or Jimmy Joe?*

"On liquor he got from Sam Blackburn," the other boy said.

Grandpa Bud turned to Sam Blackburn, who still sat with the shotgun across his knees. "Are you selling whiskey?" he asked.

"Liquor's illegal," Sam Blackburn said. "They're just trying to shift attention from themselves." He made a snorting, mocking sound. "Of course, we all know Cliff Peel is a drunk. But he don't get it from me. Heaven knows we've tried to help the family. We've been giving May work now for years, even though she's lazy and never earns half of what we pay her."

"Liar!" Eddie exploded off the couch and leaped at Sam Blackburn.

"Hold it, son." Grandpa Bud grabbed the back of Eddie's overalls and stopped him. "Sit down now." He guided Eddie back to the couch. "I think we can get to the bottom of this all right." He turned to Sam Blackburn. "Put that shotgun over there by the door before someone gets hurt, and let's hear your side of the story."

A glint of anger sparked in Sam Blackburn's eyes, but he leaned his gun in a corner without protest and turned back to face Grandpa Bud and the Peels.

"Edna thought she heard the chickens making a big fuss this afternoon," he began. "I figured there was a coyote around, so I let the dog out. He ran off a ways. He was gone quite a while, but he never did bark. So I never thought any more about it.

"A couple of hours later, Edna went out to feed them and noticed some were missing. I went out and found this nice trail of blood." He pointed to the bandaged foot. "This fool stepped on a nail."

He paused, his eyes shifting to Mrs. Peel. "She's likely to have doctored it up with flour to stop the bleeding, but if you unwrap it and wash it off, Sheriff, I expect you'll find a nail hole clear through his foot, and," he swiveled around to look all around the room, "a shoe here somewhere with a hole to match."

For a moment he kept looking around as if expecting to see the shoe. Then he looked at Grandpa Bud again. "I still can't figure the dog. Whatever they did, they made him worthless, and when I get home, I'll have to shoot him."

Brady saw Eddie's face go white at Sam Blackburn's words, and he knew Eddie had been there, for the dog hadn't barked. The dog liked Eddie.

"Anyway," Sam Blackburn continued. "I found them all out back here, butchering chickens for all they were worth. May even had a skillet on the stove, frying a couple of them." He lifted his chin and jerked it toward the kitchen range. "The evidence is right over there and out back by the chopping block."

Grandpa Bud looked at Mrs. Peel. "Is that right, May?" he asked.

She nodded. "I just couldn't see letting them go to waste now that the boys had them. I don't condone stealing, but the boys thought they were only taking what was due us. Edna ... Mrs. Blackburn decided not to pay me anything at all this time."

"Is that why you boys took the chickens?" Grandpa Bud shifted his gaze to Eddie's brothers.

"As you know, we just got home a couple of days ago," one of them spoke up. "There was nothing in the house to eat. We had a dollar between us." He nodded toward his brother. "We spent that on groceries. Mom said she would get paid yesterday, but, like she said, she didn't. There was nothing left in the house." He shrugged. "Lilly was hungry and Mom was crying."

"Mom said Edna Blackburn said she hadn't done a good job at all." Eddie's other brother continued the story. "Said the wash was dingy, and the clothes looked like she'd never touched an iron to them. She says that to Mom when she wants to deduct Pop's liquor from her pay, but Mom keeps track of that and knew she had already paid it. So T.J. and I," he indicated the boy beside him, so now Brady knew the boy speaking was Jimmy Joe, "decided to take some of their chickens for Mom's pay. We would have gotten away with it, too, but Blackburn here doesn't run too tidy of a farm. He left a board with a big nail in it, and T.J. stepped on it and ran it all the way through his foot,"

"Jimmy Joe had to lift me up under my arms and stomp on the board to get me off," T.J. said. "It hurt like the very devil."

"We had the chickens in a sack," Eddie began. Both brothers turned on him, scowling. "Shut up, Eddie," they said and turned back to look at Grandpa Bud. Jimmy Joe spoke. "He thinks if we're in trouble, he ought to be, too. But he wasn't there, Sheriff. He's making it up."

"But, I ..." Eddie began.

"Think of your mother," Grandpa Bud said. "Your brothers are in a lot of trouble. They will have to go before a judge. Who knows then what will happen. Your mother needs you here, son."

"Hey," Sam Blackburn said, "that little whelp was there, too. I saw three sets of footprints. The blood made it easy. You go take a look, Sheriff. You'll see."

"Well, we'll have to check your place for illegal whiskey," Grandpa Bud said. "So I'll take a look at those footprints then. Okay, Sam?"

Sam Blackburn muttered something, but even in the small room and standing right behind him, Brady couldn't make out what he said.

"Well," Grandpa Bud said. "I think we have enough of the story for tonight. Boys," he nodded at Eddie's two brothers, "tell your mother good-bye and come on into town with me." He turned to Mrs. Peel. "I'll let you know how things turn out as soon as I can, May. Try not to worry."

"What about the chickens?" Raymond Blackburn spoke for the first time since he had entered the house. "Can we take them home? Mom can get them canned tonight."

"Oh, I believe we'll leave them here," Grandpa Bud said. "It's kind of late. Your mother isn't going to be too happy about canning this late at night. Let's do her a favor, shall we?" He smiled and clapped Raymond on the back, at the same time pushing him toward the door.

"Can you walk on that foot, all right, T.J. ?" Grandpa Bud asked, turning back as Eddie's brother stood up.

"Yeah," T.J. said. "Jimmy Joe will help me."

Brady stepped back so he would be the last one out the door. He wanted to say something to Eddie, something to make him feel better, but all he could think of was, "Come over sometime."

Eddie just nodded and then looked away, his eyes following his brothers out the door.

"Could you give us a lift, Sheriff?" Brady heard Sam Blackburn ask as he stepped out of the house.

"That would make the car pretty crowded," Grandpa Bud answered. "It's a pretty night, not too warm now. I expect you and Raymond will enjoy the walk."

For a second Sam Blackburn's face darkened with anger, and then he smiled and turned to Raymond. "Come on, son," he said. They turned away and disappeared in the gathering dusk.

Grandpa Bud had T.J. and Jimmy Joe sit in the back seat. Brady watched to see if he put handcuffs on them. He didn't.

Back at Sentinel, instead of driving to the jail, Grandpa Bud drove to his house and parked the car in its usual place beside it. Looking around at Eddie's brothers, he said, "Come on in, boys. Let's see if the lady of the house has a bite for us to eat."

Aunt Tilly set out bowls of potato soup and thick sandwiches of roast beef and cheese for their supper. A fresh batch of cookies cooled on the kitchen counter. They were all hungry, and for a while no one spoke. Then Grandpa Bud began asking about the boys' travels. Where they had been and if they had had any luck finding work.

They told him they had been to California and about everywhere west and south, and as far east as Chicago. They had liked California the best, especially the ocean.

Brady listened intently as they told of the orchards of fruit trees and the vegetable fields and how sometimes a fella could get work in them, but usually there were more men waiting to do the work than there were jobs to do, and the wages were awfully low.

Brady hoped his dad had found something by now and the ocean air was making his mom well again. If only they would write. Just a postcard ... anything.

Later that night Grandpa Bud took Eddie's brothers down to the jail. "I hate to do this, boys," he said. "But I can't bend the rules too much."

13

THERE WAS NO EVIDENCE of bootleg liquor when Grandpa Bud and his deputy, Pete Peters, searched the Blackburn place the next day.

"I knew it would be gone," he said that evening at the supper table. "But it looks like he keeps it in the storm cellar. He has a latch on the door with a hasp closure for a padlock."

"Why did you give him time to hide it?" Aunt Tilly asked, frowning. "Why didn't you go last night?"

Grandpa Bud picked a toothpick out of the glass holder on the table and chewed on it for a while before answering her.

"You know how folks are about this, Tilly," he said. "Prohibition was repealed in '33, and most of the states went wet. But Kansas stayed dry. Dozens and dozens of folks are buying boot-leg whiskey from Nebraska or making their own home brew. They are good folks, Tilly. They don't see it even as really breaking the law, and they don't want their supplies dried up. It would be political suicide to go on a liquor raid."

"But it is the law, Bud," Aunt Tilly persisted. "I'm ashamed you would think of your own personal gain ahead of the law."

Grandpa Bud's face reddened. "I run a good office," he said. "I try to do what I can to help folks. Just like the Peel boys. They shouldn't be locked up, and I wouldn't have done it if Blackburn hadn't pressed charges. Now the judge will sentence them for stealing. They're too young for jail, so he'll send them to a boys' home for a few years. And it might be best." He shrugged. "Who knows. It's probably better for them than riding the rails. I hear they came back just to take Eddie with them."

"No," Aunt Tilly gasped. "He's so young."

"No younger than they were when they started."

"I suppose not." Aunt Tilly sighed. "But they shouldn't be locked up. If Edna Blackburn would have just paid May like she should have ..."

"I know." Grandpa Bud leaned back on the kitchen chair, rubbed his eyes and stifled a big yawn. "I had hoped Blackburn would show a little compassion and decide not to press charges after all. That's another reason I let him have time to hide his whiskey. I thought if I would go easy on him ..." He made a funny, helpless sound and looked down at his hands before looking at Aunt Tilly again. "Stealing is breaking the law," he said. "And yet, I would let those boys go if I could. And you would, too, wouldn't you?"

"Yes," Aunt Tilly said. "But I don't feel quite so charitable about folks running bootleg liquor. Clifford Peel might be a decent sort of man if liquor hadn't pickled his brain."

"He used to be." Grandpa Bud pushed back from the table and stood up, stretching. "But it won't do any good to cut off his supply now. I think he's too far gone, unless you could get him into a hospital. Those that want it are going to get it. The Cliff Peels who crave it so much they would sell body and soul to get it, and the regular Sallys and Joes who just like it once in a while. Maybe when they have folks in for a game of cards, or if they're going to a dance."

"I suppose," Aunt Tilly said. "Still it bothers me, Bud."

"It does me, too, Tilly. But I can't put half of the county in jail. And that's about what I'd have to do if I locked up those who are selling it and those who are buying it. You know yourself I've got about all I can handle with the miseries of this depression. Robberies and petty theft are almost an everyday occurrence any more ... Folks are getting desperate to feed their families ... The drought's getting worse ... Farms are failing ... A lot of folks lost all they had when the bank closed that time. I've got folks thinking suicide and some, like Anna's Carl, doing it. Folks without enough to eat and no prospects for the future. Even if I was so inclined, I've not got the time to run down every bootleg runner and buyer in the county. I just wish the voters would vote to have it sold legally in controlled establishments." He sighed heavily, yawned again and wiped his eyes. "But right now, Tilly, I'm not going to worry about it. Right now I'm going into the other room and listen to the radio."

Brady had sat still through the whole conversation, afraid that if he even so much as moved a muscle, they would decide they shouldn't be talking in front of him.

He hadn't thought much about liquor before, except to wish that Eddie's dad didn't drink it. He wondered if his mom and dad ever did. He sort of remembered when they used to go to dances. His mom would be all sparkling and pretty, and his dad excited and laughing about everything. But that had been before Sarah ... before the drought and before his mom got sick.

He wondered if Grandpa Bud and Grandma Barbara had ever gone to dances and maybe had a drink or two, and he wondered about Aunt Tilly. He looked at her now, clearing away the dishes from Grandpa Bud's supper, and tried to imagine her acting silly and stumbling about the kitchen. He grinned, and then the memory of Eddie's dad staggering down the street popped into his head. The grin died on his lips.

He got up from the table and went in to listen to the radio with Grandpa Bud. For a while, he puzzled over why people would be against Grandpa Bud arresting folks for illegal whiskey and then not voting to make it legal, but soon the antics of Amos and Andy was making him laugh and pushing aside such serious thoughts.

T.J. and Jimmy Joe spent a week in jail waiting for the judge to hear their case.

"Mrs. Peel and Lilly come every afternoon to see them," Grandpa Bud said several days after Eddie's brothers were arrested. "Eddie comes in the evenings. I noticed the boys have been sharing their dinner with their mother and sister and their supper with Eddie."

"Oh!" Aunt Tilly's hands flew to her mouth. "Why didn't I think of that! I'll start fixing more food. Oh, my, I worried so about how they were faring, but I never once thought of that. I had so hoped Eddie would stop by here so I could at least feed him. Oh, poor May!" Aunt Tilly began heaping more potatoes in the sink to peel, shaking her head and murmuring under her breath.

A big grin came over Grandpa Bud's face, and he looked over at Brady and winked.

Brady returned his grin, a glow of warmth spreading through him.

The judge sentenced T.J. and Jimmy Joe to two years in the Boys' Industrial School in Topeka. That evening Grandpa Bud was late getting home with the news of the judge's decision, and Brady went to the window so often to look for him that Aunt Tilly said he "about wore a path."

Grandpa Bud left early the next morning to drive the boys to Topeka. Brady waited all day for Eddie to come by, but he never showed.

He waited all the next day, too, certain that at any moment he would hear Eddie's footsteps on the porch or Blackie's loud call or the flapping sound of his wings. Finally he could wait no longer.

Going into the kitchen where Aunt Tilly was washing their dinner dishes, Brady took a deep breath and said to her back, "I'm going over to see Eddie."

"Why, I think that is a wonderful idea." Aunt Tilly swung around, smiling, her hands dripping soapy water. "I'll fix a basket for you to take to May." She hurriedly dried her hands on her apron and reached to pull a large, woven basket down from the cupboard. "It's easier to go calling on folks who are hurting if you have something in your hands."

Brady felt conspicuous carrying the basket, heavy with food, but he couldn't have refused to take it. Not only would he be depriving the Peels, but he would also be hurting Aunt Tilly's feelings. Besides, she was probably right. It probably would help to have something in his hands and something to say, especially if Eddie's dad opened the door.

Brady's stomach felt tied in knots by the time he reached the Peels' home. He hoped Eddie or Mrs. Peel would answer his knock, but visions of Eddie's dad standing in the doorway, wobbly and bleary-eyed, kept popping into his head. The vision was so real that when Mrs. Peel answered his knock, he just stood there, speechless.

"Is something wrong? Did your grandfather send you?" Her voice trembled and the lines in her forehead deepened.

Brady could hear the fear in her voice, and quickly he shook his head. "No, no, no, ma'am," he stammered, holding the basket out toward her. "Aunt Tilly just wanted me to bring this to you."

"Oh!" Mrs. Peel gasped like someone had knocked the air out of her. Then she took a deep breath and reached out to take the basket from Brady's hands. "Thank you," she said. "Please tell your aunt we appreciate her kindness so very much."

Her smile untied the knots in Brady's stomach. "Is Eddie here?" he asked.

"I'm not sure." She sighed. "He's feeling so blue and lonely. I wish you could see if you could find him. I think he needs you."

Suddenly the loud, rasping cry of a crow filled the air. Brady swung around to see Blackie flying toward a dilapidated outbuilding, and a quick glimpse of Eddie's blond head ducking behind it.

He turned back to Mrs. Peel, uncertainty making him hesitate.

She nodded. "Please, go to him," she said.

His heart hammering in his chest, Brady slowly walked toward the building he now saw was an old wood and coal shed. Beyond the building was the Peels' outhouse. Eddie had probably just come from there and, seeing him, had tried to hide.

Brady found him slumped down on the ground pulling up the weeds that grew around an old rain barrel set up against the building. Twisting and tearing the weed stems and tossing them into the barrel, he did not look up as Brady approached.

Perched on top of the barrel beside Eddie, Blackie eyed Brady as he came near, his shiny black head cocked to one side.

Clearing his throat, Brady said, "Uh ... hello, Eddie."

Eddie kept his eyes on the twisted weeds in his hand

"Hello, hello," Blackie said.

Brady grinned. "He's sure got that word down pat, doesn't he?"

"Yeah." Eddie raised his head a little, "he sure does."

Brady squatted down, and taking a button from the bib pocket of his overalls, laid it flat in the palm of his hand. "Come here, Blackie," he said. "Come see what I have for you."

The day had started off hot. Although Brady had worn his overalls all morning without a shirt, Aunt Tilly had suggested he wear one to call on the Peels. "It just lends more dignity," she'd said. The button had popped off when he'd put on the shirt, and he had stuck it in his bib pocket to give to Aunt Tilly later. Now he doubted if she would ever see this particular button again.

"Caw! Caw!" Blackie said and swooped down from the barrel to the ground. Eyeing the button in Brady's outstretched hand, he came closer and closer, his neck bobbing and stretching, his head cocked first to one side and then the other.

"Here you go," Brady offered, moving his hand toward Blackie. The crow stared at the button a moment longer and then snatched it up in his beak and flew to the top of the old shed.

"He'll put it with his other stuff," Eddie said, for the first time looking at Brady. "You won't get it back unless we can find out where he is stashing his things."

"Let's follow him and see where he takes it." Brady said.

Eddie gave a little snort of a laugh. "You don't think I haven't tried?" But he got to his feet, dropping the twisted weeds and dusting off the seat of his ragged overalls.

They stood side by side watching Blackie stalk across the roof of the shed, the edge of the button barely showing in his beak.

"I'm sorry about your brothers," Brady said, his voice changing on him so he hardly got the words past a whisper.

"Thanks," Eddie mumbled.

They stood awhile in silence, watching Blackie, and then Eddie said, "I was with them. I should be going, too."

"I know," Brady said. "I knew it the minute Blackburn said he let the dog out and it didn't make a fuss. I knew you had to have been there."

Sudden tears welled up in Eddie's eyes. "It's my fault he's dead now."

"Do you think Blackburn really shot him?" Brady asked, surprised.

"I know it," Eddie said, gritting his teeth. "I wish I could have gone there and gotten him away, but I couldn't." He spread his hands open in a helpless gesture and then clinched them into tight fists, his face a mask of anger and tears.

"Too bad we can't dump out all of Blackburn's liquor," Brady said, the idea just coming to him.

Eddie brightened. "We could fill the jars with water.

Wouldn't that be a joke? He'd be selling ol' Oscar Stephenson water for booze, and boy, would there ever be some mad customers." He frowned and his teeth chewed on his lower lip. "I guess we'd be dumping out Pop's, too, and he'd be awfully mad."

"But we have to have a key," Brady said. He was glad that they didn't have one, and half sorry he had even mentioned dumping the liquor. He hoped he hadn't given Eddie some crazy idea about going there to look for a key. He sure didn't want to be messing around the Blackburn place ever again.

"We'd need a key, all right," Eddie said. "So I guess we can't. But it would serve him right if we did it." He grinned at Brady, "And he wouldn't be able to report it to your grandpa, either. I bet it would make him half crazy."

"Wouldn't it," Brady said, a sudden lightness spread warmth inside his chest. Things would be okay now. He and Eddie would be friends again, just like before. He started to ask if Eddie wanted to go out and shoot the slingshots again when Eddie laughed and pointed up at the roof of the shed.

"Hey," Eddie said. "Blackie's gone! This time he fooled both of us!"

14

"MAYROSE AND HER HUSBAND came and took Mom and Lilly home with them yesterday," Eddie said as he sat down on the back door steps beside Brady. "That's why I didn't come over."

"Grandpa Bud said he saw you had company," Brady said. "Did they come all the way from Missouri?"

"Yeah, I hope they get back okay. Their car rattles something awful, but Buck, Mayrose's husband, says it can rattle until Hell freezes over for all he cares, as long as the motor stays good. Oh, excuse me, Aunt Tilly." His face reddened. "I didn't mean to say, you know, that word."

Aunt Tilly laughed. Seeing him, she had come to the back door with a plate of cookies and two glasses of milk. "You're forgiven this time," she said as she opened the screen door and handed them the milk and cookies. "Why didn't you go with your mother and sister?"

"I couldn't," Eddie said. "They don't hardly have enough for themselves as it is. Buck's pants are about as ragged as mine, and Mayrose's dress was so patched and faded and old you'd probably use it for rags, Aunt Tilly."

"I'm sorry," Aunt Tilly said.

"Maybe you could have found a job," Brady said. He didn't know why he was saying it, except maybe because it was safe now that Eddie hadn't gone. "Maybe things are better in Missouri," he finished lamely. Of course, *things weren't any better in Missouri.*

"From what my sister and brother-in-law say, it doesn't sound like it," Eddie said. "I don't think things are good anywhere."

"I guess not," Brady said, and the worry about his folks wormed its way back into his mind. Lately he had been trying to shut out all thoughts about his parents, but he wasn't having much luck, especially at night in his dreams.

"Would you like to stay with us?" Aunt Tilly asked. "Brady can share his room, and we would be glad to have you."

"Thanks," Eddie said. A light came into his face, and Brady was sure he was going to accept Aunt Tilly's offer. He wondered what Grandpa Bud would say about having another boy in the house.

But the light went out of Eddie's face almost as fast as it had come, and a somberness replaced it. "Thanks, but I can't, Aunt Tilly," he said. "I can't leave Pop."

"I see," Aunt Tilly said gravely. "Well, if you change your mind ..."

Suddenly Eddie grinned. "Maybe I can come by once in a while at suppertime."

"You certainly can, Eddie," Aunt Tilly said. "Anytime you want to. I can send something, now and then, to your father, too."

"Oh, don't worry about Pop. He mostly drinks his meals anyway." He gave a little snort of a laugh. "He has a job for that now, you know."

"No," Aunt Tilly said. "We didn't know." She turned toward Brady. "Did we?"

Brady shook his head. "What's he doing?" he asked.

"Blackburn has him shoveling out his chicken house. It sure made him mad, too. At least until he drank what Blackburn gave him and passed out."

Brady had hated to tell Eddie that his Grandpa Bud hadn't found any liquor at the Blackburn place.

"I didn't think he would," was all Eddie said, but he had sounded angry. Brady wondered if his anger had been at

Blackburn or at Grandpa Bud. Probably at both, he decided. Maybe that was why he didn't want to stay with them.

Eddie found odd jobs now and then, and Aunt Tilly hired him to help Brady hoe and water the garden, which was producing a little, but nothing like it had earlier, as the weather had turned blistering hot.

Because she was paying Eddie, Aunt Tilly insisted on paying Brady, too. Although he had protested, saying they were giving him room and board and that should be pay enough. But Aunt Tilly insisted. "A boy ought to have a little change to rattle around in his pockets," she said.

It was hot everywhere and when the boys walked uptown on errands for Aunt Tilly, even the wooden sidewalks seemed hot, but the few new cement ones actually burned their bare feet.

Brady went barefooted most of time now, but for rabbit or squirrel hunting with Eddie or walking the railroad tracks picking up "clinkers," he still needed shoes. He didn't think his feet would ever be as tough as Eddie's.

Sometimes they met other boys, who, like Eddie, killed small game for food. Some boys and a few girls walked the railroad tracks picking up the small pieces of coal they called clinkers for their family's heating stoves. Eddie said the clinkers, coal that hadn't completely burned in the train's furnaces and had dropped through the grates of the passing trains, was about all the fuel his mother had ever used in her cookstove.

Storm clouds often rumbled in overhead, and people stopped whatever they were doing to look up at the sky. They hoped and prayed and begged for the clouds to drop some rain, and occasionally they did, cooling the air momentarily and washing it free of dust. But usually only a few drops fell. The sprinkles of rain made little plops in the dirt and sent out the pleasant aroma of dirt and rain. Sometimes storms of dust and dirt and cyclone-like winds sent them running to their homes or cellars.

Aunt Tilly kept the house closed up, the curtains drawn against the heat and dirt. One afternoon they took shelter in the storm cellar behind the house. Later they heard that the cyclone, or tornado as folks often called it, had been spotted heading straight toward Sentinel but had lifted up into the air at the last possible moment.

Brady liked to lie on the cool linoleum in the darkened dining room when he came in from outside. Often he and Eddie cooled off in the shallow waters of the creek, staying downstream several miles from the Blackburn place.

The last day of June, they were out hunting when they noticed dark clouds gathering overhead. "Looks like rain," Brady said.

"But it probably won't," Eddie answered.

They had ranged out farther from town than usual and were now doubling back. They had seen only a couple of rabbits and no squirrels, and they had missed both rabbits.

They watched the dark mass of clouds gathering overhead, and when the wind picked up and began blowing dirt, they started at a run for home.

By the time they neared Eddie's house, the wind was blowing hard, filling the air with dirt and whipping around small twigs and other debris that stung their faces and shirtless bodies. But it was the sudden drop in temperature that scared them.

"It's a cyclone!" Eddie yelled. "We'd better take cover!"

"Where?" Brady cupped his hands to be heard above the howl of the wind.

"My house is closer!" Eddie yelled back. "We've got a cellar!"

They raced across an open field of blowing dirt, dodging Russian thistles and other flying debris, their watering eyes mere slits. They ran on instinct as much as sight, thankful the wind was at their backs and pushed them along instead of trying to drive them back. But as they ran across Eddie's yard, the wind suddenly whipped around in front of them and they staggered against it the last few feet.

"Pop!" Eddie called as he flung open the door. "Where are you?"

Receiving no answer, Eddie turned to Brady and pointed toward the kitchen. "The cellar door's in the floor. I've got to find Pop!"

In the kitchen, Brady lifted the cellar door and looked down into the dark coolness below. The house shuddered as if it might fly away at any minute, but Brady waited. "Hurry! Hurry, Eddie!" he whispered tersely, every part of his being wanting the safety of the cellar.

At last Eddie appeared in the kitchen, looking perplexed and scared. "I can't find him!" he cried, his voice almost lost in the roaring wind that battered the little house like a raging beast wanting in. "What'll I do?"

"Maybe he's at Blackburns' place," Brady shouted. "Or uptown getting his cigarette makings. Come on, the house is about to fall in. Wherever he is, someone will take him in." He thought of what Grandpa Bud often said, "God *takes care of fools, drunks, and babies.*" But he didn't say it and he knew it wasn't true, leastwise not so a person could tell anyway.

"I guess you're right," Eddie said and followed Brady down the steps of the cellar, closing the door over their heads.

They sat down on the bottom step, their eyes growing accustomed to the darkness. From the cellar, they could only hear the wind faintly moaning. They waited for what seemed to them a long time until, at last, there was only silence.

A shaft of pale sunlight shining through the dusty windowpanes greeted them as they lifted the cellar door and stepped into the kitchen.

Outside, they scanned the clearing sky and the rooftops of the Peels' house and outbuildings for signs of Blackie. The bird had been with them when the storm began, but there was no way of telling where he might be now. Then the crow's familiar call reached their ears, and in a few seconds the bird landed at their feet. "You rascal, you," he said, pacing back and forth in front of them.

They laughed and Blackie cocked his head to look up at them. "Hello," he said. "Hello."

The buildings still stood, but the wind had torn away all that was loose and weak, and scraps of tarpaper, old boards, broken sticks and other debris littered the ground around them. They were still surveying the damage when the door of the outhouse opened and Eddie's father staggered out, his face as pale as a ghost's.

"He was in the outhouse all the time," Brady whispered. "Is he all right?"

"I don't know," Eddie said. "But he looks okay." He moved toward his father and touched the sleeve of his ragged shirt. "Are you okay, Pop?"

"All right," his father mumbled, and brushed past Eddie. He walked with just a slight stagger toward the house. As he passed Brady, he gave him a slight nod of his head.

Eddie's eyes filled as they followed his father. Then he turned away, and Brady saw him brush a hand across his face.

"I guess I'd better get home so Aunt Tilly will know I'm still in one piece," Brady said, working on lightening the tone of his voice. Eddie rewarded him with a slight grin.

"Yeah," Eddie said. "She probably thinks you've been blown over into the next county."

"Probably so," Brady answered. "I'll see you tomorrow." He broke into a dog trot that took him around the house and behind the back of the shed where Eddie had tried to hide from him that day. As he went by, his eye caught the glint of sunlight shining on something on the ground. He stopped and picked up a silver key.

"What's that?" Eddie asked, coming up beside him.

Brady showed him, and then they noticed several clothespins and a spoon lying on the ground nearby. "These are probably my mom's," Eddie said.

He swung around, a puzzled expression on his face. "Look!" He pointed to where the old rain barrel beside the shed had collapsed in the force of the wind, the slats sagging crookedly on the steel rims that had bound it together. Three of the wooden slats had been blown several feet away, and one was stuck up on end in the ground.

It took both of them to pull the slat out of the ground.

"That had to be a twister," Eddie said, his blue eyes registering his awe at the wind's power.

They tossed the slats back beside the barrel. One slat hit the barrel, and a clothespin and a large red button dropped from the barrel to the ground. Eddie suddenly laughed. "I bet we just found where Blackie's been stashing his loot!"

At the bottom of the barrel was a small pile of bottle caps, clothespins, a small comb, buttons, including the one from Brady's shirt, and a tangled red hair ribbon. They laughed about the hair ribbon, and wondered aloud if Blackie had pulled it out of the girl's hair.

"Looks like we found your stash," Eddie said, looking up at Blackie who was pacing back and forth across the roof of the shed and looking down on them. "I guess you'll have to find a new spot now."

"Hello, hello," Blackie said.

Suddenly Eddie frowned and turned to Brady. "Let me see that key you found," he said, holding out his hand.

Brady pulled the silver key from his pocket and dropped it into Eddie's hand. He knew they were thinking the same thing. This was the key Edna Blackburn had lost. Despite the heat, a shiver of cold coursed through him. He *hoped Eddie wasn't thinking crazy. He hoped he'd forgotten all about dumping out Blackburn's liquor, but he knew he hadn't.*

Eddie squinted up at him. "I bet it's Blackburn's," he said. "I bet Blackie took it. Maybe I'll try it some day and see if it fits."

He would try it, Brady knew. No maybe about it, the

question was *when?* And would he ask him to go along?

Except for a few broken tree limbs and scattered litter, Brady saw little evidence of the storm on his way back to Grandpa Bud's house. Later he learned that the storm had taken off a barn roof north of the Peel place and had snapped off a few trees, but otherwise had done no real damage. The storm had also blown some limbs from the hackberry tree down on Aunt Tilly's garden. Some of her tomato plants and cucumber vines were mashed, but most of the rest of the garden had survived. "Still enough to have to be hoed," she said, smiling at Brady.

15

JULY BROUGHT NO LET-UP in the heat. On the Fourth, Brady and Eddie went uptown to watch the parade on main street. Grandpa Bud and his deputy had marked off the parade route by parking their cars across each end of the street. Aunt Tilly decided to stay home with Sarah. "She might get a little upset with all the noise and goings-on," she said. "We'll just wait and go later to the park."

The parade was led by the veterans of World War I and the Spanish-American War, and one old man wearing his blue Civil War uniform who rode in Sam Blackburn's gleaming black Plymouth.

Brady saw Mary, the girl who had swung at the rabbits with tears in her eyes, and David Hager, the boy from across the street. They both smiled and said "Hi" to him and Eddie.

At noon everyone gathered at the park to eat picnic lunches and hear special musical numbers from local singers, fiddlers and guitar players.

After they had stuffed themselves with Aunt Tilly's fried chicken, potato salad and apple pie, Brady and Eddie walked across the park to where Mr. and Mrs. Grebe, who ran the cream station, were selling ice cream, scooping it out of gallon containers wrapped in burlap and set in huge tubs of ice. The ice cream melted almost as soon as it was dished up, but it tasted cool and sweet.

As they started back across the park, they saw Edna Blackburn and another woman sitting on a park bench eating some of the Grebe's ice cream. Sam Blackburn stood near the bandstand talking with two men. Raymond and his cronies were nowhere in sight.

Seeing the Blackburns sparked an anger in Eddie, and his words in answer to anything Brady said were clipped and short. For a while they watched some boys play baseball. Brady longed to play, but when the inning was over and David Hager, who had been put out at third base, called to them to come join the game, Eddie shook his head and walked away, so Brady shook his head, too, and followed after him.

They walked around the end of the empty grandstands and squatted down in its shade. Two high school boys back in under the grandstand dropped cigarettes, ground them beneath their heels and walked past them into the sunlight.

A loneliness came over Brady. He and Eddie had only each other for friends. At home Jim Conners had been his best friend, but they'd both had other friends. He wondered if Eddie would understand if he tried to explain. But maybe one friend was enough for Eddie, just as he had thought it would be enough for him while he lived here. But it wasn't. He knew that now.

Across the park Brady could see Aunt Tilly sitting on a blanket spread out under a tree. Two other ladies sat with her, fanning themselves as they talked. Sarah was standing and turning in circles, her little hands flapping in front of her face. Although he was too far away to hear her, he bet she was making her usual clicking sounds.

Not far from Sarah and Aunt Tilly, a crowd had gathered to watch some men pitching horseshoes. Raymond Blackburn, his friends Roscoe and Freddie, and another boy Brady knew as Frank, were among the crowd. As Brady watched, the four boys, with Raymond leading, left the group and walked across to where Aunt Tilly and the other ladies were sitting and watching Sarah. Brady looked around for Grandpa Bud, but he was nowhere in sight. Raymond stood in front of Aunt Tilly and said something. His henchmen waited behind him, their hands in their pockets.

"Come on, Eddie," Brady said grimly. "Raymond Blackburn's talking to Aunt Tilly and her friends and probably saying something about Sarah."

Raymond and his friends must have seen them coming, for as they drew near, Brady heard Raymond tell Aunt Tilly goodbye. Then with his three toadies following, Raymond started across the grounds toward them. Brady steeled himself for the encounter, grateful for Eddie's presence beside him. He would not turn away, and neither, he knew, would Raymond.

They met face to face. "What a pair," Raymond said, his face matching the tone of his low mocking voice. "One has an idiot sister and the other has an idiot old man."

Brady saw red. Nothing else existed in his world but a blinding, red rage. With a bellowing cry, he leaped at Raymond and grabbed him about the neck, twisting him down to the ground in a bone-wrenching jolt that jarred them apart. Brady scrambled to his knees and flung himself on Raymond's prone body, battering him with his fists.

"Hey!" Grandpa Bud had a hold of his shirt collar and was pulling him off Raymond.

Yanking him to his feet, he glared at Brady. "What's gotten in to you, boy?" he growled, his pale blue eyes snapping with anger.

Grandpa Bud's anger only added fuel to Brady's, and he pulled away, fists balled and teeth gritted. But his anger lifted, and a satisfied feeling of joy flushed through him when he saw Raymond's friends helping him to his feet. One of Raymond's black eyes was swelling shut, and a huge bruise covered half of his chin.

Brady turned to look up at Grandpa Bud, unable to hold back his grin of satisfaction. But Grandpa Bud had turned away and was kneeling beside Eddie, who sat on the ground holding his right arm and grimacing with pain. Brady swung around to face Raymond, but he and his friends were retreating.

Grandpa Bud took hold of Eddie's arm. "Can you move it?" he asked.

"No," Eddie spoke through clenched teeth. "I think it's broken."

"All right. Let's get you on your feet. I think Doc Griffey is here. We'll have him take a look at it." Grandpa Bud pulled Eddie to his feet, and holding him by his good arm, propelled him across the park to where the doctor sat listening to a man play a lonesome-sounding song on a mouth organ.

"It's broken, all right," Doctor Griffey said, after examining Eddie's arm. "I'll take him to the hospital and put a cast on it."

Grandpa Bud helped Eddie into the doctor's car and then turned a stern face to Brady. "You stay with Aunt Tilly. And stay out of trouble. Pete here will see that you get home." He nodded toward the deputy and turned to his own car.

For a second Brady thought his Grandpa Bud had meant for the deputy to take him home ... back to the farm ... and then he realized he'd meant back to his house. But he bet Grandpa Bud wished he could send him back to the farm, drop him off and forget all about him. And probably Sarah, too.

"You've got a cut over your left eye," Aunt Tilly said, shaking out the blanket she and Sarah had used to sit on, "I'll put something on it when we get home."

"It's all right," Brady muttered, anger and shame twisting inside him. "He said Sarah was an idiot and Eddie's dad was, too."

"I'm not surprised," Aunt Tilly said. "From the questions he was asking me about Sarah, I thought he was putting me on, pretending to be concerned. He was just a little too fawning to be sincere."

"Mrs. Johnson." The voice startled them both, and they swung around to see Sam and Edna Blackburn standing before them. Behind them, Raymond, despite the blackened eye and bruised face, looked smug and confident.

"This is the second time your ward has picked a fight with our son." Sam Blackburn's deadly quiet voice seethed with anger. "I want you and the Sheriff to talk to the boy, because if we have any more trouble with him, I shall be forced to press charges." He drew himself up in even more of a self-righteous pose, Brady thought, and added, "I should this time. But I'm going to let it go."

Aunt Tilly stood with her hands on her hips all the time he was talking. She was as tall as Sam Blackburn, and beside the dowdy little Edna, who looked, Brady thought, like a puffed-up toad in her frilly green dress, she appeared ten feet tall.

"We will be discussing this," Aunt Tilly said in a cool, even voice. "Have no fear about that. And I would suggest that you and Edna do the same concerning your son. Now..." she seemed to stand taller, straighter, "if you have nothing further, please allow me to get our things together so we can go home." She nodded to Pete Peters, who had driven around so he could park closer to them and was standing by his car waiting. "I see our ride is here."

Sam Blackburn smiled a cold, hard smile, and without even tipping his hat, turned and strode across the park to his car. Raymond and Edna scurried along behind him.

Grandpa Bud brought Eddie home to stay overnight.

"Doc says it's a simple break." Grandpa Bud said in answer to Aunt Tilly's question. "But I thought it best if he bunked with Brady tonight." He spoke in short, tight sentences, so Brady knew he was still angry. "While you're rustling up some supper for us, Tilly, I'm going in the other room and listen to the radio. Call me when it's ready. Oh, yes." He turned back at the doorway. "The boys can help you. Eddie broke his right arm, but he's left-handed. Lucky, isn't he?" he added dryly.

After supper, Eddie approached Grandpa Bud about

going home. "Please, sir," he said. "My arm feels fine now."

Brady knew Eddie wasn't exactly telling the truth. He could tell by his face that his arm still hurt. He wondered if he wanted to go home because Grandpa Bud was still so cranky, or if he was worried about his pop, as he called his dad.

Maybe Grandpa Bud decided the same thing because his voice softened a lot when he told him he'd better stay here anyway so Aunt Tilly could keep an eye on him, and that he'd go over and tell his dad.

"It won't matter to him," Eddie said. "He probably won't even notice I'm gone."

"I'll go anyway," Grandpa Bud said.

Brady was glad to hear Grandpa Bud's voice sounding normal again. He sure hoped he was over being mad. He hated how low and worthless he felt when Grandpa Bud was mad at him.

Eddie's shirt was torn and dirty from the fight, and the doctor had cut the sleeve to get it off over his broken arm. "I'll wash it tonight and mend it in the morning," Aunt Tilly said as she helped Eddie out of it.

"Thanks, Aunt Tilly," Eddie said. "I'm sorry I'm such a bother."

"Oh, yes," Aunt Tilly said with mock severity. "You are such a bother." Then she laughed and flapped her apron at him. "Now, shoo!" she said. "Get out of my kitchen both of you, and upstairs to bed."

Upstairs, Brady shucked out of his shirt and overalls and lay down on the bed in his shorts. Eddie walked over to the open window. "Are you okay, Blackie?" he called softly.

A faint muttering sound answered him.

At Aunt Tilly's suggestion, he and Brady had built a large cage for Blackie from a roll of chicken wire and old lumber that had been stacked behind the shed. "The coop is too small to leave him for any length of time," she'd said. "And sometime you may want to leave him all day or night."

Blackie seemed to enjoy his cage. They had built two shelves on the sides and a roosting stand in the middle. Aunt Tilly gave him several empty spools and small scraps of cloth from her sewing basket, a couple of spoons, a clothespin and some other things to amuse him.

He especially liked a cup in which he put buttons and bottle caps. He spent hours, plucking them from the cup, hiding them on one of the shelves under a scrap of cloth and then returning them again to the cup. And all the while he "talked" his learned human words and his own crow talk.

Eddie stayed at the window a long time and Brady drifted off to sleep. Something woke him in the night, and in the dim moonlight shining through the window, he saw Eddie lying beside him, still in his overalls.

"You awake?" he whispered.

"Yeah," Eddie said.

"Is your arm hurting?"

"Some." Eddie shifted on the bed. "It's hard to get comfortable."

He was silent awhile and then he said, "I've been thinking. Remember when we talked about dumping out Blackburn's liquor and filling the jars with water?"

Something lurched in Brady's stomach. "I remember," he said.

"I tried the key," Eddie said. "It fits."

"When did you do that?"

"A couple of nights ago. I couldn't sleep. Pop was ranting and raving about Mom leaving and reminding me what a worthless nothing I am to him. I went outside so I couldn't hear him. The moon was full ..."

In the dim light Brady could not see Eddie's tears, but he could hear them. "Aren't you hot in your overalls?" he asked for something to say, something to make Eddie's voice sound normal again.

"I'm all right," Eddie said.

"But you've got to be hot," Brady insisted. "I'm hot even

in my shorts. Come on, Eddie."

"Quit pestering me," Eddie said, grinding out his words through gritted teeth, and in a quick, angry motion, he turned his back to Brady. "I don't have any shorts."

The anger in his voice, mixed with the thickness of tears, confused Brady. Why was he so upset?

Brady got up off the bed and rummaged around in a drawer until he found a pair of his shorts. He tossed them over in front of Eddie. "Wear these," he said.

Eddie swung his legs off the bed and slipping off his overalls, put on the shorts. It took awhile with one hand and Brady almost offered to help him and then decided against it, afraid Eddie would just get angrier. After all, it wasn't Eddie's fault that his arm got broken today. He hadn't started the fight.

Suddenly Eddie laughed a low, chuckling sound. "Look at this," he said standing up.

In the dim light, Brady could see the white shorts start a downward slide before Eddie grabbed for them.

Brady laughed and rolled off the bed to find the safety pin he had seen earlier on top of the dresser.

They lay back on the bed and Brady closed his eyes, hoping Eddie wouldn't say any more about dumping out Blackburn's liquor, but he knew he would.

"You don't have to go if you don't want to," Eddie finally said. "But I'm going to do it."

"With a broken arm?" Brady asked.

"I'll wait until it heals. Doc Griffey thought it would take about six weeks. I can wait that long, I guess, if you're afraid to go."

"All right," Brady said. He felt like he had just dived into a bottomless pool. A pool in which he would drown. "When can we do it?"

"Tomorrow, if we want to."

"Tomorrow?" Brady swallowed. *Tomorrow!* He wasn't quite ready to do it tomorrow.

"The sooner the better, Eddie said. We can take some gunny sacks to carry the jars down to the creek and back again to the storm cellar."

"They're going to hit against each other and make a noise," Brady said.

"We'll stuff other gunny sacks around them. We've got some, and I saw some in your grandpa's shed out back."

"Maybe Blackburn's got a new dog by now," Brady said, a shiver running through him.

"I didn't see or hear one when I was there," Eddie said.

The matter seemed settled to Eddie's satisfaction, and Brady couldn't think of anything that would change his mind. After a while he could hear Eddie's even, steady breathing and knew he was asleep.

But Brady slept fitfully, waking often with visions of snarling dogs, and of himself and Eddie staring down the barrel of Blackburn's shotgun.

16

AT AUNT TILLY'S INSISTENCE, Eddie stayed with them two more nights. Up in Brady's room they discussed their "raid," as they began to call it, and finally decided on Sunday night.

"I think the fella from Nebraska brings the stuff on Thursday," Eddie said, "and I bet Oscar Stephenson picks his up before Saturday for the people who like to celebrate a little on Saturday night. If we go Sunday night, there won't be so much to empty and refill, but still enough to upset Blackburn and make him good and mad."

"What if Oscar Stephenson takes it all?" Brady asked.

"He won't. Blackburn will have his own personal stuff, I bet, and some just to give away, and Pop's will be there, too." Eddie paused and looked at Brady. "That's good enough, don't you think?"

Brady nodded. None would be even better, he thought.

By Saturday, Brady was so jittery that Aunt Tilly felt his forehead several times during the day, certain, she said, that he was coming down with something.

Brady wished he was and that Aunt Tilly would send him to bed with aspirin and maybe even call the doctor. Eddie wouldn't think he was a coward if Doc Griffey came to see him and if Aunt Tilly was hovering over him with spoonfuls of medicine. Maybe Aunt Tilly would think he was getting polio and wouldn't even let Eddie in the house. Just like his mom, Aunt Tilly worried a lot about polio. And just like her, she thought summertime was the worst. Summertime and swimming pools.

She and Grandpa Bud had been sitting on the front porch one evening, and Brady had started to push open the screen door and step out to join them when he heard Aunt Tilly mention the word polio. His hand on the screen, he had waited, listening.

"I'm glad Sentinel doesn't have a swimming pool," Aunt Tilly said. "But I guess if we did, the town would have to close it, wouldn't they?"

"Only if we have a case of polio. Otherwise, it's not dangerous for folks to be swimming in the same water."

"Kind of like closing the barn door after the horse has been stolen, isn't it?" Aunt Tilly said.

" I suppose. But we can't live in fear of what might happen, can we?"

"I never feared at all for my boys. Never dreamed ... I wish I had worried more."

"It wouldn't have changed things," Grandpa Bud said.

"If I had just thought that day that the boys might drown ... I knew they were going swimming."

"Would you have called them back?" Grandpa Bud said, the gentleness in his voice surprising Brady.

"Maybe ... at least I would have told them to be careful."

"Don't torture yourself, Tilly. It wasn't your fault."

"I know. I think of folks like Clifford Peel throwing away his life ... his family ... he has no more idea than nothing of the treasure he has in that family of his. The ignorant ..." Aunt Tilly's voice ended in an angry-sounding sputter.

"It's the alcohol, Tilly," Grandpa Bud said. "It changed who he was. I remember when he was a school boy. He looked a lot like T.J. and Jimmy Joe do now. I think Eddie favors his mother. Anyway, Cliff was a good boy, bashful as all get out. But he grew up and fell into a bottle and couldn't, or wouldn't, get out, and it made him its slave. Which is like being a slave to the Devil. It's too bad, but there's nothing we can do about it. Maybe nothing any more that Cliff can do about it either."

Grandpa Bud had gone to the office then to see that everything was all right for the night. In his mind, Brady followed him, seeing him pick up his hat, step down off the porch and walk to his car. He saw the flash of headlights as Grandpa Bud backed out and drove through the town to the courthouse. Inside the courthouse, he walked down the steps to his office and the jail. He saw him go back to the cells where Eddie's brothers had waited to be sentenced. He saw him look through the bars at him and Eddie ... He shivered and tried to shake the image from his mind.

On Sunday, Brady sat through church and dinner and, in the afternoon, hoed all of the garden that Aunt Tilly had coaxed back to life after the storm. After supper, he listened to the radio with Grandpa Bud and Aunt Tilly, but even Amos and Andy didn't seem funny, and he had to force his laughter.

At dusk he went out to sit on the back steps. Fireflies flitted through the air, and the locusts had set up their steady droning song. It was still hot and the slight breeze only stirred the hot air.

After a while he went back inside and up the stairs to his room. He lay down on his bed. The clock on his dresser seemed to tick louder and louder while the minute hand seemed to stand still. But at last, it was time. He got up off his bed and slipped out through the open window and into the branches of the hackberry tree.

Eddie waited in the shadows. Without a word, he handed Brady some gunny sacks and padded barefooted ahead of him, a silent ghost of a boy in the dark night.

As they walked out of town, past Eddie's house and along the well-worn path through the open fields and the plum thicket, Brady kept up a silent chant. *Don't let us get caught. Please, don't let us get caught.*

When they reached the creek, a faint trickle of sound in

the darkness, an owl hooted softly. Eddie jerked around, his face pale beneath the billed cap he wore. "It's an owl," he whispered.

"I know," Brady said. It didn't help any to know that for all his brave talk, Eddie was a little scared, too.

They waded the creek, the water barely to their ankles, and climbed the bank to peer across at the Blackburn house. A light shone in an upstairs window. They sat on the ground and waited.

When the light went out, Eddie gave a little grunt and started to his feet.

"Wait," Brady hissed. "Give them time to go to sleep."

Eddie settled back.

A bird twittered sleepily in a bush nearby, as if momentarily awakened. Overhead, stars twinkled in the black sky. Brady looked for the Big and Little Dippers, the only constellations he knew. He tried to pick out other shapes in the stars, but he couldn't make pictures out of any of them. Intent on the stars, he jumped when Eddie touched his arm.

"Let's go," Eddie whispered.

His legs suddenly weak, Brady forced himself up off the ground. He took a deep, ragged breath and followed Eddie's shadowy form moving toward the row of lilacs.

At the door to the storm cellar, Brady fumbled with the padlock and in his nervousness almost dropped the key.

The cellar walls were whitewashed so it was easier to see, but they still had to feel along the walls as they crept down the steps.

"Here's the matches," Eddie whispered, touching Brady's arm. "I can't light them with one hand."

Brady took a match and struck it on the buckle on his overall straps. In the flare of light from the wooden match, they could see several empty bushel baskets and a sack of potatoes. The walls were lined with shelves full of quart jars filled with canned vegetables and fruits, and small pint jars of jams and jellies sealed with paraffin. It reminded

Brady of the preserves his mother used to make, and how he'd loved to chew on chunks of the sealing wax.

The match burned low and too close to his fingers. He shook it out and lit another. Still they couldn't see anything that looked like liquor, and Brady was suddenly hopeful. But on the third match, Eddie spied four wooden crates hidden behind several large crocks and a stack of gunny sacks.

"Here it is," he whispered. "I bet he keeps it in these crates so he can move it in a hurry."

In the light of the next match, Brady saw him grin. "Lucky for us, too," he added. "Now we won't need our gunny sacks."

Brady blew out the match and they lifted a crate, each taking a hold of the wire handles.

As soon as they came out of the cellar, Brady looked quickly toward the house. All was still and dark. They carried the crate down to the creek and Brady unscrewed the lids and passed the jars on to Eddie who poured the potent-smelling liquid out on the ground.

As the jars were emptied, Eddie squatted at the water's edge and filled each one with creek water. Then he handed them back to Brady who screwed the lids back on and put them back in the crate. Once in his nervousness and haste, Brady let go of a jar before Eddie got a grip on it and the whole jar of alcohol spilled out on both of them.

"We'll have to wash our overalls out in the creek to get the smell out," Brady said. "As hot as it is, they'll be dry by the time we get home."

"Yeah," Eddie said sniffing the bib of his overalls. "We smell just like Pop."

Each time they carried a crate of water-filled jars back to the storm cellar, Brady kept his eyes on the Blackburn house, certain that at any moment the lights would come on and a door would fling open and Sam Blackburn would come running, shotgun in hand. But as they started out with the last crate, Brady began to lose some of his fear.

He was unscrewing the cap on the last bottle when Eddie said, "I thought I'd be able to tell which ones Blackburn sold to Pop, but I can't see any difference, can you?"

"No," Brady said. He held the jar up and turned it around in his hand. "This one looks just like all the others." He brought the jar up to his nose and sniffed. "It smells just as bad as the others, too. I wonder what it tastes like. Have you ever tried any, Eddie?"

"No," Eddie said. A smile barely visible in the darkness flashed across his face. "Shall we take a little taste?"

For an answer, Brady tipped up the jar and gulped a big swallow. The liquid shut off his air as it burned like a roaring fire down his throat. Dropping the jar, he bent over gasping and coughing, tears streaming from his eyes.

When he finally got himself under control and could breathe again, he wiped his eyes and nose with his hand and gasped out in a choking whisper. "Don't take a big drink! It'll kill you!"

"It's mostly all spilled out anyway," Eddie said, picking the jar up off the ground. "But there's a swallow or two left."

Through watering eyes Brady watched Eddie tip up the jar and take a small sip, grimace, and then take a bigger one and begin to cough and choke as Brady had done.

"Geeze," Eddie said when he finally found his voice. "That is some really bad stuff! It must be what Pop drinks. It tastes like rotgut to me!"

Brady grinned. The liquor inside him had cooled, making a warm spot in his stomach. Taking the jar from Eddie, he squatted and filled it with creek water.

They put the last crate back in the cellar and, climbing the steps, closed the door. Brady slipped the padlock out of his pocket and reached up to slip it through the hasp.

"Hurry," Eddie whispered.

Then another voice cut through the darkness. *"Don't move an inch or you're dead."*

Brady's stomach dropped to his toes and his heart

lurched upwards into his throat. His fingers dropped the padlock and key.

And then Eddie was gone in a quick, scrambling, running sound. A gun fired, a heart-stopping, booming sound. Brady dropped to his hands and knees and began scrambling away on all fours. He heard a man swear and running footsteps coming after him. He leaped to his feet, tripped over something and fell flat. And then someone was straddling his back and, pulling his head back by his hair, began banging his face into the ground.

"Okay, Raymond," a man's voice said. "I've got him covered. He won't get away now."

Raymond hesitated a second and, before getting off him, slammed his face once more on the ground. This time Brady tasted blood.

"Roll over," Sam Blackburn said, prodding Brady with the toe of his boot. "Strike a match, Raymond. Let's see this fella's face."

Brady rolled over and looked up into a faint yellow glow backed by two dark figures.

"It's that Foster boy." Brady heard the gloating sound in Raymond's voice. "We've got him dead to rights, Dad."

"It looks like it," Sam Blackburn said. "Not only trespassing, but stealing, too, I bet. Bud Lewis will have a time getting him out of this." Sam Blackburn prodded Brady again with his boot. "Come on, get up. Let's get you to the house and get your granddad called. And don't forget, like your friend did, that I have the shotgun on you. I missed him, but I won't miss you."

He turned to his son. "Get on up to the house and get some lights on, and tell your mother to stay upstairs." Turning back to Brady, he gestured toward the house with the barrel of his shotgun. "Get moving, boy," he said.

The lights came on in the house as Brady forced his weak, wobbly legs to climb the steps of the Blackburns' back porch. Raymond opened the door to their kitchen, holding it wide, a pleased smile plastered all over his face. Brady noticed with some satisfaction that the bruises from their Fourth of July fight were still visible. But his satisfaction dissolved into fear at Sam Blackburn's next words.

"Hold the gun on him, Raymond," he said. "I'll get Central to ring up Sheriff Lewis."

"Sure thing, Dad." Raymond narrowed his black eyes to gleaming slits. Pretending, Brady figured, like he was one of J. Edgar Hoover's G-men, or some tough guy from the picture shows, like Edward G. Robinson. Pretending, but dangerous all the same.

Brady held his breath, afraid to even move while Raymond strutted around waving the shotgun in front of him. "You're not so smart now, are you, boy?" Raymond ground out the words through his "tough man" teeth, a sneer curling his lip.

Brady didn't answer. Fear prickled his scalp and dried his mouth so he wasn't sure he could speak even if he wanted to. He stared at Raymond's shoes and waited. He could hear Sam Blackburn on the telephone, but he couldn't quite make out the words. Finally, Raymond's father came back and took the shotgun from Raymond's hands. Brady breathed a sigh of relief.

"Sit." Sam Blackburn waved the gun barrel toward a chair at the kitchen table. "Your granddad's ..." he broke off, swinging around, as a knocking came at the door. "What the ..." he frowned and jerked his head toward Raymond. "See who it is," he said.

Raymond opened the door a crack and then pulled it all the way back. "Look who's here, Dad," he said grinning. "It's the one that got away. The stupid jerk came back."

Raymond stepped aside and Eddie came into the room. He looked at Brady and tried to grin, but the grin was crooked and soon slipped from his face.

A mixture of relief and anger washed over Brady. Eddie had gotten away scot free. Why had he come back? Did he think he would tell on him? But he was glad Eddie had come back. He didn't feel so alone and scared with Eddie here.

"Well, get over here," Sam Blackburn said, motioning Eddie to a chair beside Brady. "Pull a chair over here for me, Raymond," he added. "We might as well be comfortable while we wait for the sheriff."

Sam Blackburn sat down on the chair Raymond brought him. "You know trespassing is against the law, don't you?" he said, his black eyes cold as ice.

They both nodded, but neither spoke.

"So what were you boys doing?" The icy black eyes shifted to Brady. "Were you going to help Peel here steal my wife's canned goods?"

"No," Brady managed to say past the paralyzed muscles of his throat.

Suddenly a look of surprise crossed Sam Blackburn's face and he stood up and came close, bending down, he sniffed at them. "You boys been in Peels' liquor?" he asked.

Not waiting for an answer, he turned and motioned Raymond with a quick incline of his head. They both moved to the door, whispered back and forth, and then Raymond went outside, closing the door behind him.

Brady looked quickly at Eddie, who nodded, a small glimmer of light coming into his eyes. Raymond had been sent to hide what had once been illegal liquor and was now harmless creek water. It would have been funny at some other time. But not now. Not with Blackburn's shotgun leaning in the corner and Grandpa Bud due to arrive at any moment, and probably mad enough to bite nails in half.

Raymond was gone twenty minutes or longer. He had just stepped back into the kitchen when the lights of a car flashed through the window.

"That ought to be Sheriff Lewis," Sam Blackburn said.

Brady bit down on his lip, his insides tightening into a hard knot, and a cold shiver of dread spread though him. *Grandpa Bud was going to be really mad.*

When Grandpa Bud entered the room, Brady knew that Sam Blackburn hadn't told him who he had caught on his property. The big man's face went slack and his whole body seemed to shrink, and then he was himself again ... and the law. His presence and his tall, large frame filled the room and dwarfed even Sam Blackburn. "What's the problem here?" he asked.

"Raymond and I caught these two sneaking around the place." Sam Blackburn shook a ready-made cigarette from the pack in his pocket and lit it, drawing the smoke deep into his lungs before blowing it out into the room. "Since one's a Peel, I suspect they were planning on stealing something. They've been drinking. They smell like it anyway. I suppose they got into Cliff Peel's sauce and that gave them courage."

"Drinking?" Grandpa Bud frowned.

"Smell them," Sam Blackburn said.

"Is that true, boys?" Grandpa Bud's pale blue eyes narrowed.

"N ... no," Brady managed to stammer.

"No, what?"

"We weren't stealing and we weren't drinking," Eddie said. And then as if suddenly remembering he added, "Well, just a swallow."

"We dumped it out," Brady said, finding a new steadiness in his voice.

"Yeah." Eddie pointed at Sam Blackburn. "We dumped out his bootleg liquor and refilled the jars with creek water. We spilled some on our overalls. We did take a drink, but just a little one ... to see what it was like."

Sam Blackburn laughed a loud, scornful laugh. "Lies," he said. The truth doesn't exist for a Peel." He smiled at Grandpa Bud. "You're welcome to search the premises like you did before, but I can tell you it's a waste of time." He stubbed out his cigarette in a small ashtray. "We caught them getting ready to go into our storm cellar. Mrs.

Blackburn has all her canned goods there, and we also have a few sacks of potatoes." His expression and tone of voice suddenly filled with compassion. "I expect the Peel boy does get pretty hungry with his dad drinking up everything they have. But your boy, Sheriff..." He shook his head. "I wouldn't have thought it of your boy." He frowned. "He's Lydia's boy, I understand. Perhaps he has more Lee in him than Lydia." He sighed. "You did have a time with Lee, didn't you, Bud?"

Grandpa Bud looked at Sam Blackburn. "That was a long time ago, Sam."

For a moment the two men locked gazes, then Sam Blackburn turned to Brady and Eddie. "So you weren't stealing," he said, "but you were drinking. I expect if we look around we'll find an empty bottle. Right, boys?"

"No, sir," Brady said. "We put them all back in the cellar."

"You brought Peel's liquor and put it in my cellar?" Sam Blackburn faked a puzzled look. "I think you boys must have had quite a bit to drink to come up with that story."

"No, sir," Brady said. "We just had a swallow."

"A swallow?" Sam Blackburn raised his eye brows as if in disbelief. "And you spilled the rest on your overalls? Sure, you did. I'm glad I told Mrs. Blackburn to stay upstairs. She would have been so offended by your smell."

Across the room Raymond, lounging against the wall, got a smirky grin on his face.

"All right. Let's go look things over." Grandpa Bud spoke as if everything was all settled and there was no need for more words of explanation. "It's nearly daylight, but you had better bring a lantern, Sam."

They filed out into the pale gray dawn. No one spoke as they approached the storm cellar. The door was latched, but there was no padlock. Brady wondered if Raymond had found where he'd dropped it when he went outside to move the water-filled jars. The jars the Blackburns had thought were full of illegal liquor.

As they all knew, except maybe Grandpa Bud, there was no evidence of the crates in the cellar. Only the rows of canned food, sacks of potatoes, crocks and empty bushel baskets remained.

"Show me where you dumped it by the creek," Grandpa Bud said.

"Where they say they did," Sam Blackburn said.

Grandpa Bud studied the ground beside the creek, walking slowly and holding the lantern low. "All right," he said straightening up, "I guess I'm done here."

They walked back to the Blackburns' front yard before he spoke again. Looking at Sam Blackburn, he said, "Well, there doesn't seem to be any harm done. Suppose I take these boys home and give them something to think about for a few days? My office and the jail hasn't been scrubbed thoroughly for a long time. Leo Shiller does a good job, but a thorough cleaning won't hurt."

"I guess that would be all right," Sam Blackburn said. "But if I catch either one of them on my property again, I will have to press criminal trespass charges." He looked at Raymond. "Do you agree with that, son?"

Grandpa Bud frowned.

Raymond grinned. "I guess that would be okay." He nodded toward Eddie. "He's a little handicapped with that broken arm, but..." He paused, his face taking on the false, thoughtful look he used on adults, "they probably drank enough of Mr. Peel's liquor to have a headache for most of the day. That should be a good lesson as well."

"Okay, boys, get in the car." Grandpa Bud turned to them without acknowledging Raymond's words. They hurried to get in the back seat. Brady knew they had gotten off easy, and he hoped Sam Blackburn wouldn't change his mind. He wondered if Grandpa Bud had been able to tell where they had poured out the alcohol. Had the ground been too dry and the weather too hot to leave any moisture?

Grandpa Bud opened his car door and put a foot up on

the running board. Looking over the top of the car, he seemed to be waiting for the sun, which was just beneath the horizon but sending up fingers of color across the eastern sky. Then he turned to the Blackburns and spoke quietly, "I would call my supplier, if I were you, Sam. Tell him you've just gone out of business."

17

By SEVEN O'CLOCK, Aunt Tilly had Brady's overalls washed and out on the line. She had sent him to the bathroom to wash as soon as Grandpa Bud dropped him off and went on to take Eddie home. Now she set a plate of bacon and eggs and toast on the table in front of him and sat down to watch him eat.

"Your grandfather is pretty upset," she said. "I hope you can keep yourself out of trouble from now on."

"Yes, ma'am," Brady murmured around a mouthful of eggs. He was just about too tired to even eat. His eyes, scratchy from lack of sleep, kept wanting to close, and his whole body ached. He longed to go to his bed, but a long day of cleaning Grandpa Bud's office lay ahead of him first.

"You look a sight," Aunt Tilly had said after Grandpa Bud left to take Eddie home. It was true, he did. His bottom lip was split open and his face was bruised and dirty from Raymond banging it into the ground. But other than that comment and the admonishment to stay out of trouble, she never mentioned it again.

Eddie was waiting by the courthouse steps standing close to the building in a narrow strip of shade. The sun was already too hot for comfort. The ragged overalls he wore were too big for him, and he had crossed the straps several times and rolled the legs to expose his bare feet.

"Aunt Tilly sent you some breakfast," Brady said, handing Eddie the bacon and egg sandwich she'd wrapped in waxed paper.

"Thanks," Eddie said. He ate the sandwich quickly. "We'd better get to your grandpa's office," he said around the last mouthful.

Grandpa Bud was the only one in the office when they entered. He looked up from his desk where he'd been writing something and jerked his head toward a small door. "Buckets, mops, all you need are in there," he said, and went back to his writing.

Not sure exactly where to begin, they took out a couple of brooms from the closet and began sweeping the office floor. As they worked, first sweeping and then mopping, several men came in to talk to Grandpa Bud. Each time, he sent the boys outside to wait until the men left. It was mid-morning, and they were sitting in the shade of a locust tree in the courthouse yard waiting, when Blackie flew in and landed beside them.

"There you are," Eddie said, a grin lighting his face. He turned to Brady. "He was gone when I left this morning. I wonder how he knew I was here."

At noon Grandpa Bud took them home for dinner. Blackie followed the car, flying behind it. Eddie shut him up in his cage, and he began to walk about saying, "Hello, hello," as if greeting his toys.

Grandpa Bud got a telephone call before he finished dinner and left with the food on his plate half eaten. "You can send the prisoner's dinner with the boys," he called back to Aunt Tilly as the screen door slammed behind him.

That was the first they realized there was a prisoner in the jail, and they asked Aunt Tilly about him. "I don't know who he is or why he's there," she said. "I just know I have to feed him." She handed Brady a quart jar of milk and gave Eddie a sack of sandwiches. "Broken arms can't be trusted to handle jars," she said with a smile.

Grandpa Bud was still out when they arrived at the office. Deputy Peters was sitting on a corner of his desk waiting for them. "Your grandpa said to start wiping down the walls here in the office," he said, taking the food and disappearing down the narrow hallway that led to the cells.

Brady tore an old towel into two pieces and filled a bucket with soapy water to wash down the walls. When Deputy Peters came back to the office, Brady asked about the man in jail.

"That's quite a story," the deputy said, laughing. "Seems this fella stole a car up in Nebraska and was heading for Colorado. He ran it out of gas west of town just as George Fennessey happened along. Seeing the car, George stopped to see if he could be of help. Well, the fella jumped up on the running board, pulled a gun, and ordered George to drive him to Colorado." Deputy Peters took a drink of the coffee he'd poured while he was talking and then chuckled, "Aren't you boys forgetting something?" he said.

Caught up in the story, they had stopped wiping the walls and were standing with the soapy rags dripping from their hands. Grinning at each other and Deputy Peters, they turned back to their work.

"What the guy didn't know," Deputy Peters continued," was that George was on his way to the filling station, and George was so scared he forgot all about being on empty and ran out of gas about five miles out of town. The fella jumped out of George's car and took off running. George hoofed it back to town to tell us. We found his car-stealing gunman about a half mile farther up the road, trying to thumb a ride."

"He didn't try to shoot you and Grandpa Bud, did he?" Brady asked.

"Nope. Gave himself up right away. I guess he figured the luck he was having, he might just as well give up his life of crime before he got into any more trouble. He's wanted by the law up in Nebraska, so they're sending someone for him tomorrow."

Eddie grinned. "He sounds about as lucky in crime as Brady and I were."

"Just about," Deputy Peters said. His eyes twinkled and a grin stretched across his face. "But we hope you two won't be repeat offenders."

After supper, Grandpa Bud took Eddie home, and as he did before, Blackie followed the car.

Brady fell into bed and slept until Grandpa Bud called him the next morning.

They had just finished the walls in the office and had started on the hallway when a deputy sheriff from Nebraska arrived for his prisoner.

A cheerful looking man, he kidded them about their "booze raid." Pete Peters chuckled along with him, but Grandpa Bud never cracked a smile.

After he left with the prisoner, Grandpa Bud had them sweep and mop both cells, wash the gray walls and run a wet rag over the iron bars. It was cool back inside the cells, but an odor like sweat mixed with urine and the small confining space gave Brady the willies, and he hurried as fast as he could to finish the work.

"Your granddad put Pop in jail once when I was in the third grade," Eddie said suddenly after a long silence. "He stole a sack of Bull Durham tobacco from the grocery store and got caught." He turned from running his rag over the bars and looked at Brady. "I bet your granddad thinks I'm not much better than my old man."

"I think he thinks you're more like your mother," Brady said.

Eddie flashed him a grateful smile and later began to whistle a cheerful tune.

They were nearly finished with the jail cells when the telephone rang in the office. They paused to listen, but could only make out a few words. "Do you think your grandpa is bringing in another prisoner?" Eddie asked.

As if in answer to his question, Deputy Peters came down

the hallway. "Hurry it up, boys," he said. "We're about to have company."

Fifteen minutes later they were back in the office when Grandpa Bud entered with two ragged old men. The old men peering out of dirt-blackened faces stumbled along as if they were almost too weak to walk.

"You can leave your bundles here in the office," Grandpa Bud said. They dropped their filthy bedrolls and turned back to him. "Deputy Peters will show you to your cells so you can get some rest, and we'll rustle you up some chow as quick as we can."

He swung around to Brady and Eddie, who stood beside the closet where they had just put away their bucket and rags. "You boys run on home and tell Aunt Tilly we need some sandwiches and whatever else she has on hand. These men have just come in on a freight and they need rest and food, and they need it now. So hustle!"

They ran all the way, taking shortcuts through alleys and across several yards, arriving sweat-streaked and out of breath.

"Grandpa Bud wants some food right away!" Brady gasped out. "He's got two old bums in jail. They came off a freight and they're really old."

Aunt Tilly had been to the clothesline and had a stack of freshly dried clothes in her arms. "It'll be suppertime in a couple of hours," she said. "Can't they wait?"

"I don't think so," Brady said. "They're sort of staggering and they don't look so good."

"I think they're awfully hungry," Eddie said quietly.

"Well, in that case I'll see what I have."

Aunt Tilly made several thick sandwiches and added two apples and a dozen cookies to the sack before she handed it to Brady. "I'm out of milk," she said. "Grandpa Bud will just have to give them some of his coffee or let them drink water."

Grandpa Bud glanced at the clock as he took the sack

of food from Brady. "It's four o'clock," he said. "You boys might as well call it a day."

"What will you do with those old fellas?" Brady asked.

"In the morning we'll get some breakfast in them and send them on their way. I expect they'll catch a freight before noon and travel on. God only knows where."

"At least they have a bed for the night and a full stomach to start out on tomorrow," Deputy Peters said. "That's more than a lot of their fellow travelers will have."

"I expect so," Grandpa Bud said.

In the night, Brady heard the telephone ring and, a little later, Grandpa Bud leave the house and start up his car. He went back to sleep. He dreamed his dad was shaking him. *"Wake up! Wake up!" his dad shouted at him.* Brady's eyes snapped open. Grandpa Bud was leaning over him, shaking him. "Wake up, Brady," he said. "There's been a little trouble tonight, and I'll have to be gone a few days."

Brady blinked his eyes in the gray morning light. He could still see his dad's face in his dream. His dad had been crying, his face twisted in pain.

"Are you all right?" Grandpa Bud asked.

"I'm all right." Brady managed to keep the quiver out of his voice.

"A man tried to kill his wife and children last night," Grandpa Bud said. "I'm taking him to Larned."

"To Larned," Brady echoed stupidly. His dad's face was fading, but the fear clutched at him so he could hardly think.

"The State Hospital," Grandpa Bud said. "I also have to go on down to Johnson county and pick up a couple of runaway boys and drop them off on the way home."

"Okay," Brady said. He sat up in bed, fully awake now, but the dream still haunted him.

"You and Eddie keep up your work at the office," Grandpa Bud continued. "And stay out of trouble. Aunt Tilly has enough to do without having to ride herd on you boys. Whatever she tells you to do, you do it. Understood?"

"Yes, sir," Brady said.

"All right then. I'll see you when I get back," Grandpa Bud said.

Brady sat up in bed. He was conscious of Grandpa Bud's footsteps on the stairs, but his thoughts were still on his dream. *"Wake up! Wake up!"* his dad had called. His voice so urgent ... so troubled ... had something happened to him ... or to Mom? Had his dad somehow called to him? Or was it just a dream? Sudden tears scalded his cheeks, and he grabbed up a pillow and rolled over to muffle the sound.

Sometime later the need to use the bathroom drove him out of his bed and down the stairs. At the kitchen door he stopped to wipe his eyes and heard Aunt Tilly speak his mother's name. He waited, listening.

"I hope a letter comes while I'm gone." Grandpa Bud's voice carried clearly to Brady's ears. "I'm afraid something has happened. Maybe to both of them. It's not like either one of them not to let us know."

"I know," Aunt Tilly said.

"I hope history isn't repeating itself." Grandpa Bud's voice sounded harsh to Brady's ears. "I hope we don't have two more abandoned children here."

"Hush," Aunt Tilly said. "They aren't abandoned."

"No, not in the true sense of the word. I don't suppose Lee and Lydia's folks abandoned them on purpose either. I just hate to think of trying to raise Brady. He reminds me so much of Lee."

"We'll get along all right," Aunt Tilly said. "Don't you worry, Bud."

Brady heard a deep sigh, and then Grandpa Bud said, "I hope you're right, Tilly. But Brady's gotten into a lot of scrapes since he's been here, and if he loses hope of his parents ever coming back ..." Brady heard another hard, deep sigh before Grandpa Bud continued. "I can hardly bear the thought of raising another angry boy."

Brady sat on the bottom step and waited to use the bathroom until Grandpa Bud left and Aunt Tilly went back into her bedroom. Now he knew what Grandpa Bud thought of him, and the knowledge formed a hard, angry shell around his heart.

If he wasn't wanted, he wasn't going to stay. Trains left here every day. Before Grandpa Bud came back, he'd be on one, headed west. West to California to look for his mom and dad.

18

BRADY HARDLY SAID A WORD at breakfast. "Don't you feel well?" Aunt Tilly asked as she filled a sack with egg sandwiches for the two old men Deputy Peters would be sending on their way this morning. She had also made a sandwich for Eddie.

"I'm fine," he said, taking the two sacks she held out to him. "Just tired, I guess."

Deputy Peters took the men's food and sent the boys outside to pull the straggly weeds that grew along the back side of the courthouse. "Then if you'll clean the toilet and the sink here," he gestured toward the small room off from the office, "you'll be done."

While they pulled weeds and dug up the roots with his pocket knife, Brady told Eddie of his plan to run away.

"I knew you had something on your mind," Eddie said. "I guess I would go, too, if I thought I wasn't wanted. Which," he said ruefully, "I guess I'm not. Not by Pop anyway."

"Why don't you go with me?" Hope pushed back the fear and worry that had been building since his decision. "It would be great traveling together."

Eddie shrugged. "With this cast on my arm, we would always have to find either stopped trains or really slow ones, so I could get on board."

"I'm going on the one that comes in at midnight," Brady said. "Remember, you said they change crewmen then so it stops for quite a while."

"Yeah, that would be the one to take. The one going west."

"So you'll come with me?" Brady tossed a weed over on the small pile they had collected.

Eddie frowned. "I can't. Not until T.J. and Jimmy Joe get out of that place in Topeka. They said they would come for me just as soon as they'd served their time. We'll travel together, like we planned before." He sighed and gazed at some distant point beyond them. "I hope some of those trains go by where Mayrose lives. I sure do miss Mom and Lilly."

They were still pulling weeds when Deputy Peters opened the back door of the courthouse for the two old hobos. "You two boys take care of yourselves now," he called, before stepping back inside.

They did not answer him, but one of them raised an arm overhead in acknowledgment.

They watched the two old men move off, walking taller, straighter than when they'd come into the jail. Suddenly it occurred to Brady that they could tell him about traveling on the rails. "Hey, wait a minute," he called and jumped up to run after them.

The tallest one turned back, raising a hand to shield his eyes against the glare of the sun. His companion took another step or two before turning to wait, too, his cap pulled low, shielding his face.

As Brady came up to them, the tall one waited silently, but the shorter one demanded, "What do you want? We served our time, didn't we?"

"It wasn't time. It was generosity," the tall one said before turning tired dark eyes on Brady. "What do you want, son?" he asked.

"I just wondered ..." Brady hesitated. He wasn't sure what he did want to know.

"The camps," he began again. "You know ... the camps where you fellas stay. How do you find those camps?"

"Most times they're along a river or a creek so you look for trees in this country. They're often down over a bank or under a bridge, but usually not far from water." He paused and squinted at Brady. "You ain't aiming to take up traveling, are you?"

"I was just wondering," Brady said.

"You go running off, you'll get yourself into a pile of trouble." The shorter one blinked cold eyes beneath the bill of his cap.

"You meet up with all kinds of folks in these camps," the kind one said. "Most are just ordinary folks who've fallen on hard times, but there's mean ones, too. Ones you need to be wary of. Traveling the rails is an education, but not one I'd recommend."

"The braggarts are the ones I can't stomach," the cross one moved a step closer and glared at Brady as if seeing one of them in him. "They sit around in camp fingering the fancy label in their coats and acting like they were once right up there with the Rockefellers and Roosevelts."

"You miss my point," the kind one said. He sighed and looked back at Brady. "There are lots of folks on the road. Quite a few are youngsters ... boys, even girls..."

He shook his head. "It makes a fella's heart ache to see youngsters with no place to go." He looked at Brady a moment and then added, "Think long and hard, son, if you're thinking of taking to the road. If you've got a place to sleep and eat, you'd better stay put."

He turned away and spoke to his companion. "Let's go," he said, "we've got a train to catch."

Brady watched the men cross the street and disappear down the alley between the barber shop and Cope's Hardware store.

"What did they say?" Eddie asked, coming up behind Brady.

"The camps are usually near water ... a river or something..." Brady shrugged. "Not much else."

By late afternoon they had finished their work, and Deputy Peters dismissed them. They walked back to

Grandpa Bud's and flopped down in the dry grass beside Blackie's cage. The crow peered at them through the chicken wire before going back to resume tugging on an old rag Aunt Tilly had tied to his perch to amuse him.

"I sure wish you were going with me," Brady said after a long silence.

"I wish I could, too," Eddie said

There was an awkwardness between them now. Once they would have talked about everything. But now it was like all their thoughts and words had just dried up.

Eddie refused to stay for supper. He was anxious to see if a letter had come from his mother, so Aunt Tilly sent some sandwiches home with him.

After supper, Aunt Tilly sat down in her chair and picked up a pair of overalls to mend. Brady tried to read and then tried the radio, but he couldn't concentrate on either, his mind was so jumbled with his plans and fears.

His nervousness increased with each hour that passed, and he began to wish there was some other course to follow. But he needed to find his parents, and it was plain that Grandpa Bud didn't want him. He was too much like his Uncle Lee to suit Grandpa Bud.

He wished Eddie would go with him. But maybe he could find another boy to travel with him. That old bum said there were a lot of boys on the road. But even if he didn't find someone, and even if he was scared, he was still going. When Grandpa Bud got back, he would be long gone. He wouldn't be a burden to him any more.

He'd take Sarah, too, if he could. But that was impossible. There was no way he could get Sarah on a train. Aunt Tilly didn't seem to mind looking after her, though, and Grandpa Bud hadn't said anything about Sarah, so he probably wouldn't care if she stayed. He looked at the clock on the wall. It was only a little after seven o'clock, nearly five more hours before he'd have to leave. He sighed and picked up a magazine and leafed through the pages.

Aunt Tilly looked up from her sewing. "Are you all right, Brady?" She asked. "You seem restless tonight."

"I'm okay," Brady said. "But I think I'll go up to my room."

"I've just been mending these overalls for Eddie," Aunt Tilly said, holding up the pair she held on her lap. "Mrs. Rice gave them to me along with a shirt and a pair of shoes. Her grandson outgrew them and she was going to put them in the church's charity box."

She picked up a blue-checked shirt and held it up for Brady to see. "This will look nice on Eddie, don't you agree?"

Brady nodded, not trusting himself to speak for the emotions rolling around inside of him. He wondered if Aunt Tilly would take Eddie in after he was gone. Maybe Grandpa Bud wouldn't mind having Eddie around.

"It'll be light for quite a while yet," Aunt Tilly said. "I'm so anxious for Eddie to have these things, I wondered if you would take them to him tonight. I think he would accept them better coming from you. But," she hesitated, "if you'd rather wait until tomorrow."

"I'll take them," Brady said. *He wouldn't be here tomorrow.* Besides, he would like to see Eddie one more time. He missed him already. Just as he was already missing Aunt Tilly ... and surprisingly, Sarah.

A few minutes ago, Sarah had stood up and begun her odd little dance on her toes, her hands fluttering, a barely audible hum accompanying her dance.

Watching her, Brady remembered how sometimes, although very rarely, Sarah would come up to him and caress his face with her tiny hands. If he stood still and didn't try to touch her, she would stay for several seconds and look at him as if really seeing him, as if for the moment she had broken the chains of whatever held her prisoner.

But thinking about Sarah only made him feel worse. He couldn't, no, *wouldn't* back out now.

Aunt Tilly put the clothes and shoes for Eddie in a sack, and Brady, making the excuse that he wanted to be sure the window in his room was open to catch the cooling evening breeze, hurried to his room to add to Eddie's sack two pairs of his own socks and a pair of his undershorts. He smiled as he added the safety pin Eddie would need to hold the undershorts up around his skinny waist.

The sun shimmered on the horizon, a brassy ball radiating its last heat waves for the day, as Brady hurried along the dusty path, the shortcut to Eddie's house. He hoped Eddie wouldn't mind that he had added his underwear and socks to the clothes Aunt Tilly had sent. Maybe this way he could let Eddie know how much he appreciated him for being his friend when it seemed that no one else would.

As he came in sight of Eddie's house, a sudden scream ripped through the air, following by a crow's harsh, cawing cries. Brady stopped, rooted to the spot, and gooseflesh raised hairs at the nape of his neck and along his forearms. Then a window exploded with a bang and a shatter of glass. The crow's cries grew more urgent, and Eddie's voice yelled, "No, Pop! No!"

The sack of clothes dropped from Brady's hand and he was up the steps, yanking open the sagging door.

The first thing he saw was Eddie's dad, a roaring, screaming madman, ragged clothes flapping, face twisted and eyes wild with fury. He was swinging a stout club, one Brady recognized as one of the clubs he and Eddie had used at the rabbit hunt. The club in Clifford Peel's hand was toppling chairs, smashing windows and sending pots and pans and plates flying about the room, where they crashed against the walls and dropped, broken and bent, to the floor.

Tearing his eyes from the sight of the raging man, Brady saw Eddie crouched in a corner, his face contorted with fear. Blackie flew from place to place, landing on upturned chairs and on window sills and on the table tipped over on its side, and then up on top of the stove and a cupboard and back again, all the time crying his hoarse, rasping crow cries.

Suddenly Eddie's dad stopped and, lurching slightly,

began to look around the room as if searching for something more to overturn or smash into pieces. But as far as Brady could see, there was nothing left.

"Pop," Eddie said hesitantly and slowly eased his way out of the corner.

Clifford Peel swung slowly around until his mad-looking eyes rested on his son. "You little snot-nosed brat," he muttered through gritted teeth. "Poured it out, did you? Can't get no more."

"Blackburn," Eddie said.

"My gout's hurting me something awful," Clifford Peel whined. "Gotta have relief." He seemed calmer now, almost crying, a limp, miserable lump of a man.

"I'm sorry, Pop." Tears glistened in Eddie's eyes.

At those words, Blackie ceased crying and flew to Eddie's shoulder. From this vantage point, he eyed Clifford Peel. "Hello, hello," he said.

The crow's words seemed to rekindle the madness in Clifford Peel and, raising the club, he lunged forward. "I'll kill that stupid crow!" he screamed.

"Fly! Fly!" Eddie yelled and pushed the bird from his shoulder, turning just in time to miss being struck with the club. Sprinting across the room, he fell against Brady, who tumbled backwards out the open door, his hands clutching the straps of Eddie's overalls and carrying him out with him.

They staggered down the steps, and Eddie fell to his knees. Hugging his arms across his stomach, he doubled over, his blond hair falling in the dirt.

Tears welled up in Brady's eyes. He shivered, chilled, although the evening was still warm. He listened for sounds inside the house, certain that at any minute Eddie's father would tear out of the house wielding the rabbit club. With an eye out for Clifford Peel, he knelt beside Eddie.

"Come on," he said. "You can't stay here. Come with me."

Eddie allowed himself to be pulled to his feet, and as he stood up, Blackie flew to his shoulder. He reached up, patted the bird, and without protest walked back to Grandpa Bud's with Brady.

"Can Eddie stay overnight?" Brady asked Aunt Tilly. She sat in the living room embroidering a red flower on a piece of white cloth and listening to music on the radio. "His dad's a little upset."

"Of course," Aunt Tilly said. "Can I fix you a bite of something?"

"I don't think so," Brady said. "We'll just go upstairs."

"If I can help," Aunt Tilly said, a soft, worried look coming over her face, "do let me know."

Assuring her he would, Brady went upstairs where Eddie lay on Brady's bed, staring up at the ceiling. Brady stretched out on his back beside him.

"I'd like to go with you," Eddie said, "but I need to see my brothers. Would you go there with me first, and then I'll go west with you?"

"Sure," Brady said, relief flooding through him. "But what train can we take to go east?"

"There's a freight at four in the morning," Eddie said. "It slows to a crawl on an upgrade in those limestone hills near the Blackburn place. T.J. and Jimmy Joe say a fella can get on easy there."

"That's what we'll do, then," Brady said.

They lay awake side by side through the night, hearing the long, drawn-out cry of the midnight freight and the other night noises. In his cage below the window, Blackie muttered sleepily.

Brady took the clock from the dresser and held it in his hands, periodically squinting at the time as the hours passed.

The clothes and shoes had fit and Eddie wore them now. A slight grin had touched his face when he'd pinned up the shorts. His old clothes were rolled in a bundle and tied with a piece of twine from the cardboard box of clothes Brady had brought from home. Brady had sharpened his jackknife and had slipped it and the whetstone into his overall pockets. His change of clothes was in a bundle, identical to Eddie's, except his also held the slingshot Eddie had given him.

When it was time, they picked up their bundles and climbed out into the branches of the hackberry tree.

19

BLACKIE DID NOT WANT to come out of his cage, and he muttered sleepily in response to Eddie's coaxing. Finally Eddie had to reach in and pull him off his perch, which caused the crow to make a loud, sputtering sound of protest.

A light went on in Aunt Tilly's bedroom, and the boys ducked down beside the cage and waited. Eddie smoothed the crow's feathers and whispered softly to him. At last he settled down, cradled against the cast on Eddie's arm, and Aunt Tilly's light went out.

"Let's go," Brady whispered.

They hurried through the dark, silent streets and out across the dusty fields toward the limestone rock ridges where the freight, according to T.J. and Jimmy Joe, would slow to a crawl. As they walked, the sleepy Blackie sputtered an occasional protest.

When they reached the train tracks on the crest of the ridge of hills, the slim quarter moon was riding the western sky and a fresh freeze was blowing.

"I hope we won't have any trouble getting on," Brady said as he and Eddie dropped down on the ground to wait.

"My brothers say the best way to get on is to run alongside an open box car, toss in your bundle and then grab hold of the box car's door or ladder, and swing yourself up inside." Eddie smiled at Blackie still dozing in his arms. "I guess I'll just give you a toss, too, you big sleepyhead."

"I'd better throw Blackie and your bundle," Brady said. "With your arm, you'll have enough trouble getting on as it is, and I'm not going without you. So don't try to sneak away now." He hoped he'd gotten the light-hearted sound to his voice right. The truth was, doubt and fear had about a million butterflies all fluttering around in his stomach. Butterflies so thick he could hardly breathe.

Maybe they should go back to Sentinel. Back to Grandpa Bud's. Eddie could move in with them. But what if his mom and dad never came back? What then? Grandpa Bud had made it plenty clear that he didn't want to raise another boy. And Eddie would make it two boys. No, they had better go on. Probably everyone was a little scared the first time they hopped a freight. It wouldn't be so scary after the first time.

"It's coming," Eddie spoke suddenly. Brady could see him quite clearly now, his body leaning slightly forward, his head cocked to one side as he listened. Brady had been surprised at how well his eyes had adjusted to the dark. It eased the worry he'd had that in the dark they'd not be able to tell which boxcars were open and which were not.

They stood up holding their bundles. The crow stirred, muttering.

The sound of the train grew louder as it drew closer. The thundering pulse beat of it filled the night. By the labored sound of its engine, they knew when it reached the ridge and began to climb. They moved forward and waited. When the oncoming lights shone against the sky, Brady took Eddie's bundle and held it with his own.

The train topped the crest of the ridge, barely moving. Its wide beam of light caught them for a moment and then slid past, moving on.

They began to trot beside the train. A boxcar rolled by before they realized the door was open, but behind it came another, both sides open so the lighter darkness of the night contrasted clearly with the deep blackness inside the car.

Brady grunted as he threw his and Eddie's bundles. Then he reached for Blackie and tossed him inside the slowly moving boxcar. But Blackie's wings fluttered and flapped, and he took flight, disappearing through the opposite door and out into the coming dawn.

"Come on," Brady yelled, looking back at Eddie, as he grabbed for the open door and swung himself up into the boxcar. "He'll find you!"

But Eddie hesitated and then a voice snarled out of the inky blackness of the car. "Blast it, kid! Jump on if you're going to!"

The voice spurred Eddie into action and he leaped forward, catching the ladder as the train pulled away and began to pick up speed. He swung his legs up, missed and fell back again, his shoes dragging along the tracks. The train went faster. Again he swung his legs and again he missed. The cast on his arm making one hand useless, the other desperately gripping the ladder, he was dangling helplessly, his wide eyes filled with terror.

"Hang on!" Brady yelled and dropped to his knees. Hanging on to the door frame, he reached out a hand. "Swing your legs up again," he cried. "I'll try to grab them!"

"Here, I'll get him." The rough, angry voice came out of the darkness, and a hand pushed Brady aside. The figure leaned out from the boxcar and grabbed Eddie, pulling him up into the car and dropping him on the floor in a crumpled, gasping heap.

"Thanks, Mister," Brady said. His voice trembled so he could hardly get the words out. "We're much obliged."

A grunt answered him, and the dark figure retreated back into the shadows of the car.

"You okay, Eddie?" Brady asked just as a sudden, swinging motion of the train knocked him off his feet. He fell hard, his teeth snapping together.

The train was moving fast now, the dark landscape a blur from the open doors.

Still breathing heavily, Eddie sat up. "Boy, I about didn't make it." Suddenly he lifted his head and looked around. "Blackie," he said. "Did Blackie come back?"

"I don't think ..." Brady started to say when the flap of wings flashed past his head and the crow landed on the floor beside them.

"You rascal, you," the crow said, stalking back and forth in front of them. "You rascal, you!"

They laughed and Eddie drew his crow to him in a one-armed hug.

The boxcar rattled and banged and shook as the train raced across the land. Wind whipped in through the open doors and beat against them until they crawled back into a corner. They sat with their backs pressed against the walls of the boxcar, but still they bounced around, barely able to keep their balance.

The stranger sat in the opposite corner, unseen and silent except for an occasional cough. Brady wondered about him. So far they had seen nothing but a huge, dark outline of the man. Had heard nothing except those few words. He wondered if he was asleep or awake. Was he watching them from the dark depths of the car? Waiting for them to sleep so he could rob them of the dollar they each carried in their pockets? Would he then push them out the open door? Would he do it soon, or wait for daylight to come? He had saved Eddie, but was it so he'd have someone else to rob and kill?

Brady reached inside the pocket of his overalls and fingered his pocket knife. It wouldn't hurt to have it in his hand, the blade open, just in case. He thought of the slingshot he'd put inside his bundle, but it was useless without rocks. Besides, the train was swaying and bouncing too much to take aim, even if he had some rocks. No, he would just hold on to the knife and stay awake.

But he dozed off, despite his worries and the jarring motion of the train. When he woke, he vowed not to sleep again, but he was so tired.

He awoke with a jolt, the gray light of dawn filling the boxcar. He jerked his head toward the man in the opposite corner. He was still there, a dark figure, knees drawn up and hat pulled low.

The train whistled and began to slow. Panic seized Brady. What were t*hey supposed to do now!*

"You going north or east?" The voice came from the hulking figure now rising to his feet.

"E ... east," Brady stammered.

"Get off then. They switch the eastbound off onto another track. This one goes north."

"Thanks, Mister," Brady said. But the man didn't answer. He stood at the door of the car looking out, his clothes like a scarecrow's tattered rags flapping in the wind.

The train slowed and the man jumped. One minute he was there and the next, he was gone.

"We'd better jump off now, too," Eddie said. "Besides I've got to go bad."

"Me, too," Brady said. "But let's wait a little bit so we won't see that man."

Tossing out their bundles, Brady took Eddie by the hand and they leaped together as the train chugged to a stop. They ran down an embankment out of sight of the train and anyone who might be coming in from the town. They stood side by side and released two steady streams of urine into a patch of dust-covered weeds.

"Do that off a train and you're hooked," a deep voice said.

They swung around. Later Brady would notice that in his haste he had dribbled a little on his overalls.

"Who said that?" Brady asked, peering in the direction of the voice but seeing no one. His hand slipped inside his pocket and clutched at his knife.

A deep, rumbling laugh answered him, and a red-bearded man rose up out of a stand of tall weeds and came toward them. "You boys new to the road?" he asked.

Up close, the man looked friendly with twinkling, blue

eyes and a warm grin on his face. Brady relaxed his grip on his knife. "How did you know?" he asked.

"Not quite dirty enough for one thing. Faces too clean. Hair too short."

The sun, moving up in the eastern sky, was beginning to heat up. Standing in the full sun, Brady could feel the rays burning the back of his neck.

"Another thing that points you out as greenhorns is not doing your business off the moving train. You travel long enough, you ain't going to be holding it 'til your feet are on solid ground. But I gotta warn you, boys." He leaned in closer to them and chuckled. "If you do, you'll be hooked. Staying in one place won't ever be as satisfying again." For a moment his grin disappeared and his eyes took on a faraway look. "I wish I hadn't done it," he said. Then he laughed, and at that moment Blackie flew down over the bank and landed beside them.

"Hello, hello," he said.

"Well, I'll be ... A traveling, talking crow!" The red-bearded man admired the bird aloud and then asked, "Where're you boys headed?"

"Topeka," Eddie said, and Brady nodded.

"You had better get a move on, then. That train's about to pull out now. Come on." He jerked his head toward the tracks. "Follow me."

The red-bearded man seemed suddenly particular about which car they should ride in, and they passed up several as they moved along the tracks beside the waiting train. Finally the man said, "This is the one you want."

"Why this one?" Brady asked. He had begun to grow suspicious of the red-bearded man. Did he have a buddy in there ready to jump them and take their money?

"This is an empty between two loaded ones," the man said pointing a finger toward the boxcars in front and back of the one they stood beside. "It'll ride smoother. The full ones tend to hold the empty one down. A bad boxcar will beat you half to death."

"I think we just got off one like that," Brady said and made a show of rubbing his tail bone.

The red-bearded man laughed and then turned suddenly gruff. "Get on now and stay out of sight until the train's moving. This town probably ain't big enough to have any bulls, but watch out when you get to a city."

"Bulls?" Brady asked puzzled.

"Railroad detectives," Eddie said. "My brothers told me about them. The railroad hires them to keep folks from hitching rides on their trains. Some are real mean."

"Your brothers are right. So get on and be quiet. Here, son." He turned to Eddie and gave him a boost up into the car.

Brady swung up after him and stood looking down at the red-bearded man. "Aren't you coming?" he asked.

"No. I'm heading west. See what they've got in California."

Brady's heart skipped a beat. Califo*rnia!* For a fraction of a second he forgot about Topeka and Eddie's brothers, and he almost asked if they could travel with the red-bearded man. Instead, he said, "My folks are in California. Their names are Jack and Lydia Foster. If you see them, tell them their son, Brady, is coming to California soon. Real soon."

"I will," the man said gravely, and with a wave of his hand he disappeared back over the embankment and into the weeds.

They had just settled down on some flattened-out pieces of pasteboard when the side doors of their car suddenly slid shut, startling them. They waited, wondering, until the train began to move. "We won't have the wind whipping things around, anyway," Brady said.

As the red-bearded man had said, the boxcar rode quite smoothly, and they slept peacefully on their sheets of pasteboard. They woke sweating and parched with thirst in a roasting oven of a boxcar. Scrambling to their feet, they pushed on the sliding side doors, first one, and then, in panic, across the car to the other. Neither would budge.

They looked at each other and sat down again. They knew they could do nothing but wait and hope. Hope that the train would stop before they died of heat and thirst. And hope that when the train did stop, they could somehow open the doors.

"I'm so thirsty," Eddie mumbled some time later.

"Me, too," Brady said. He mopped his sweating face with the dirty handkerchief he had stuffed in his back pocket and tried to work up some saliva to moisten his mouth.

"I'm worried about Blackie," Eddie said.

"I know," Brady said. The crow was panting heavily, his narrow tongue protruding from his open beak. "I hope it isn't much farther."

Sometime later, Eddie spoke again. "I'm dizzy," he said.

They lay on the smooth pasteboard and waited.

What seemed to Brady like hours later, Eddie said, "If I don't make it, keep Blackie for me. My brothers don't much care for him and I know he likes you."

Despite the heat, Brady felt a chill. "You'll make it," he said, his voice a dry rasp of a whisper. His mouth was so dry he no longer had enough saliva to even wet his lips. But even as he croaked out his words, he felt the train begin to slow. "It's stopping," he whispered.

They sat up as the cars jerked and banged and finally settled to a stop, Brady staggered to his feet and pulled Eddie up beside him. "Maybe we can get the doors open now," he said.

The words were hardly out of his mouth when one of the doors began to slide open and an unshaven face peered in at them, and as quickly withdrew. By the time they got to the door, there was no one in sight.

They all but fell out of the boxcar, Eddie going down on his knees and Brady staggering a few feet before he could get his balance.

"There has to be water here somewhere," Brady said, squinting into the sun as he looked up and down the tracks. "There'll be some at the depot, and it must be ahead a little ways." *But would someone see them? Maybe the railroad detectives? The bulls?*
Brady focused his gaze on the town. It looked like a big town. It had to be Topeka. There had to be water here somewhere. Then he saw a line of grayish green. *Trees.* He blinked and looked again. They were still there. He reached out and gripped Eddie's arm.

"Trees," he said, pointing a shaking finger. Trees just over there. There must be a creek or a river for trees to be growing. And a camp. That old hobo, Grandpa Bud had in jail said the camps were by water."

They crossed several tracks and came out on a street. A car horn blared at them, but they kept moving forward, their eyes fastened on the trees. The sun beat down, its heat waves shimmering before them as they stumbled along.

Blackie, flying ahead a few feet, landing and taking off again, suddenly lifted up in the air and headed straight for the stand of trees. The boys began a weaving, stumbling run.

At the edge of the trees, they stopped short. The place was alive with people. Little camps were set up everywhere and around them men and women and children sat or moved about. Scraps of conversation filled the air. One woman, stirring a steaming kettle set over a fire, ran a bare forearm across her sweaty face and peered up at them.

"You boys all right?" she asked.

"Water," Brady croaked, feeling tears gather in his eyes. *How he could possibly make tears?* "Water," he croaked again, as beside him Eddie fell to his knees, his head falling forward in the dirt.

Then the woman was beside them, tipping a cup of water to Brady's lips. He gulped a swallow, and she moved the cup to Eddie. Squatting, she lifted his head and cupping her hand under his chin poured the rest of the water in his mouth and over his face.

"Joe," she called, twisting around in her squatted position. "Come help me!"

Before he blacked out, Brady saw a thin, dark-haired man move toward them. When he came to, he was lying flat on the ground and the woman was wiping his face with a wet rag.

He struggled to sit up, and the woman moved back to give him room.

"Feeling better?" she asked.

He nodded and looked at Eddie sitting beside him, his face as pale as his white-blond hair.

"I expect you boys are hungry," the woman said. "We don't have much, but you're welcome to what we have."

The odors from the steaming kettle set over the fire brought a rush of saliva to Brady's mouth. Swallowing, he looked around, noticing for the first time two solemn-faced, ragged children, a boy and a girl. They peered shyly at him and Eddie. Brady thought their brown eyes looked too big for their small, thin faces.

The little girl held something in a soiled blanket. Brady thought it was a doll until it moved in the little girl's arms and made a soft, mewing cry, like a kitten.

Brady turned from the children and the baby and looked up at the parents. Looked at their gaunt, tired, worry-lined faces, and his hand went into his pocket. "We can pay," he said, and was rewarded by the sudden flash of joy in the woman's eyes.

20

"YOU CAN SLEEP HERE by us tonight," Laura Gaines said, nodding towards Eddie who was already asleep, sitting straight up with his chin sunk down on his chest. "Your friend looks about all in."

"We'd sure appreciate it, ma'am," Brady said. He and Eddie had eaten with the family, sharing a thin mixture that could hardly pass for soup, Brady thought, remembering his mother's and Aunt Tilly's thick, rich soups.

Eddie had fallen asleep as soon as he had eaten, but Brady sat with the Gaines family as the night closed in around them, bringing the loud, droning cadence of the locust and the fluttering moths drawn by the lights from the campfires.

"The locust puts me in mind of my grandmother," Joe Gaines said. "She used to say the later in summer, the louder the locust. Warning us ..."

"... of the cold to come," his wife finished.

Joe Gaines looked at her and then out at the dark shadows moving about other campfires.

"I wonder where we'll be when the cold comes," Laura Gaines said softly. "Where will all these folks be?"

"Somewhere south," her husband said. "Somewhere south."

Brady asked where the family had lived before they came to this camp, and he learned that Joe Gaines had lost his job six months ago. When they could no longer pay their rent, they were put out on the street with their belongings piled around them.

Brady was horrified. "Even with the baby?" he asked.

"We didn't have Jeffy then," Laura Gaines said. "He was born three months ago in a camp in Missouri."

"But your other children aren't very big either," Brady said.

Mrs. Gaines smiled, but it wasn't really a smile. Her lips stretched in a smile, but her face stayed sad. "Raymond is eight and Susie is six. No, not very big at all."

"I guess it's really hard to find work," Brady said, his thoughts on his parents somewhere in California.

"Once in a while I can pick up an odd job or two," Joe Gaines said. "Chopping wood, carrying water, digging ditches, but it's getting harder to find even those jobs. Too many folks on the road and not many jobs."

"Susie's good at begging," the boy, Raymond, spoke before warning looks from his parents hushed him, and he ducked his head and began to poke in the dirt with a stick he held in his hand.

Mrs. Gaines stood up abruptly. "I think we'd all better turn in for the night," she said.

Brady woke with the first rays of light and lay listening to the awakening sounds of the camp or jungle as Joe Gaines had informed him it was called. "These jungles are all over the country," he said. "Jungles and Hoovervilles. Jungles are more transient, whereas Hoovervilles with their tar paper and pasteboard shacks and lean-tos are pretty much permanent residences."

Brady had known about Hoovervilles and hobo camps, but he had never heard of the camps being called jungles. He had asked Joe Gaines if he knew why.

"I don't know," Joe Gaines had answered, "unless it's because every species of man is represented in these places. The good, the not so good ..." He'd shrugged. "This depression has no favorites."

A brisk, cool morning breeze suddenly swished through the tops of the trees over Brady's head, carrying with it the varied smells of the camp. A girl walked up from the river. She struggled to carry a bucket that was too full and two heavy for her. Little splashes of water slopped over the edge with each step. Brady started to his feet to help her, hesitated and let her go on by.

He scratched a mosquito bite. It was cool now, but the sky was clear, so it would probably turn off hot in a few hours. He and Eddie had been dumb as anything not to have brought food and water along. They could have died shut up in that boxcar. When they started for California, they would be a whole lot smarter about traveling the railroads.

Eddie, still slept, sprawled out on his back. Joe and Laura Gaines were up, but the children still lay nestled together like peas in a pod, the baby snuggled up against the little girl. Overhead, Blackie gave out one of his loud, harsh caws and flew to the low branches of the tree where he had roosted through the night, and then down to land on Eddie's stomach. "Hello, hello," he said, treading the full length of Eddie's body, up and down and back again.

Eddie reached out a hand and stroked the bird. Then he rolled over to face Brady. The crow had to back-track to stay aboard Eddie's narrow side. "Some alarm clock, isn't he?" His mouth spread as if in a grin, but it looked more like a grimace than a grin.

"Are you okay?" Brady asked.

"I'm okay," Eddie said. "Do you think we can see T.J. and Jimmy Joe this morning?"

"Sure," Brady said. "Maybe Joe can give us directions."

After thanking the Gaines family and wishing them luck, the boys set out in the direction Joe Gaines had told them was the business part of town. "Someone there should be able to give you directions to the school," he said.

"I'm sorry not to offer you breakfast," Mrs. Gaines said, "but except for the baby, we try not to eat more than one meal a day. We'll buy the baby some canned milk with your dollar." A quick start of tears misted her eyes. "Thank you so much," she said.

"That's okay," Brady mumbled, feeling embarrassed. He wished he could call Aunt Tilly and have her bring this family some of her fried chicken and potato salad. He felt ashamed of himself for taking all the good meals he had eaten for granted, even when he knew that Eddie had sometimes gone hungry. Well, one thing for sure, he'd never do that again.

As they cut through the jungle, heading toward town, Brady took along the faces of the Gaines family. He tried not to think of what might happen to them. He was glad he had given Mrs. Gaines the dollar in his pocket. Eddie had one left, and they would have to buy something to eat with a part of that. Then he wasn't sure what they would do. He wished he had saved more of the few dollars Aunt Tilly had paid him for hoeing the garden. Eddie, of course, had had to spend his for food, but he had spent his on comic books and candy bars and root beer floats. He'd only had the two dollars left when they had decided to go on the road. He had insisted that Eddie take one in case they got separated or something.

"Hey, boys, look at that crow!" The loud, mocking voice came from one of a group of dirty, ragged men lounging around on the ground before a small fire. "I hear crow meat is right good."

"Makes mighty good stew," another rough voice said, and one of them laughed.

"He's a pet," Eddie said, reaching up to touch the bird riding on his shoulder.

"Not for long," a voice behind them said, and a long, dirty arm snaked past them, grabbing for the crow.

"Fly! Fly!" screamed Blackie and lifted off Eddie's shoulder and into the air, barely escaping the grasping hand.

Eddie whirled to face Blackie's assailant, a leering,

ragged, glittering-eyed man. "Don't you touch my crow," he said, glaring at the man. "Don't you ever!"

The men around the campfire were all laughing now. "You've gotta be quicker than that, Windy," one of them yelled. Several others hooted and flapped their arms and made loud, cawing sounds. The man, Windy, looked over at his companions and then back at Eddie. "All right, kid," he said. "Don't get all huffy."

Brady grabbed Eddie's arm. "Come on, let's go."

"I'm coming," Eddie said, taking a couple of backward steps facing the man before turning to join Brady.

They found a small grocery store at the edge of town, and while Eddie stayed outside with Blackie, Brady went in and spent a quarter for two thick slices of cheese and some crackers. The owner, a heavy-set, balding man, knew exactly where the Boy's Industrial School was, having, he said, visited that institution when his wife's son by her first husband had served time there for robbing a blind man and stealing his cane. "He panhandled folks all over town pretending to be blind. The stupid boy."

When Brady came out of the store, he found that Blackie had attracted a small group of admirers. Eddie was squatted on his heels, and the bird was strutting back and forth spouting off his whole vocabulary. "Hello, hello. You rascal, you. Fly! Fly!" and even "I'll kill the stupid bird," which Brady remembered had been Clifford Peel's words the night of his rampage.

Brady wondered if Eddie was remembering that night, for he didn't look so good. He was grinning, but it looked forced, like he was just pulling his lips back from his teeth. His eyes looked funny, too, like they'd sort of sunk back in his head, and his face was an odd chalky color.

Worried, Brady took a step toward Eddie and then stopped at the sudden silence of the crow. Just as if he had finished a planned performance, Blackie closed his beak and refused to utter another word.

"I guess that's all for now," Eddie said, stroking the crow's shiny black feathers and looking up at the crowd.

Blackie tilted his head, opened his beak and laughed. At least it sounded like a laugh.

That pleased the crowd even more, and they laughed and clapped until Blackie suddenly flapped his heavy wings and flew to the roof of the store.

"Here, son." A man stepped forward and handed Eddie a dime. Others began digging in their pockets and pocket books, bringing out dimes and nickels and pennies. Then the crowd drifted away and left them standing in front of the store.

"That's some bird you got there," the store owner said, grinning at them from the doorway. "You boys hang on to him and you'll soon be rich."

"Won't we, though," Eddie said his forced-looking smile fading from his face as he turned toward Brady. "Did you get the directions?" he asked.

The Boy's Industrial School, a huge brick building, was an imposing structure. Brady was kind of glad not to have to go inside with Eddie. The man who had tried to snatch Blackie had made Eddie afraid to leave his crow to wait alone in the branches of a nearby tree, so Brady waited with him.

In the shade of the tree, Brady dozed and woke and dozed again. The sun rose higher in the sky, and Brady thought an hour must have passed when he woke again. He hadn't expected Eddie to be gone that long, and he was beginning to worry when finally he appeared and, crossing the grounds, flopped down beside him.

"There's no fences around this place," Eddie said. "They could walk away from here if they wanted to, but they won't. I tried to talk them into going to California, but you know what they said?"

"What?" Brady asked.

"They said that for once they were getting enough to eat and they had a place to sleep, and folks were generally pretty good to them."

Eddie paused, his eyes following Blackie, who had flown down from the tree and was pecking around in the sparse, yellowing grass.

"They said they want a clean record when they leave here." Eddie paused again and rubbed at his eyes, a deep frown wrinkling his forehead.

"Does your head hurt?" Brady asked.

"A little," Eddie said, "but I'll be okay."

"What else did they say?" Brady plucked a strand of grass and offered it to Blackie.

The crow cocked his head and gazed up at Brady as if to say, "*I don't eat grass.*"

"They said they knew it was stupid to steal those chickens of Blackburn's, even if they did cheat Mom. And they said I should call Mayrose and her husband to come and get me. They said you should call your grandpa."

"What about finding my folks?" A sudden flush of anger mixed with fear made his words loud and harsh. *Eddie was not going with him! He'd have to go alone!*

"They said California is a long ways away, and it's a big state. And chances are you won't find them. They said it's not easy being on the road. They said lots of things can happen." He paused, sighing, and rubbed his forehead. "They made me promise, Brady. I'm going to call Mayrose. I have to. I promised."

"*Didn't you promise me?*" he wanted to say, but his anger cooled at the sick look on Eddie's face. They'd go back to camp, back to the Gaines family, and think it over. Thanks to Blackie, they had some extra money and they could stop at the store and buy some bread and meat, and maybe even a can of fruit ... peaches or something to share with the family. After they had eaten and Eddie was feeling better, they would talk about it again.

Avoiding the area where the man had tried to grab Blackie, they hurried through the camp. Brady was anxious to share their bounty from the grocery store, but when they arrived at the campsite, the family was gone.

Eddie sat down beside the cold ashes of the campfire and dropped his head in his hands. A low moan escaped his lips.

"Still hurting?" Brady asked.

"Yeah, a little. I'm kind of tired. Maybe if I sleep some."

"Don't you want to eat first?" Brady asked.

"You go ahead," Eddie said. "I'm not hungry right now. "I'll eat later." He lay down and curled up on his side, shoving his bundle under his head for a pillow.

Brady dug out the bread and a thick slice of bologna from the sack of groceries and, sitting cross-legged on the ground, washed the food down with a bottle of Orange Crush. As he ate, he tore off small pieces for Blackie. He hoped Eddie would feel better after he slept. He needed to eat, too. It had been quite a while now since they'd wolfed down the cheese and crackers.

Brady didn't mean to sleep, but his stomach was full and the afternoon was hot, and the flies droning about him was a lazy summer sound.

When he woke, the sack of food they had used all their money to buy, the food they had planned to share with the Gaines family, was gone.

"Eddie! Wake up!" Brady scrambled over on his hands and knees and shook Eddie. "Wake up! Wake up! Someone's stolen our food!"

Eddie groaned and rolled over on his back. "I don't feel so good," he moaned. "My throat hurts." Suddenly he turned on his side and vomited a spew of clear, slimy liquid on the ground.

"Water," he gasped reaching back a hand toward Brady.

"I don't have any, but I've got your soda. Do you want that?" For an answer, Eddie retched again, but nothing came up. "Water," he whispered and rolled over on his stomach. "Water."

"I'll get some," Brady said. He touched Eddie's shoulder

and felt the feverish heat of his body. Jumping up, he grabbed up his empty soda bottle and raced toward the river.

They stayed in camp all night. Eddie moaned in his sleep, waking Brady from frightening, confusing dreams. Each time he woke, he felt Eddie's forehead. It was always hot. In the early morning light, he went back down to the river and refilled the soda bottle. Tearing off a piece of his shirt tail, he bathed Eddie's face and arms. Eddie's skin just seemed to get hotter.

Fighting tears, Brady remembered that his mother had always given him aspirin for a fever. If he could get some aspirin, maybe Eddie's fever would go away and he'd get better.

He wished they hadn't been so foolish as to have spent all their money, but they had both thought they could earn more by getting Blackie to perform again. The trick, they had decided, was in getting a crowd to watch him perform.

Brady wondered if he should take Blackie and try, but decided against it. Without Eddie, Blackie might refuse to talk at all, and he would be wasting valuable time. He thought of the grocery store owner. He had been friendly and had put in an extra can of fruit when Brady had told him about the Gaines family. He might let him have a couple of aspirins for Eddie.

He hated to leave Eddie alone, but there was nothing else he could do. His decision made, he squatted beside Eddie and touched his shoulder. "I'm going to get you some aspirin," he said. "I'll be back as soon as I can."

Eddie opened his eyes and tried to speak, but the words came out so garbled and low that Brady could not understand him. Eddie's breath was coming in short, rasping gasps, and he moaned constantly now, his face twisted with pain.

Brady looked up at Blackie perched on a tree limb. Tears clouded his eyes so the crow was just a hazy, black blur. "Please watch over him," he whispered, and getting to his feet he set off running through the jungle.

21

BRADY BURST THROUGH THE DOOR of the little grocery store and stopped in sudden bewilderment. Behind the counter stood a thin, sharp-faced woman. She looked at Brady, her cold eyes peering at him through narrow, dark framed spectacles.

"Yes?" she said.

Brady was suddenly conscious of his appearance. Of the sweat trickling down his face and his dirty hands and grimy overalls. "Where ... where's the man?" he stammered.

"My husband?" The woman's smile was as cold as her eyes. "Oh, he's under the weather today. Always has some kind of an ache or pain, and me with so much to do." She sighed heavily. "So what do you need?"

"I ... I ...," Brady began, swallowed and started over. "I need aspirin. My friend is sick. I don't have any money, but I'll pay you as soon as I get some."

"Sure you will," the woman sneered.

The heat rose up in Brady's face. "I will. I promise."

"What is the problem?" Brady turned at the sound of the soft voice to see a tall woman standing behind him. She carried a shopping basket over one arm and beside her stood a girl about his own age. The girl's eyes were clear and blue, the color of her dress and the ribbon that held her tumble of shiny brown curls away from her face.

"Are you in some sort of trouble?" the woman asked in her gentle voice.

"My friend ..." he started to say, swallowing tears that threatened to surface, but the sharp-faced woman interrupted.

"This little beggar thinks he needs some aspirin," she said. "Chances are he's trying to pull a fast one." She sighed. "We get them all the time any more. Although usually there are two of them. One to plead a hard luck story while the other steals us blind."

"Honest, ma'am," Brady said, his face hot with embarrassment. "My friend really is sick. He got sick yesterday. I tried to get his fever down with cool water, but I couldn't. I ..." Another lump rose up in his throat and shut off his words. He had never felt so alone, so scared, so helpless.

"Emily," the girl's mother turned to her. "Would you get a bottle of aspirin off the shelf for this boy?" She turned back to the woman behind the counter. "Put it on my bill, if you please." Brady felt his bones dissolve into jelly. He put his hand on the counter to steady himself. "Th ... thank you, ma'am," he managed, while fighting the tears that were stinging his eyes.

"You are very welcome." The woman smiled and turned to the girl she called Emily. "Give him the aspirin, dear," she said.

"I hope your friend gets well soon," Emily said, her blue eyes solemn. Her clean, soft hand brushed his dirty one as she handed him the bottle.

"Thank you," Brady said. He stood still staring at the girl, the aspirin bottle in his hand all but forgotten. Little fluttery wings stirred in his chest.

"Go," Emily's mother said gently. "Your friend is waiting."

"Oh, yes. Thank you, ma'am." He backed to the door. Emily and her mother watched him. "Thank you," he said again. He turned, opened the door and stepped out into the warmth of the morning.

Breathing in a gulp of air, he gripped the aspirin bottle

and began to run. For a moment the vision of the girl called Emily went with him, and then all of his thoughts flew to Eddie.

As he ran he imagined Eddie sitting up, smiling and saying he was feeling fine. But Eddie still lay where he'd left him, curled up and moaning. Blackie walked back and forth beside Eddie, making his loud, raspy, cawing sounds.

Brady knelt and touched Eddie's shoulder, and a cold wash of fear flooded through him. Eddie was shaking like he was freezing cold, but he was still burning hot to the touch. "It's me," Brady whispered through choking tears. "I brought you some aspirin."

But Eddie seemed not to hear him, or to understand. He opened his eyes briefly, but they looked clouded and unseeing.

Frantically, Brady open the bottle, spilling some of the white tablets out on the ground. Finally his shaking fingers held one and holding Eddie's jaw with one hand, he tried to push the pill into his mouth. But Eddie's teeth were clenched tight and the pill crumpled and dissolved against them. He tried again and again, but Eddie would not, or could not, unclench his teeth so the pill could slip through.

Brady rocked back on his heels and stared around the camp, fighting the panic engulfing him. *What was he to do? Was there anyone here who could help them? They needed someone!*

He wished he could get Eddie's brothers to come, but even if they could, he didn't dare leave Eddie again. Not without getting some aspirin in him anyway. There must be someone here who could help him do that.

Early this morning he had noticed a new camp, a small canvas shelter, set up near a few straggly-looking bushes. Someone who had come in during the night. Now he saw that they had strung a clothes line between two trees and several small shirts hung from the line. Maybe there was someone there who could help him get the aspirin down

Eddie. Maybe a mother. She would know what to do. Visions of his own mother filled his head, but he shook them away before his tears could fall.

"Hello."

The man stepped out from under the small canvas shelter at Brady's greeting, and smiled. "Hello," he said. Beside him, a small boy with oddly round and slanted eyes, a retarded boy, Brady suddenly realized with a jolt, smiled, too, a sweet, loving smile.

The smile tore away the tentative grip Brady had on his emotions, and his vision blurred with tears. "Please," he choked out, "I need help."

In one long stride the man was beside him. "What's the trouble?" he asked. "What can I do?"

As Brady explained in a shaky, crackling voice, the little boy came up and slipped his soft little hand into Brady's. "Poor boy," he said, bringing Brady's hand to rest against his smooth round cheek. "Poor boy."

When they got back to Eddie, the man whose name was Alvin knelt for a moment beside him. Then he rose, shaking his head. "I don't know what the problem is, but it's serious, I know that. I think you had better get him to a doctor."

A doctor! "Can't we just give him some aspirin? I don't know how to find a doctor." Panic made his voice quiver and he added through clenched teeth. "I don't have money for a doctor."

"There are hospitals that will take him even if you can't pay. You just need to get to a telephone and call one." He paused and looked past Brady, a startled look on his face.

"Is that your bird?" he asked.

Blackie had flown down from the tree overhead and with his head cocked to one side and his bright, black eyes on Alvin's little boy, spoke. "Hello, hello," he said.

Dropping down on his little bottom in the dirt, the smiling boy patted his out-stretched legs in an invitation to Blackie. The crow eyed him for a moment and then hopped up on his lap. "Hello, hello," he said, and the little boy nearly fell over backwards laughing.

With Alvin's help, Brady finally got two aspirins inside Eddie's mouth. But his groans grew louder and his legs and arms began twitching so that Brady was afraid they had hurt him.

"The aspirin should help even if he didn't swallow them," Alvin said. "They'll dissolve and some will get down his throat. But you've still got to call a doctor. There will be a telephone at the depot. I'd try that first since it's closer. I'll stay here until you get back."

Brady ran all the way. The last few feet he was gasping for breath and doubled over with a stabbing pain in his side. He burst through the door of the depot, wishing he could see a sheriff, a policeman, anyone who could take charge. But the few people there were travelers, an old Negro man pushing a broom, and a gray-headed man at the ticket window. One of the woman travelers turned, and for a moment Brady thought she was Aunt Tilly. His heart smacked against his chest and then dropped again in despair. He'd give anything to see her and Grandpa Bud, too, but they wouldn't be here, even if they were looking for him. The note he'd left pinned to his pillow said he and Eddie were headed for California. Taking a deep breath, he squared his shoulders and walked up to the man at the ticket window. "Will you call a hospital for me?" he said.

Two white-coated men were loading Eddie into an ambulance when Brady got back to the trees leading into the jungle.

"The fellow back there with the boy said you'd be the one to take with us," one of the men said when Brady explained who he was. "You can ride up front with the driver."

Inside the hospital, Eddie was whisked away and a white-capped nurse began to ask Brady all kinds of questions about Eddie. When he had answered them all, he went out into the summer afternoon and, sitting on a bench on the hospital grounds, let the tears fall.

"You rascal, you," a rough voice said, and Brady looked up to see Blackie strutting around on the ground in front of him. B*lackie! He had forgotten all about Blackie!*

He laughed through his tears and knelt down on the ground beside the bird. He must have followed the ambulance like he used to do Grandpa Bud's car.

"Are you Brady Foster?" a voice said.

Brady looked up to see a man in a white coat standing before him. A stethoscope dangled from around his neck.

"The nurse said I might find you here. Mind if I sit down?"

Brady shook his head, started to get up off the ground and then sat back again. His legs felt as weak as a newborn kitten's. Beside him, Blackie cocked his head up at the doctor. "You rascal, you," he said.

"He's Eddie's crow," Brady said to the doctor's questioning look. Usually Blackie made people laughed when he talked. The doctor did not even smile. "How's Eddie?" Brady asked.

"Your friend had polio. We've called for his brothers. Do you have someplace to go?"

Brady's heart lurched and went still. *Had polio?* He looked up questioningly at the doctor, tried to speak, but no words came.

"I'm sorry," the doctor said. "He didn't make it, son. He died about a half hour ago."

Brady stared at the doctor. "I ... I ..." he began.

"I know. It's a shock. I'm sorry." With a deep, heavy sigh, the doctor got to his feet.

"The nurse will call your folks for you, if you'll give her the number."

Brady stared dry-eyed at the doctor's receding back. "Wait!" he suddenly shouted, leaping to his feet. "Can I see Eddie when his brothers get here? Can I see Eddie with them?"

The doctor turned back, frowning. After a moment's

pause, he said, "I'll see what I can do."

Brady nodded, not trusting his voice. He was scared to see Eddie, but he had to know for sure that Eddie was gone. His eyes followed the doctor until he disappeared through the hospital's door; then his tears gathered, fell and gathered again. Finally he rose and, warning Blackie that if he moved from this spot he would wring his scruffy black neck, he went inside the hospital and up to the nurse's desk.

She smiled at him. He tried to smile back, but nothing came of it. "The doctor said you would call my family," he said.

22

"BRADY!" GRANDPA BUD'S VOICE came thundering over the line. "Where are you! Oh, Lord, Brady! Aunt Tilly is nearly frantic with worry. Where are you, son?"

In a slow, shaking voice, Brady told him.

"Aw ... Brady, I'm sorry," Grandpa Bud said as soon as he had finished telling him about Eddie. "We'll be there as soon as we can. A friend of mine, Ken Koller, lives there. Have the nurse call him. He and his wife will gladly put you up for the night. We'll leave first thing in the morning." He made a small sound like a chuckle and added, "If your Aunt Tilly can wait. She has missed you so." Then his voice husky and gruff at the same time, he said, "I missed you, too, Brady."

"Thanks, Grandpa," Brady managed to whisper, but the line had already gone dead.

Brady wiped the back of his hand across his nose and rubbed the tears from his eyes before turning around to give the nurse his Grandpa Bud's instructions.

Brady stood at her desk, listening to her make the call. "Mr. Koller said he would be here just as soon as he can," she said, smiling at him as she replaced the receiver. Then she looked past Brady, and her soft smile faded.

Brady turned to see the doctor behind him.

"Eddie's brothers are here," the doctor said. "They want you to go with them to see Eddie."

Brady's eyes blurred for a second, and a buzzing began in his head. He could hardly hear the doctor's words, and he had to blink his eyes to keep him in focus.

"Are you all right, son?" The doctor stepped closer and put a hand on Brady's arm.

Brady forced the dizziness from his head. "Yes," he said.

He followed the doctor down a long hallway to a small waiting room where T.J. and Jimmy Joe waited. Eddie's brothers were slumped in large orange chairs, their faces showing their grief. They jumped up as Brady and the doctor entered the room.

"I'm sorry," Brady said. He felt suddenly shy and afraid.

"I know," T. J. said, his voice so soft and kind Brady felt tears sting his eyes. *They weren't blaming him at all!.*

"I didn't mean ... mean ..." he began, trying to explain. *He didn't mean, what? To run away? For Eddie to get so sick?* "We didn't have any water in the boxcar ..." he tried again. "I got some aspirin ..."

"We know," T.J. rescued him from his jumble of words. "Eddie thought the world of you." A shimmer of tears gathered in T.J.'s eyes and he looked away.

"It helped Mom when she had to leave to know you were his friend," Jimmy Joe said, his hand going to his brother's shoulder.

"Oh ..." T.J. gave a little moan and put his head down in his hands. "Oh, I wish we didn't have to tell Mom."

They stood in awkward silence, and then the doctor cleared his throat and spoke. "Because we don't know what causes polio and your brother had polio, I can't take you into the room to see him. But you can see him through a window."

T.J. and Jimmy Joe nodded. "We understand, Doctor," T.J. said.

Eddie lay on a narrow cot, a white sheet pulled up to his chest. He was wearing an odd-looking green shirt. "It's a hospital gown," the doctor said when Jimmy Joe asked.

Eddie's eyes were closed as if he were sleeping, and his white-blond hair was parted on one side and combed in a wave over his forehead. The cast had been removed and his arms were straight at his side. He looked like Eddie and yet he didn't.

"Good-bye, Eddie," Brady whispered, touching his fingers to the glass. Beside him T.J. and Jimmy Joe began to cry.

Later, his good-byes said to Eddie's brothers, Brady went back outside to get Blackie and wait for Grandpa Bud's friend. But Blackie was not by the bench where he'd left him, nor had he flown up to settle in the tree. In wave after wave of panic, Brady crossed and re-crossed the hospital grounds calling for the bird. He was about to give up hope when he heard the familiar call and the quick rush of wings, and Blackie landed at his feet.

"You scared me half to death!" Brady yelled at the bird. "Don't you ever do that again. Do you hear me?"

Blackie cocked his head and looked up at him a moment before flying up to balance on the back of the bench. His anger at the bird spent, Brady sit down to wait.

A layer of gray clouds had moved in, cooling the air, but it was still warm. Brady's throat felt parched and dry. He thought of Eddie and fresh tears gathered behind his eyes.

He blinked them away and tried to think of other things. He didn't want his eyes to look red and swollen when Mr. Koller came for him.

Grandpa Bud's words over the telephone about Aunt Tilly missing him echoed again in his ear, and Grandpa Bud's, "I miss*ed you, too, Brady.*" But these thoughts, too, brought tears to his eyes.

He turned his thoughts to the man in the first boxcar. The nameless, faceless man who had pulled Eddie inside the boxcar. The red-bearded man ... Joe and Laura Gaines, and their children, Raymond and Susie, who had not run about or played, but had sat so quietly, their big, brown eyes watching. And the baby, Jeffy, who lay listlessly in his family's arms, rarely crying and never making those happy, cooing baby sounds. He was glad he had given them the dollar. He wondered how much canned milk cost, and he hoped there had been a little left over for Raymond and Susie. An orange to share maybe, or even a potato.

He thought of the men who had tried to grab Blackie for meat for their stew. And he thought of Alvin. Alvin and his little retarded boy. He had never learned the boy's name or where his mother was. Like Sarah he was so different, but unlike Sarah, he liked people. Brady could almost feel again the warm little hands in his and hear his sweet loving voice saying over and over, *"Poor boy. Poor boy."*

His thoughts drifted from the sweet little boy to the sharp-faced woman in the grocery store and then to Emily in the blue dress and hair ribbons and her gentle-voiced mother. It seemed like with people, kindness and meanness often lived side by side.

Then he thought of Eddie's father and Sam Blackburn ... and Raymond. Raymond with the same name as the Gaines boy, but worlds apart. He wondered if Raymond would try to make his life miserable at school when it started this fall. That is, if he stayed ... if his folks... he turned his mind from that worrisome thought and let it drift back to the farm in the days before the dust began to blow. Those days when the wheat grew ripe and rippled in golden waves under a deep blue sky, and his mother sang as she worked and his dad smiled to hear her.

A place where he had friends and a dog. .. a place where he roamed the wide open fields with Taggart at his heels.

Blackie hopped down from the bench, and Brady's vision faded. The crow moved about, poking his beak in the dry grass.

It was dry here in the eastern part of the state, but nothing like back home where mounds of dust covered the land. Even Sentinel didn't have it as bad as southwest Kansas, although the dust did blow pretty hard sometimes, and the ponds and streams were either dry or drying. Nowhere that Brady knew of had there been enough rain for a decent crop.

The Depression had hit everywhere. Almost everyone had to work extra hard to make ends meet, even those with a roof over their heads. But lots of folks, like the Gaines family, were homeless and hungry. Some had other problems, too. Some had children like Sarah and Alvin's little boy to worry about ... and Eddie had had his pop. The farm sale lady, Anna, had a husband shoot himself over these hard times, and that one old lady, when they first came to Sentinel, he'd forgotten her name, had died because there was no food in the house.

He doubted if there was anyone with no problems at all. And if he had to choose, wouldn't he choose his own over some other people's problems? Maybe ... But maybe not. He would have to look at everything connected to the problem. Maybe then he would change, or maybe just keep his own and just do the best he could.

"You must be Sheriff Bud Lewis' grandson." The deep, pleasant voice brought Brady quickly to his feet. "I'm Ken Koller," the man said holding out his hand. "Your granddad said I'd find a boy here, but he didn't say anything about a crow. Is he yours?"

"I guess so," Brady said shaking the man's hand. "He used to belong to my friend."

Ken Koller was a small, thin man with a cheerful face and dark, friendly eyes. On the way back to his house, he talked about a pet crow his cousin had had when he was a boy. On one street they passed, he pointed out the state capitol building, and then he told Brady how Grandpa Bud had kept him from taking a wrong turn in life. "I owe your grandpa plenty," Mr. Koller said. "I lived in Sentinel as a boy and I got into a spot of trouble, and your grandpa went to bat for me." Brady tried to listen, but he was so tired the words flowed over him in faint waves of sound.

He thought Blackie was tired, too. His body quivered

like he was cold. His eyes closed and opened and closed again. Brady wondered if Blackie could somehow know that Eddie had died. That they would never see him again.

When they arrived at the house, Mr. Koller took Brady around to the back to a small screened-in porch. Against one wall was a stack of boxes. Mrs. Koller, a short, heavy woman with a round, pleasant face, brought out some newspapers and laid them on the boxes for Blackie to use for a roost. The bird seemed strangely passive to Brady and still quivering and unsteady on his feet. He set the crow up on top of the boxes, and Mrs. Koller went back into the house and brought out a bowl of water and a mixture of bread and milk. Blackie ignored it all and settled down on the newspaper, his feet tucked under him, and closed his eyes.

Brady hated to leave him, but he had no choice. He couldn't let him go free for fear he'd fly back to the hospital, or maybe even back to the camp, looking for Eddie. And he sure couldn't bring him into the Koller's house. Blackie was a neat bird, but he wasn't housebroken.

After Brady washed up, Mrs. Koller directed him to a chair at their kitchen table and placed a heaping plate of mashed potatoes, ham, peas and cornbread in front of him.

For a moment the odor of the food sickened him, but when he took a bite, he was suddenly ravenously hungry.

23

BRADY TOSSED AND TURNED in a kind of half sleep, with dreams bringing him bolt upright in bed with a trail of tears on his cheeks. Once he dreamed of Eddie lying on the cot in the hospital, peaceful and still, and then again saw him huddled by the ashes of the camp fire, moaning with pain. Sometimes Grandpa Bud and Aunt Tilly appeared in his dreams, as did his parents and the crow. Once he saw Blackie in a kettle of steaming water, the bird struggling to escape.

He woke at dawn, the windows above his bed letting in the morning breeze and the cooing voice of a mourning dove. He listened for sounds that would tell him the Kollers were up and about, but all was silent, and he slept again.

This time he dreamed Eddie stood on a slight rise of ground, his white-blond hair shining as if caught in the rays of the sun. He heard Eddie laugh and saw him turn and look upward. And as he did so, Blackie flew down and landed on his shoulder.

"Brady," Mr. Koller stood beside his bed, "it's ten o'clock. You'd best get up, son."

Brady tumbled out of bed, bleary-eyed and staggering. "Oh," he cried, "I slept too long. I forgot about Blackie."

"I checked on him early this morning," Mr. Koller said. "I don't know what happened, but he's gone."

"Gone?" Brady asked puzzled. "Gone where? He couldn't get out, could he?"

"No. He didn't get out," Ken Koller said. "He died sometime in the night, Brady."

"He went with Eddie," Brady said, his eyes filling with tears. "I guess I knew he couldn't leave Eddie."

Blackie was still where Brady had put him the night before. When Brady touched him, he was stiff and cold.

"He didn't eat a bite of his food," Mr. Koller said. "I think he might have been poisoned. Someone's been setting out poisoned bait and killing cats and dogs all over town. If they ever catch the person responsible I hope he gets the book thrown at him."

Maybe that was what happened, Brady thought. Maybe when I couldn't find him by the bench at the hospital. Maybe he got hungry and went to find some food. But maybe he knew Eddie was gone and he wanted to go with him. But how could that be? No, Mr. Koller was probably right. Birds didn't die of broken hearts, did they?

"I'd like to take him back to Sentinel?" Brady told Mr. Koller. "I think Eddie would like him buried under the hackberry tree in Grandpa Bud's yard."

"I bet he would, too," Mr. Koller said. "I'll help you build a box for him, and we'll see if Mrs. Koller has some nice cloth for a lining."

It bothered Brady that he felt no sadness over Blackie's death. Somehow it seemed a natural thing that the crow should be with Eddie.

When the box was finished, Brady laid Blackie in on the soft white cloth Mrs. Koller had furnished. Then he picked up Mr. Koller's hammer and nailed on the lid.

It was late afternoon when Brady, sitting on the front porch waiting, saw Grandpa Bud's car pull up. He met them in the yard and was soon in Aunt Tilly's warm and wonderful, comforting embrace.

When she released him, Grandpa Bud put both of his hands on Brady's shoulders and squeezed. "It's good to see you, son," he said, smiling.

Sarah, who had climbed out of the car after Aunt Tilly, was doing her little tiptoe walk across the yard, her hands fluttering their butterfly dance. She looked so sweet, so cute to Brady, that he almost reached out and hugged her.

On the way back to Sentinel, Brady sat in the front seat beside Grandpa Bud. Aunt Tilly had put Sarah in the back seat and had climbed in herself as if she had always ridden there.

For the first few miles they talked of the weather and things back at Sentinel, and then Brady began his story. He told of overhearing Grandpa Bud and Aunt Tilly and about Eddie's dad tearing up the house and trying to hit Eddie. He told of the man in the boxcar and the red-bearded man. He told about nearly dying of heat stroke and thirst, locked up in the boxcar, and he told about the Gaines family, Alvin and his sweet little son, and even about the men who had wanted Blackie for their stew. He told about the storekeeper and his sharp-faced wife, about the mother who bought the aspirin, but he didn't mention Emily, the girl in the blue dress.

Grandpa Bud and Aunt Tilly listened until he had talked himself out and fell silent. And then Grandpa Bud began to talk about Brady's mother and his Uncle Lee.

"I was just plain scared of taking you in, Brady. I tried to be a father to your Uncle Lee, but we could never ..." He shook his head, his hands tightening on the steering wheel. "I don't know ... I guess he just felt too abandoned ... maybe he thought I'd abandon him, too."

Again silence fell over them, and they rode several miles before Grandpa Bud spoke again. "Your problems with Raymond Blackburn had to do with me ... and your mother. Sam Blackburn came to town when your mother was seventeen years old. He took her out a few times over my objections. He was quite a bit older and slick even then. One night he got rough with her, and she came home crying. When he came by the next day, he was all apologetic, but I wouldn't let him in. Men like that cry about how sorry they are, but most times they'll do it again. Anyway, I turned him away at the door. He's hated me ever since. I'm sure he encouraged his son's attacks on you."

Grandpa Bud suddenly braked and shifted gears as the driver of a car ahead of them signaled a turn and slowed down. When they passed the car, he glanced at Brady.

"I went to see Eddie's father last night, to tell him about Eddie. The poor man broke down and cried. He's nothing but skin and bones now. I expect he'll end up drinking himself to death. He has a new source, I hear. Lenny Tucker is a little simple and he's lonely, too. He'll do anything for attention, and Cliff will do anything for a drink. Lenny gets it from Oscar Stephenson, I'm sure. I could stop Lenny, and maybe I should, but he doesn't drink it himself, and Cliff's too far gone to help now."

Brady hardly heard the last of Grandpa Bud's words. He was still puzzling over the first part. "He cried?" he said. He could hardly believe the man who had torn his house to shambles and tried to club his own son could have cried. "I thought he didn't care," he said.

Grandpa Bud shrugged. "It's the alcohol that doesn't care," he said.

Back in Sentinel, Grandpa Bud opened the trunk of his car and handed Brady Blackie's wooden box. "You'd better bury him now," he said gently. "Do you want me and Aunt Tilly to help?"

Brady nodded, not trusting himself to speak. Now that the time had come to bury Blackie, he was feeling the sadness that had eluded him earlier. Maybe I was just numb, he thought.

Grandpa Bud brought Brady a shovel to dig the grave. Afterwards he helped him put Blackie's cage in the shed. Wild sunflowers had come up along the fence by the garden, and Aunt Tilly used Brady's knife to cut a thick stalk.

"I'm going to miss you, you old bird," she said as she

bent to lay the yellow flower on the grave.

Brady slept late again the next morning, untroubled this time by dreams. When he came downstairs, Aunt Tilly fixed him a breakfast of bacon and eggs. As he ate, Raymond and Susie Gaines' big, brown eyes followed his every bite.

He had just finished eating when Grandpa Bud burst through the door, waving a letter.

"It's from Jack and Lydia," he shouted, his face beaming with joy. "They are all right! But here, Brady, you read it!"

Brady looked down at his father's handwriting, his eyes blurring so the words swam in and out of his vision. Wordlessly, he looked up at Aunt Tilly. She took the letter from his trembling hands.

"Dear Bud, Aunt Tilly, Brady and Sarah," Aunt Tilly read aloud. *"I'm sorry I haven't written before this, but Lydia was so ill. She's been in the hospital for months. I got a job in the fields picking vegetables. I worked days and sat with her through the nights. I knew you were worried, but I thought if I wouldn't write what the doctor kept telling me was true, that she couldn't get well, then it wouldn't happen. And praise be, it didn't. This week has been a big turnaround for her. The doctor is amazed. He says now she is going to get well!*

"Please write soon. Send your letters in care of the hospital. My love to all, Jack."

Smiling, Aunt Tilly lifted a corner of her apron and wiped at her eyes.

They looked at each other with huge smiles lighting their faces while unshed tears choked back their words of overwhelming relief and joy. Then Grandpa Bud pulled a penny postcard from his shirt pocket and handed it to Brady. "This must be from a friend of yours," he said, a twinkle shining in his eyes.

The card was from Jim Conners. *Dear Brady,* he read. *We're in Oregon, as you can see by the postmark. Dad's got a part-time job and I'm selling the Saturday Evening Post. My new friend sells it, too.* Jim had signed the postcard and then had added his address and the words, *please write back right away.*

"Good ol' Jim," Brady said grinning. Then he told them about his friend and the time they had put the snake in Mrs. Guilder's desk.

The rest of the day they all went around with smiles on their faces, and their talk centered most of the time on Brady's parents.

The telephone rang in the night, and Brady heard Grandpa Bud get up and leave the house, driving away in the dark. In the distance he heard the wailing cry of a train and then, closer and mixed with the train's whistle, the clanging bell of a fire engine.

Grandpa Bud brought them the news late the next morning, but they had already heard it from the neighbors and Aunt Tilly's friends. "Cliff Peel's house burned last night," he said. "Cliff didn't get out."

"Does May know?" Aunt Tilly asked.

"I had the sheriff there in Missouri notify her. I told him to ask about Eddie, too. She said that because he had died of polio, he was buried that same day in Topeka."

"I wonder if T.J. and Jimmy Joe will stay in Topeka when they get out," Brady said. He hoped they would so Eddie wouldn't be all alone.

"I don't know," Grandpa Bud said. "But I've been thinking. Maybe we could go to Topeka and see about having a stone put on Eddie's grave."

"I'd like to do that," Brady said. "Thanks ..." He hesitated and then added, "Grandpa."

"Hey," Grandpa Bud's voice turned husky, "I'm thinking you and me could be quite a team." He grinned. "Now that we've got the kinks worked out." His grin broadened. "In fact, I've got to see a man tomorrow about his dog. Seems it insists on reducing the neighbor's chickens to a pile of feathers. How about riding along?"

"Great," Brady said.

The days passed, some so slow Brady thought they would never end. Other days, usually the days he spent down at his grandpa's office or riding with him around the county, went swiftly by.

There were still funds enough to open school after Labor Day, now just two weeks away. He had grown taller during the summer, and Aunt Tilly insisted he have new clothes for school. Instead of overalls, she bought him pants and a brown leather belt. But the new clothes didn't help to ease his dread of starting back to school. He had hoped his mother would be well enough to come back home, but his dad had written that it might be months before she would be strong enough, and the drought was still hanging on. He couldn't bring her back to the dust that had started it all in the first place.

Maybe we'll sell the farm and move to California, his dad had written in one of his letters. *Or maybe we'll come to Sentinel to stay if the drought lets up there first.* The thing was, right now, his dad just didn't know. They'd just have to wait and see. But Brady guessed, the waiting wasn't so bad. His mom was getting well and his dad had a job, and as for him, well, Grandpa's house was beginning to feel a lot like home.

Still he was lonely. He missed Eddie more than he could ever have imagined.

Sometimes he saw David Hager across the street in his yard or walking up town with some other boys. When he saw them, he would duck back inside the house.

"You'll never make a new friend if you keep hiding yourself," Aunt Tilly said to him one day. "Go out when David is in the yard. Just say hello. That's all you have to do."

He tried several times before finally getting enough nerve to stay out in the yard when David came out of his house.

"Hey, Brady," David called, and crossed the street toward him.

"Hey," Brady said, but the word came out so weak he

wondered if David had heard him.

"Are you staying and going to school here?" The tall, brown-haired boy was smiling, his blue eyes shining with good humor.

"Looks that way," Brady said.

"I wanted to tell you I was sorry about Eddie." David's face sobered, and he looked down at his feet and then up again at Brady. "Some of us fellas feel kind of bad now for not being friendly to him. He was a good boy. We just never got to know him."

"He was a good friend," Brady said. "You'd have liked him."

"Ahh …" David looked away and then back again. "Do you want to go to Porter's Drug for a soda?"

Brady was startled. "What about Raymond Blackburn?" he said.

"A bunch of us fellas have been talking. We've decided that Raymond Blackburn's not going to rule us in high school. If we all stick together, he's not going to give us too bad of a time."

A warmth spread through Brady. "I bet he'd think twice before taking on a bunch of us, all right."

David grinned. "Yeah. Or three or four times. Anyway we can't be pushovers all our lives." With a mock scowl, he thrust his chest out, and in an exaggerated tough voice, said, "Hey, it's time we started acting like men."

Brady laughed. "I guess we have to grow up someday," he said. "We can't stay boys forever."